THE TARTAN RINGERS

The playground was a screaming turmoil. Through the railings I said to a snot-riddled urchin, 'If I give you a million zlotniks, will you give Miss Ross a message?'

'Piss off, Lovejoy.'

I sighed, and looked about. Most of the little psychopaths are from my village and believe I'm a bum. 'Lottie,' I called. One of the tinier girls skipped closer, pigtails flying with each bounce. I used to babysit her.

'Salt, mustard, vinegar, pepper', she chanted breathlessly.

'I'm going to elope with Miss Ross,' I said. 'Say I'm here.'

Also in Arrow by Jonathan Gash

FIREFLY GADROON
GOLD FROM GEMINI
THE GRAIL TREE
THE JUDAS PAIR
PEARLHANGER
THE SLEEPERS OF ERIN
SPEND GAME
THE VATICAN RIP
THE GONDOLA SCAM
MOONSPENDER

THE TARTAN RINGERS

RINGERS

A Lovejoy narrative

JONATHAN GASH

ring'er: a person or thing very like another
Dictionary definition

ARROW

This edition published by Arrow Books Limited 1987

5 7 9 10 8 6

© Jonathan Gash 1986

First published in the United Kingdom in 1986 by
William Collins Sons & Co. Ltd.

Random House, 20 Vauxhall Bridge Road, London SW1V 2SA

Random House Australia (Pty) Limited
20 Alfred Street, Milsons Point, Sydney,
New South Wales 2061, Australia

Random House New Zealand Limited
18 Poland Road, Glenfield
Auckland 10, New Zealand

Random House South Africa (Pty) Limited
PO Box 337, Bergvlei, South Africa

Random House UK Limited Reg. No. 954009

A CIP catalogue record for this book
is available from the British Library

ISBN 0 09 948210 X

Printed and bound in Great Britain by
Cox & Wyman Ltd, Reading, Berkshire

To
The ancient Chinese God Wei D'to, Protector of books against
unscrupulous borrowers, indolent librarians and other forms of
corruption, this book is humbly dedicated.
Lovejoy

For
A story for Lal and Richard, Our Kid and his, and Susan.

CHAPTER 1

This story starts with criminal passion in a shed. It descends into sordid corruption. But all along just remember one thing: love and antiques are the same. Hatred and evil are their opposite. I'm an antique dealer, in bad with the law, and I should know.

There's nothing antique dealers hate worse than fog and rain. Ellen agreed.

Three o'clock in the morning on a foggy rainy bypass Ellen was tired—only the same as anybody else daft enough to be awake at this ungodly hour, but women are very self-centred.

'How much longer, Lovejoy?' she moaned.

'Couple of minutes.' I'd been saying this since midnight.

We were in Ben's hut. He's the vigilant nightwatchman hired to watch for thieves who habitually steal the roadmenders' gear. He's never caught any because he mostly kips in front of the portable telly his daughter bought him last Easter. Me and Ellen had made love and the old bloke hadn't even stirred from his glowing stove.

'I'll get into trouble,' Ellen whimpered.

I quaked. 'Er, your bloke isn't . . . ?'

'Of course not. I've got a meeting tomorrow. That old bitch from the vicarage has a filthy mind.'

Ellen's husband is heap big medicine, being a Customs officer. Mercifully a kind Chancellor had sent him to patrol the coasts and keep a lookout for dark deeds. Meanwhile my own particular dark deed was thrombosing in the fog while Ben snored his old head off and me and Ellen swilled his rotten tea. Who'd be an antique dealer? I ask you.

'What *are* we waiting for, a fake, Lovejoy?'

'A reproduction bureau,' I corrected coldly.

Ellen shivered, a lovely sight even when she's indianed in a moth-eaten blanket. 'Why couldn't they send it by train?'

She'd reached the repetitive stage. I sighed wearily. Women get like this. They believe that if they say something often enough it becomes true. 'Nobody in their right mind sends antiques by proper transport. The whole bloody kingdom uses a night lorry.' For a few quid on the side, of course.

'But isn't that illegal?' the poor little innocent asked, turning her beautiful blue eyes on me. Old Ben broke wind, as if in criticism.

'It's safer, and surer.' Most antique dealers have their barkers down on the bypass all over the country collecting and loading up. This fraudulent system has the merit of being beyond the reach of tax.

Huddled over the brazier, we waited dozily for the signal from out in the rain-soaked night. I thought of her and me.

Men are amateurs; women are professionals. And that's in everything: love, life, greed, hate, all the emotions. And why? Because we blokes have animal souls. Oh, I don't deny that every so often some bird thinks she's educated us out of being primitive, but it's only imagination. Women never seem to realize this. Like now.

'We could be somewhere warm, Lovejoy,' Ellen's blanket muttered. 'You make the best fake antiques. Everybody says so. What's the point of sending to Caithness?'

'Shhh.' I said. Old Ben's principal asset is that he's bent. He often helps with loading, especially when German buyers are scouring soggy East Anglia spending like drunks. His conscience only costs a pint, but I still didn't want him learning too much. I whispered, 'Nobody local'll know it's a fake, see? I'll sell it as genuine.'

'Matthew will be cross if he finds out, Lovejoy.'

See what I mean? She ignores the fact that she's literally shacked up with a grubby antique dealer riddled with lust and perishing cold. See how they shift the blame?

'Your husband can get knotted.'

'That's not a very nice thing to—'

Ben stirred, woke, spat expertly into the stove's grille. 'It's here, Lovejoy. Far side.'

There are two lay-bys down the road. They're about a mile apart. I shrugged. The lorry should have been coming from the other direction but I knew better than argue. These old roadmen have a third ear. 'Best get going, then.'

'Can we go, Lovejoy?' Ellen asked hopefully.

'No. I need your car.' It has a roof-rack. Ben's hut always holds ropes and tools for neffie schemes like this. 'Drive into Colchester, then back here and into the lay-by this side. I'll be waiting.'   •

'But it's foggy! Can't I just—?'

'No. The bloody lorry's stopped on the wrong side.'

'Stupid man.' She cast off the blanket with a whimper.

'Cheers, Ben,' I said, and opened the hut door.

'Here, Lovejoy.' Ben was listening, past me into the blackness. 'There's two engines in the lay-by.'

Silly old sod, I thought, and stepped out as Ellen's car pulled away up the gravelly path. God, but the night was opaque. The way down the long slope to the road was familiar. There isn't quite a footpath. You find bearings by hawthorns and brambles. Usually there's enough light from passing cars and the distant town's sky glow. Tonight there was only this horrible graveyard opalescence.

Ellen had thoughtlessly forgotten to bring a torch. Typical. I skittered down, brambles plucking at me, until the level road surface jarred my heel. No traffic sounds, so presumably safe to cross.

Listening nervously, I loped over, climbed the central crash barrier and thankfully made the opposite verge. Left turn, keep within reach of the grassy slope for safety, and plod until the road margin indented the steep bank. Then a huge car started at me of a sudden, roared off, all in one instant. I had a vague swirly image of two figures, one familiar, then silence. Bloody fools could have killed me.

The wagon when I came upon it looked enormous. Oddly, its lights were dowsed. I almost walked into its radiator in the damned fog. The heat-stink of the cooling engine drifted at me.

'Hello?' Fog muffles sounds, doesn't it? My call hardly went a yard. No answer. 'You there, mate?'

The cab's door was ajar. I swung myself into the driver's seat, feeling at altitude. A fumble for the keys, there sure enough, and a half-twist for beam headlights. The dashboard's fluorescence cast a ghostly apparition on the windscreen, losing me a heartbeat till I realized it was my own nervy face. A square white card was lodged in the corner of the thick glass. I turned the card over. A black capital L. My signal, so this was the right wagon. But stillness is stillness, and there was a lot of it about. The size of these night haulers is daunting. I levered down, leaving the lights on. A car swished by steady and fast heading for the coast. The driver was probably having a pee, or gone looking for me.

'Hello,' I called. My voice warbled. I cleared my throat, called again as unconvincingly. No sound. I walked the length of the vehicle. It seemed all wheels. The rear doors were unlocked, one leaf swinging ponderously open at a pull. Interior lights came on, like in a fridge. Empty.

'Hello?' I shouted. The place was giving me the spooks. Now, the one thing a night haulier never does is leave his wagon. Gulp.

A car crawled into the lay-by, spotlighted me in its beams, Ellen to the rescue at two miles an hour. 'Darling?'

I walked round and got in, trying hard to disguise my relief. 'Where the hell have you been?'

'Charming,' she said bitterly. 'It's hundreds of miles to the Marks Tey turn-off. Where's your cupboard?'

'It's four miles. And it's a bureau. Gone.'

'Then ask the driver, dear.'

'He's gone, too.' I peered uneasily into that black-grey smirch.

'How *very* thoughtless. I'll give him a piece of my mind.'

You have to forget logic with Ellen. She was moved to aggro, actually starting to get out to bollock a vanished lorry-driver, when I stopped her. 'No, love,' I said piously. 'I've kept you out in this awful weather long enough. It's time I considered your feelings.'

'Darling,' she said mistily. 'You're so sweet.'

True, but I'd better get rid of her sharpish after dawn because Liz was due about ten with a genuine pair of mid-Victorian nipple jewels, sapphires set in diamonds. I joked nervously as we pulled out. 'Promise not to ravish me again.'

'Very well, dear,' she said seriously. 'Look, Lovejoy. The lorry's left its light on. It'll waste its electricity.'

'How careless,' I said uneasily. 'No, love. Don't stop.'

Next morning I had three jobs. First was Liz, chatty antiques dealeress from Dragonsdale that I was conning into selling me those lovely nipple drops—think of earrings with bigger loops for dangling pendant-like from the pierced nipples of interesting Victorian ladies. Liz had found a set with their accompanying large gold sleepers. I'd been banking on profit from the bureau to afford them.

My second and third jobs were easy, now I was broke. Two lithophanes of erotic couples, and a pride of tortoise-shell seamstress scissors, 1840, were in the auction. I'd hate seeing them sold to some flush swine, but I could no more keep away than fly.

Ellen fried me a good nosh. She brings supplies because I'm always strapped, and leaves little labelled packets in the fridge—'Boil 10 Mins In Slightly Salted Water' and all that. I never do it, because it always goes wrong. I got shut of her at a safe nine o'clock. She always wants to strip the bed and hang sheets on the line, God knows why. What good are they waving in the breeze? I lied that I'd do it, to make her trip home to Ipswich less of a rush. She said I was an angel. Modestly I waved her off, concealing my relief, and got down to sussing out The Missing Bureau Problem.

First, however, remember this ratio: five to one. Not a Grand National bet, but the number of phoney/fake/reproduction bureaux to the genuine. Five times as many fakes as genuine. And that's here, in rural East Anglia where habits—and furniture, and paintings and porcelain—don't change. I have figures for most antiques. Jewellery is eight to one; pearls twenty; pre-Victorian oil paintings three fakes to one genuine. So, all in all, the odds are heavily against the honest buyer and heavily in favour of the crook.

It stands to reason that you're on a loser. The dice

of honesty are loaded against you, the poor unsuspecting customer.

Lately, though, I'd been having a bad patch. Even though I'm a very special type of antique dealer—tell you more in a minute—it was pathetic. Sometimes, antiques vanish like snow off a duck. Buyers evaporate. Collectors get a collective 'flu. Money zooms into the Inland Revenue's coffers untouched by human hand. In other trades things never become utterly hopeless. I mean to say, a farmer at least still has the good earth if his crop ails, and doctors can always look forward to a really great epidemic if their patients strike a depressingly healthy patch. But in the antiques game there's nothing. An antique dealer with no antiques feels a right prune. A hungry prune, because when you're broke the Chancellor simply refuses dole. No, subtract antiques from the great equation of life and all is zero.

Well, nearly zero.

Because there's fakes. And frauds. And counterfeits, reproductions, marriages, twinners, naughties, copies . . . I finally found my note about the bureau in a heap of paper clippings that makes my tatty armchair a hell of comfort:

'Jo: Teddy repro b. split m/u, Inv. T. fix Thurs. M.'

Roughly translated, an Edwardian period reproduction bureau was available. I'd agreed to divide the mark-up (i.e. my hoped-for profit) with the sender, who would ship it from Inverness, a collecting centre for the four northernmost counties by these night wagons. I'd told Tinker to fix delivery for the previous night. Jo—Josephine—had been my original contact. Tinker's my old barker, my message ferret.

I'd better try to catch Jo, then get to the town Arcade where antiques and dealers congregate.

For a second, guilt tugged. I glanced around. The cottage's interior was a mess: books, newspaper cuttings, a mouldering heap of unpaid bills, the divan bed I'd promised Ellen I'd make. I opened the door, masterful with guilt. I was actually smiling from the relief of having triumphed over housework, when my jubilation ended.

''Morning, Lovejoy.' Liz Sandwell stood there in the tiny flagged porch. Pretty as a picture. The trouble is her live-in boyfriend's one of those strength-through-joy fanatics who gasp their way through our rain-soaked countryside and finish up where they started. A tough rugby player.

''Morning, love,' I said brightly, slamming the door to edge on past.

'Well? Did it arrive?'

Blankly I stared at her. 'Eh?' I never know what the hell women are on about half the time.

'The money. From your Uncle Percy.'

'Ah.' Evidently one of my less memorable myths. Swiftly I switched to heartfelt grief. 'No, love. Uncle Percy's just sent a telegram. He's ill and needs me.'

Concern leapt into her eyes. 'Oh, how terrible, Lovejoy. Are you very close?'

Not as close as I'll be to that burke of a wagoneer who lost my bureau and disappeared, I thought grimly, but said brokenly, 'Yes. Can we postpone the deal over the nipple jewels, love? Only I'm hurrying to town to borrow the fare to, er, Llangollen.'

Liz took instant charge. 'Let me run you to the station, Lovejoy. How much is it? You can't shilly-shally at times like this.' A warm-hearted, lovable lass is Liz. Where the hell's Llangollen, I wondered, getting into her car. Let's hope it's a fair distance. Then with that money I'd have enough to split-purchase Margaret Dainty's Belleek porcelain trelliswork basket—no harp-and-greyhound mark, so post-1891, but lovely . . .

A few minutes later I was mouthing gibberish at a puzzled railway clerk while watching the reflection of Liz's departing car in the glass. She'd lent me a real handful of notes.

''Ere, mate. You going any bloody where or not?' A soldier in the queue behind me was growing impatient.

'Sorry, sorry.' Liz'd gone. I stepped aside. 'I can't leave Nellie and the little uns,' I said nobly.

Twenty minutes later the bus dropped me outside Jo's school. It was playtime.

CHAPTER 2

The playground was a screaming turmoil. Through the railings I said to a snot-riddled urchin, 'If I give you a million zlotniks, will you give Miss Ross a message?'

'Piss off, Lovejoy.'

I sighed, and looked about. Most of the little psychopaths are from my village and believe I'm a bum. 'Lottie,' I called. One of the tinier girls skipped closer, pigtails flying with each bounce. I used to babysit her.

'Salt, mustard, vinegar, pepper,' she chanted breathlessly.

'I'm going to elope with Miss Ross,' I said. 'Say I'm here.'

Lottie bounced off, chanting. I sat and waited while the playground roared on. Five minutes and Jo came, red-faced and embarrassed. She's a lovely slender faun of a woman, mid-twenties. Infants flocked round, staring.

'Lovejoy! What on earth?'

'Aren't you escaping, miss?' a kiddy asked disappointedly.

'Certainly not! And get away the lot of you!'

They dispersed with that silent scorn only infants can attain, Lottie explaining, 'I told you he tells lies.'

'That bureau, love.' I had the scrap of paper out.

'You interrupt school and make me a laughing-stock just to ask stupid questions?'

Women are always narked. You just have to ride out the storm. I nodded. 'Yes, love. Only it didn't arrive.' She'd given me the original address, an Inverness box number.

'Well, I can't help that, can I?'

'Why did you tell me instead of some other dealer, Jo?'

Momentarily she coloured deeper. 'You happen to be the first antique dealer I thought of.'

I turned to go, and said loudly, 'Pretend to start teaching, darling, then slip out. I'll be waiting—'

'Shhh, you fool.' She was trying not to laugh. A police car pulled alongside the kerb. Two Old Bill descended. The children fell silent and gathered at the railings.

'You Lovejoy?' one peeler said.

'Give over, John.' I've known Constable Doble ten years. Every Friday night I beat him at darts.

'You're under arrest,' he said. 'Get in.'

'For anything in particular?'

'Murder of a night driver,' he said. 'In particular.'

Jo gasped. Thinking quickly, I passed her the note. 'To Tinker, please, Jo.' The children's faces solemnly followed me as I crossed to the car.

Lottie called, 'I'm sorry you didn't escape like you planned, Lovejoy.' Another nail in my coffin.

'Ta, chuck,' I called back, best I could do with my throat dry.

The other bobby was already scribbling this new evidence as we drove off. Education gets everywhere these days, doesn't it.

Gaols have been great literary stimulants. John Bunyan or Oscar Wilde would have used the next dozen days to dash off a masterpiece. Me, I simply languished. Twice I was dragged out to stand before Arthur. He's our famous magistrate. He writes little stage plays about ghost trains and doubles as Judge Lynch. I was remanded in custody. I didn't claim my two witnesses because Ben's lies are notorious, and fornicating with a Royal Customs officer's wife while illegally transporting a fake antique might not stand up as a character reference.

Maslow came to see me on the first day.

'Your fingerprints are all over the wagon, Lovejoy,' he told me. 'The man was found dead a hundred yards up the bank.'

'Ah,' I said, baffled. Maslow's not a bad old stick for a troop leader, but there's only a limited amount of truth police inspectors can take. 'That explains why I couldn't find him. I wanted to give him a message.'

'At that hour in the morning? In the fog? On a lonely road?' He was beginning to glare and breathe funny. 'Ben the roadmender said he hadn't seen you, Lovejoy.'

Thank you, Ben. 'I walked to the lay-by. When I got there the driver had gone. I looked about the wagon, wondered if he was, erm . . .'

Maslow nodded, and left. Three local prostitutes work the lay-bys. Night hauliers find solace for the loneliness of the long distance wagoneer in the privacy of their own vehicles.

Three days elapsed before reassuring rumours filtered in. The driver, a big Brummie, had put up a struggle before being bludgeoned. Needless to say the peelers had taken my clothes, scraped my fingernails. The screw told me this news between bowls of porridge and atrocious jokes.

It was Monday evening before a wonderful sound floated in through the bars of my cell. I brightened, listened as a long cough began, swelled and shuddered the walls. The cough rumbled closer. I ran to the bars grinning all over my face.

'That you, Tinker?' I yelled. 'In here.'

'Wotcher, Lovejoy.'

In he came. Small, shambling, in a grimy old beret and tattered army greatcoat. An aroma of stale booze and feet wafted in as he subsided wheezing on the bunk.

'Never been in this one,' he croaked. A connoisseur of gaols. 'Did we do it, Lovejoy?'

That plural warmed me. Tinker's not much to look at, but any ally counts one. Since my arrest I'd been solo. 'No.'

'Fank Gawd,' he said, rolling a grotty cigarette in mittened fingers. 'They've been at me three frigging days. Yon Scotch tart got the paper to me in time.'

I nodded. That had warned him to disclose nothing. He gave another cough. I waited. They seem to start somewhere out to sea, like thunder. 'You'll get sprung, Lovejoy. That bird you wuz shagging in Ben's hut's seeing the Commissioner.'

I sank back, eyes closed in relief. Tinker lit up, coughing. Ellen had come to give me an alibi. 'Learn anything?'

'About the bureau? Aye. Word is that frigging Dobson creep's had it away, to frigging Amsterdam, Antwerp, one of them places through the Hook. Twinned it.'

'Jesus.' An antique which is made into two of itself is 'twinned' in the trade. If half of a piece is truly genuine antique, it becomes very difficult to dismiss it as a fake. And of course you get twice the profit. If Tinker's information was true, the only piece of evidence which could pin the killer had been destroyed as effectively as if they'd burned it to ashes. Dobson is a barker, like Tinker. He works with a pleasant youngish bloke we call Dutchie. Oddly, I thought of that familiar face in that great old car. Had it been Dutchie? Indistinct, but . . .

'How'd you know?'

'Seen down the hangars, two nights back.'

My bad luck, I thought bitterly. Anybody with stolen antiques takes them to a disused wartime airfield near here. No questions are asked down at the hangars. Jade, jewellery, silver, porcelain, complete suites of furniture, I've seen stuff change hands a dozen times an hour. Always at night. No way of backtracking there.

'Here, Lovejoy,' Tinker was grinning toothily in his fag smoke. 'If you'd not been shagging that Excise officer's missus they'd be topping you.' He really fell about at the thought of my being hanged, cackling through his brown fangs.

'They don't hang people now, stupid sod,' I said icily.

'Maslow always said he'd make you an exception, Lovejoy.' He was still rolling in the aisles, coughing himself apoplectic, when his visiting time was up and they shelled him out.

They released me on two counts. One, the big Midlander had fought his murderers, and I was unmarked. And two, a respectable lady testified that, marooned with a stalled engine on the main A12 during the night of the great fog, she had been assisted by a stranger who started her motor and drove her to safety. As a gesture of appreciation, she had insisted on driving him to his home, a thatched cottage in a little village nearby.

'How could the lady see your cottage, thatch and all, in the pitch fog, Lovejoy?' Maslow asked evenly, with that

19

threatening peace police manage so effortlessly. 'And how come you'd forgotten the entire incident?'

'I couldn't compromise a lady,' I explained nobly.

'One day, Lovejoy. One day.'

Deliberately I let the office door slam on him. I waggled my fingers at the desk sergeant.

He too warned, 'One day, Lovejoy. One day.'

'Great phrase you police've got there, Ernie,' I said. 'Stick at it. Might make a full sentence one day.'

And I left happily. In fact, super-happily, because in my languishment the penny had dropped in my cavernous skull. You never twin a fake, right? All that extra skilled labour is only worthwhile if the original piece in a *genuine* antique. The driver had been done for a valuable piece, not a cheap reproduction.

Now things made sense I began hurrying.

CHAPTER 3

Our ancestors liked to be thought fine, moral folk. Same as us, eh? Flesh being flesh and spirits being weak, they rarely made it. In fact they were as hopeless at sanctity as we are. Sadly, it bothered them more, but they were better at pretending. Look at lithophanes, for example, that I was currently angling after.

You've seen how light transluces through a lampshade? If you're a craftsman you can make porcelain thin enough to show translucency in exactly the same way. Lithophanes are small plaques of super-slender porcelain in which you see a picture when you hold them up to the light. However, naughtiness crept in to the Victorian designs. Not all the pictures hidden in the antique porcelain are pretty trees and hillsides. They are often lascivious ladies in mid-frolic, doing scandalous things with sexual abandon. Nowadays collectors pay through the nose for erotic lithophanes—purely for the art, you understand.

Tinker was in the White Hart soaking the day's calories

and coughing so well that people had given up trying to listen to the jukebox. It's where our local antique dealers gather and pretend to celebrate between failures.

'Wotcher, Lovejoy.' He jerked his chin. Ted the barman nodded and drew two pints. I paid. It's Tinker's principal method of claiming his salary from me. I've gone hungry before now to get him sloshed, because a barker's vital. He can winkle and cheat with abandon. Antique dealers must be circumspect.

'Wotcher, Tinker.' I forked out. I bought us a bar pasty in the euphoria of freedom. 'News of the bureau? Dutchie?'

'Nar. I got you Dobson.' He indicated with his eyes the tall lone figure at the bar's end. Even in a crowd the thin silent barker somehow stood apart.

Dobson's a sombre one-off. For a start, he's the only bloke I know in the trade who doesn't have a nickname. And he never says much, just hangs around listening, vigilant. Folk say he carries a knife and once did time. He looks fresh from an alley war. On the other hand I like Dutchie, a genial bloke with a word for the cat. He appears out of nowhere once every Preston Guild. He comes like a comet, handles the deals Dobson's lined up for him, then vanishes for a fortnight or so. But Dobson unsettles me. A few minutes later I was asking Dobson where his wally Dutchie was.

He never answers immediately, in case there's another way out. 'Gone on the ferry. Dunno where.'

Fair enough. 'See anything of a bureau, the night that wagon driver got done?'

'No. Sorry.' Nothing here for an inquisitive dealer fresh out of clink.

'Was Dutchie around that night?'

He shrugged after a long lag phase. Nothing. I rejoined Tinker, back to hungry reality. So I'd lost a fortune. I couldn't afford to lose still more by inactivity. 'The lithophanes, Tinker.'

'Them little pot flaps?' Tinker's way of describing artistic genius. 'Three-Wheel.'

'Three-Wheel Archie? Great. Come on, Tinker.'

He wailed, 'But I haven't had me dinner, Lovejoy.'

Fuming, I gave him two of my three remaining notes, which left me just enough to breathe. 'See me tonight, then. The Three Cups.' The sly old burke was cackling with glee as I left.

From the call-box outside I phoned Ellen to beg a lift. The glass was shattered so I had to stand in the rain and shout over the whistling gale. Unbelievably, she put down the receiver the instant she recognized my voice. Bloody nerve. Next week she'd prove to me, by complex female reasoning, that her refusal to speak was a precaution to help me in some way.

A call to the Infant School earned another rebuff, this time from Jo. A bad day for loyalty. A stranger gave me a lift in his car to within a mile of Archie's place, and told me all about astronomy.

Three-Wheel Archie gets his nickname from a tricycle he rides. He grew up in an orphanage somewhere near White-chapel. When I say grew up, I mean his head and features did, but the rest of him sort of lagged behind. Mind you, with most of us others it's the opposite, isn't it; relatively big over all but very little brain. Archie ended up a thickset titch who walks with a low swagger. He deals in engines, mechanicals, and watches, and lives alone down the estuary. I like him.

He was cleaning his dazzling new motor-car when I arrived. It lives grandly in a brick-built garage, cavity insulation, dehumidifier, air-conditioner, the lot. He'd run it out on polished lino. He lives in the near-derelict cottage adjoining.

'Sprung, eh, Lovejoy?' he panted, sprawled on the bonnet polishing like mad. 'No way a soft bugger like you could clobber a big Brummie to death. The Old Bill are stupid.'

'I've come about the lithophanes.' I walked round his car, admiring. 'Posher than ever. How old now?'

'Ten next September thirtieth. She's Libra.'

'Er, great. Still going okay?' It has one mile on the clock, in and out of the garage once a fortnight. Five yards a month mounts up.

'Brilliant, Lovejoy,' he said proudly, sliding chutewise down to the ground carrying his sponges. 'Glass?'

'Ta, Archie.' When I said new, I used the term loosely. Archie's one ambition from birth was owning a saloon car. He bought it a decade gone, and built for it that luxurious garage. Of course he's so dwarf he can't reach the pedals to drive the damned thing, but he loves it. He runs the engine every week, has engineers in to service it. Once, a local dealer laughed at Archie for having a new/old car he couldn't drive. Archie's never spoken to him since. Nor have I.

'Here, Lovejoy.' He gave me some homemade wine. 'Last autumn's blackberry.'

'Mmmmh.' I smacked my lips. Dreadful.

'The lithophanes'll cost you, Lovejoy.' We sat on packing cases beside the glittering vehicle.

'Archie. If you wanted an antique bureau twinned up, who'd you get to do it?'

'You, Lovejoy, on that rare occasion you're not dicking some bint. Otherwise Tipper Noone at Melford. He's done lovely stuff lately.'

'I mean a rush job.'

'So do I.' Archie drained his glass. He knew what I was asking, the crafty devil. 'Somebody said Tipper did one a few days back, for shipping to the Continent.'

I sighed. That's the trouble with East Anglia. Most is coast, inlets with busy little ships steaming to and fro. And continentals spend like lunatics when they've a mind.

'I'm the one who told Tinker, Lovejoy.'

Useless. That was as far as we'd got before a car pulled in and Jo descended. I introduced Archie to her. He rose, shook hands gravely. I knew she'd behave properly, thank God.

'Good of you to come, Jo.' I was mystified.

She stood in the mucky yard, hands plunged into the pockets of her floppy coat. Her collar was up, framing her face. Women stand with elegance, don't they, one foot slightly averted so they're all one lovely composite shape.

'Won't you sit down?' Archie offered her a crate. She sat

23

without a trace of hesitancy. I really like Miss Josephine Ross. More, she gravely accepted a glass of Archie's wine and said reflectively that it was possibly a little too dry, like her father's recipe. Archie adored her.

'Don't let me interrupt, Lovejoy,' she said, smiling. 'I only wanted to say sorry, cutting you off on the phone just because you'd been . . . seeing the police. It was mean of me.' Her colour was high. 'We shouldn't be swayed by public stigma.'

'Don't mix metaphors,' I said, to get us off ethics. 'Give me a lift and I'll forgive you.'

Me and Archie settled the deal over the lithophanes while Jo admired the car, wisely not touching it. She had quickly registered the difference between Archie's grotty residence and the opulent garage, but said nothing. Archie came to see us off. The swine wouldn't let me have the lithos on approval.

'Four wheels on your motor,' Jo said. 'Why Three-Wheel?'

'Come on, Jo.' I got in her car irritably.

'Tell her, Lovejoy.' Archie was grinning, saw I wouldn't budge, and walked over to a shed. He pulled the door open to reveal a beautiful tricycle with an elegant canopy.

'How lovely, Archie!' Jo exclaimed. 'Do you ride it?'

'Makes me mobile, Miss Ross. Courtesy of Lovejoy, five years ago now.'

She looked at me. 'Really.'

'Can we go?' I called wearily. 'Bloody time-wasters.'

Archie waved to us. By the time we left the yard he was already buffing the car's hubs. We drove a couple of miles before she said anything. 'Lovejoy?'

She wanted to prattle about Archie, but I wasn't having any. 'You only gave me the box number for that bureau, Jo,' I said. 'Is there more?'

She took a while to answer. 'Very well,' she said finally. 'Grammar apart, Lovejoy, you'll have to sing for your supper.'

It was Jo's free afternoon. She stayed and I made tea for

her. Ellen had washed up, so I had clean cups. I made some sandwiches and cut their crusts off to make natty triangles. A bit thick, but all the more nourishing. The tomatoes had gone pappy so I blotted them on newspaper first. I felt posh serving up, like the Savoy chef. I had to use a towel for a tablecloth because I can never find anything when Ellen's tidied.

'I'm impressed, Lovejoy,' Jo said, smiling.

'Ta,' I said modestly. I knew she would be. I can really lay on the elegance when I want. I'd even found the teapot lid.

She wore a beige twin set, tweed skirt, but mainly a black opal ring, Edwardian setting, heavy and gold. Beautiful.

'It was my friend I was at school with, Shona. We've kept up correspondence.' She coloured, proving rumour right: a farm manager, a passionate holiday affair, and her coming to a teaching job in East Anglia to be near his fertile acres.

Shona was a teacher in Caithness, which is almost as far north as you can go. In a recent letter Shona had mentioned selling some furniture. By pure chance, Jo said, carefully avoiding my gaze, my name entered the correspondence.

'It was soon after I'd met you at the Castle show,' she explained. Farmer Bob had been away. Jo and I had met on that local gala day—everybody goes to our Castle's flower displays. We saw quite a bit of each other for a fortnight until her favourite yokel homeward plodded his weary way.

'You told Shona I was a divvie?'

'I may have mentioned it. In passing.' She spoke off-handedly. 'Maybe. I can't remember. Shona insisted on selling through a box number. I passed it on to you. You wrote, and . . . and now that poor driver . . .'

My mind wouldn't stop nudging me, but I'd have scared her off if I'd started a serious interrogation.

'Wasn't it lucky, you meeting that woman in the fog?' Jo said, too casual. She'd reached the suspicion bit, about Ellen.

'A fluke,' I agreed.

'You deserved it, Lovejoy,' she said, smiling. 'For giving Archie that grand tricycle.'

'It isn't his fault his legs can't reach the car throttle.'

'Of course not.' Still smiling, she put her fingers to my face. We were suddenly close.

My hopes of examining the true worth of Farmer Bob's black opal engagement ring were dashed when Jo found her hand on a pair of Ellen's stockings. They'd treacherously crept out from behind a cushion. She was up and vehement in a flash.

'Lovejoy! And to think that I was about to . . . *oh!*'

'Honestly, Jo. They're my sister's . . .' Trala trala. Good night, nurse, with Jo storming out in a ferocious temper and me shouting invented explanations after her.

Women really get me down sometimes. They're so unreasonable. You'd think they'd learn sense, having nothing else to do all day. I watched her car burn off up the lane, then went in disconsolately.

The sight of her unfinished grub cheered me up and I sat down to finish it. My spirits began soaring. Where one valuable antique came from there was bound to be more, right? And if the sender was dim enough to send a pricey article thinking it a mock-up, I was in for a windfall.

Give Jo a day to come round, wheedle Shona's address off her, then hit the high road. Or the low road. I'm not proud.

Between mouthfuls I burst into song.

CHAPTER 4

Jill was at Gimbert's infamous auction rooms. This emporium of wonderment and infamy is lodged between a row of ancient cottages, a ruined priory, two pubs and a church. She was inspecting the assorted junk in her time-honoured way, which is carrying a microscopic poodle and trailing a knackered seaman. Jill's tastes are catholic, as they say. She wears furs, grotesque hats, rings, brooches, pearls, the lot.

I like her. She saw me pushing through the dross and screamed.

'Lovejoy *darling!*' She drenched my face with a kiss. Quickly I pulled away. Her embrace is a dead risk. Either the poodle gnaws your earhole or you stink like a boutique. 'How clever to escape from gaol! Meet . . . the name, lover?'

'Dave,' the young sailor said.

'Dave,' Jill repeated, trying to lock the name in. She always forgets. 'Dave's just into port, aren't you, honey?' In or out is her only criterion.

'Yes.' Dave was bemused, like all Jill's Jolly Jacks. Coastal ships docking at our town's minuscule port take turns lending Jill nautical manpower. The names change, to protect the innocents. I've never met the same one twice. Tinker says they don't dare land again.

'Hello, er, Dave,' I said heartily. 'Jill. You sometimes commission Tipper Noone?'

'Not lately, Lovejoy. 'I've been absolutely *rushed* off my feet!' Big Frank from Suffolk, silver dealer among the Regency ware, snickered at the unfortunate turn of phrase. A couple of other dealers up-ending furniture politely disguised their guffaws as coughs. 'Dobson gave him a twinner, Patrick said.'

Tinker's tale was beginning to sound true, despite Dobson's reticence.

'Ta, Jill. Tell him to bell me, eh?'

I evaded another soak, gnaw, and scenting by eeling among heavy suites of 1910 furniture to where Patrick stood. He always looks crazy to me—crocodile handbag, silken bishop sleeves and enough mascara to black your boots— but he's a hardline dealer. I was swiftly getting narked. This bloody drudgery's Tinker's job.

'Hiyer, Pat. Where's Lily?' Lily's a married woman who loves Patrick while her husband's away and sometimes when he isn't. I'd say more but it's too complicated and I'd get it wrong.

'Patrick,' he corrected. 'That stupid bitch brought the wrong cheque-book, Lovejoy! Can you *imagine*?' He swore extravagantly in falsetto. 'I made her go right home!'

'That's the spirit, Pat. Look. Where's Tipper Noone?'

'To each his own, dear heart. You won't find him in my boudoir.' He boomed—well, trilled—a gay laugh.

'Don't help, then,' I said evenly. 'See if I care.'

Other dealers sieving through the gunge on display paused at the implied threat. Even Patrick abated somewhat.

I may not be much to look at, but among antique dealers I'm special. Very few dealers know anything about antiques. In fact most are simply Oscar-minus actors highly skilled at concealing their monumental ignorance. Try one out, if you don't believe me. Offer an antique dealer a Rembrandt —he'll hum and ha and won't offer you more than eighty quid. It isn't because he's miserly. It's because he can't tell an Old Master from an oil slick, which is why you can still pick up fortunes hidden among loads of old tat.

Ignorance being endemic, it follows that antique dealers need somebody to help them, not only with reading and writing, but also with *knowing* antiques. I don't mean somebody who's simply read the right books. I mean somebody whose inner sense tells if that fifteenth-century Book Of Hours is a brilliant sequence of illumination from the unsullied monks of Lindisfarne, or a newspaper and starch. Easy? Yes, for somebody like me, who quivers and trembles when that Roman oil lamp radiates its honest ancient little soul's vibes out into the universe, or when that antique Chinese jewelled fingernail cover emanates gleams under the auctioneer's naked bulb.

The people distributed in Gimbert's showrooms had paused with alert interest because I'm the only divvie for many long leagues. I'm gormless with money and women, which is why I'm always broke, but I'm the only one of us who isn't gormless with antiques.

Patrick's venom is legendary. But if I called his antiques fakes he too would be broke. Mostly I'm honest because special gifts aren't for monkeying about with. So, wisely, he turned sulky and pulled his mauve silk lace gloves on.

'Don't be *nasty*, Lovejoy. I positively sweated *blood* arranging for Tipper to give me an estimate for mending a Chippendale fret. He didn't turn up, did he, Lily?' Patrick's admirer had just breathlessly returned proudly bearing her cheque-book.

'Tipper? Yes. Here you are, darling.'

Patrick dropped the cheque-book, demanding icily, 'Do I have to carry everything, silly bitch?'

Lily was picking it up, saying, 'Sorry, sweetheart . . .' as I left. They're both on a loser, but neither thinks so. It's hard proving people are wrong when they're doing what they want.

There on the pavement stood Antioch. He's a slim, quiet bloke. A friend, thank God. (You'll see later why I'm glad on that point.) He waits motionless, never lolls. He's the contact man for the night wagoneers. As I hesitated, he nodded hello.

'How do, Antioch,' I said, nervous. 'Look. That driver.'

'You're asking around, Lovejoy?' he said quietly.

'Aye. No luck so far.'

'You find out who did for him, don't do anything. Understand?'

'You know me, Antioch,' I said heartily. 'Scared of my own shadow.'

He looked into me. 'Just tell me who, Lovejoy.'

'Right, right.' I watched him go, my nape chilled.

Then I phoned Jo, trying to sound urgent. 'The police, Jo.' There was a background din. Some school. 'They pulled me in for questioning but I didn't let on about your involvement, love.'

'My involvement?' she said faintly.

'I'm just reassuring you, in case you were anxious. I've said nothing.' Pause, for her to say nice of me. Not a word. I'd have to be even nicer. 'And I'm sorry the jumble sale stuff made you mad. I've not had a minute to clear up since—'

'What jumble sale stuff?'

'Those women's clothes lying about. Old Kate brings them. I collect for the, er, hospital charity. Next time you come it'll be tidy. Honest.'

'Oh.' Uncertainty at last. Belief might not be far behind.

I gasped indignantly. 'Jo! You didn't think those under-clothes were . . .'

We agreed on the Tudor Halt restaurant, six o'clock. A bit posh for me, but I'd scrape the gelt together somehow. And Jo might give me a lift home afterwards, during which dot dot dot to the sound of the waves upon the shore, with any luck.

I don't blackwash people, because what's the use? All reputation is just whitewash carefully applied. So for me gossip, the sole means of communication among antique dealers, is valueless unless it's filtered by an expert.

Tinker, my only employee, is that all-time gossip-filtering expert. He was hard at work becoming paralytic in the Ship tavern when I arrived. I wheedled Sandra the barmaid into letting me slate his next few pints. She blames me for having stood her up once, and makes me earn my badges back every now and then. Women never forget what you owe. On the other hand they're great at forgetting repayments. Swings and roundabouts.

'Ta, Sand,' I said. 'Don't give him more than six.'

Tinker cackled. I leant away as his alcoholic fetor wafted past and moved him away from the bar. He was with a group of barkers boozily trading rumour. I kept my voice low. The barkers had shut up and were oh-so-casually inclining their ears at an eavesdropping angle.

'Tinker. Where the hell's Tipper Noone? Gimbert's viewing today and he's not showed.'

'Not been in the Arcade more'n a week.' He drained his glass. I sprinted for a refill.

'Listen. Here's what I think, Tinker. That bureau we had shipped down was nicked. The driver protested, and got done. They owffed it to the hangars. It changed hands a few times as usual. Then—'

'—Dutchie got Tipper Noone to twin it, shipped it out.' Tinker nodded. 'Benjie bought it, then Nacker Hardie, then Alison Verney, but nobody remembers how it first come.'

He'd done well to find all that out. 'Tipper's a home bird,' I reminded.

He said nothing, stared at his empty glass. Sprint, smile at Sandra, refill. Resume. 'Aye. Never goes anywhere, doesn't Tipper. But he's not in the Eastern Hundreds any more.' This was making me uneasy.

Tinker suddenly looked sober, a novel but alarming sight. 'It's bad news.' His rheumy old eyes were on me. 'Are we in trouble, Lovejoy?'

'Yes,' Maslow said, sitting down beside me. There was a faint stir in the taproom smog. I looked across. The mob of barkers had vanished as if by magic.

'Another false arrest, Maslow?'

He grinned from behind his pipe. The match tufted flame so bright I turned away. 'False arrest isn't trouble, Lovejoy. Trouble's the body of a man washed ashore off the estuary.'

I drew breath to ask the question but Tinker was clobbering my arm with his glass. I took the clumsy hint and rose for another refill.

'Some boating accident?' I said sympathetically, returning after telling myself to watch my big mouth. Sometimes Tinker's worth his weight in gold.

'Possibly, Lovejoy.' Distastefully Maslow watched Tinker slurp the ale. 'You know, you repel me, Dill. A dosshouse fusilier. I'm sick of the sight of tramps like you.'

Tinker said humbly, 'Yes, Mr Maslow.'

'Tinker's the best barker in the business,' I said. Maslow narks me.

'And you, Lovejoy. Pillock. You could have made something of yourself. Instead you haunt junkshops, shag your way through women's handbags. You're pathetic, you know that? You're too cuntstruck, Lovejoy.' He was really motoring now, glaring and practically yelling. 'You two burkes—'

'Get stuffed, Maslow.' I can bawl as good as him. 'You frigging peelers should be out there finding who drowned poor bloody Tipper Noone instead of . . .' I paused, aghast.

Tinker groaned, head in his hands. Maslow smiled.

'How did you know the body was Tipper Noone, Lovejoy?' he asked gently. 'Fancy a ride to the station?'

CHAPTER 5

They let me go, shaken but not stirred, about four that afternoon. I'd seen poor Tipper's horrendous mortal remains. A fishing line had entangled his legs. His head was stove in, but Maslow said the pathologists never learn anything from drowners. Tipper must have been in the water some days. His drifting dinghy was found a couple of miles out to sea. I'd been in clink at the time, a fact I mentioned every chance I got.

'You see, Lovejoy,' Maslow said staring morosely at the traffic from the police steps. 'This isn't a game, is it? And you're deep in because as soon as you're sprung from one problem you're asking after a furniture-restorer who lo and behold comes bobbing in without a boat.' He added his pipe's carcinogens to the lead-soaked traffic pollution. 'You're no killer, Lovejoy, not really. You fancy yourself, but you're brim full of cowardice, cant and crap. O' course you didn't do for Tipper. Never believed you did. Any more than I believe that Tipper accidentally drowned.'

He wouldn't let me reply, just reamed his pipe like they do. Pipe-smoking's a job.

'I'm telling you all this by way of warning, Lovejoy. Witnesses are a public's protection of innocence. Consequently they're at risk. They tend to get eliminated. Now you're tied in with the wagoneer's death and Tipper's. So stay in the company of friends, close to that Customs officer's pretty wife, or Mrs Dainty, or yon Scotch lass, or—'

'Here,' I said defensively. I didn't know he knew.

'And stay off the bypass. Stop contrabranding old wardrobes till I clear this up. Okay?'

Which is why I spent an anxious hour in the library with a gazeteer, and the next hour divvying for Francie to earn some money to feed Jo to get Shona's address to leave the district. A process of elimination was going on, and I wanted out.

Francie's rarely around, but always is, if you follow. She travels with her husband and sixty-seven others. They're a fairground, the sort with roundabouts, roll-a-pennies, sideshows and a Giant Caterpillar that whirls round and covers you over for a quick snog. They've even a Galactic Wheel and a Ghost Train. It's marvellous, lights and action and people. I like fairgrounds, always have. Francie collects antiques on the side, eroding the whole enterprise's meagre profits year after year. I used to make smiles with Francie before she went a-gipsy-roving.

The place they land is Castle Heath, a greensward where centuries ago some baddies shot some heroes to death, or the other way round. They come like night-thieving arabs, suddenly there in full swing. It's one of the most exciting scenes to see an early-morning fairground with wagons and tents and fanciful structures. I love their colours, for the same reason I love them on canal boats; they are the brilliance of an earlier century showing through modern grot.

Francie welcomed me as always as I shouted at the steps and climbed into her caravan, which is to say with hardly a glance. In her tribe it's an insult to dawdle at the door. She immediately put the kettle on.

'How do, love.' I bussed her and quickly sat down uninvited, another must. 'How's it among the oppressed nomads?'

'How is it among the static fascists, darling?'

'Bloody grim. Better for seeing thee, though.'

'So you got off.' That always makes me blink. The fair only arrived a day ago, but here she was knowing everything.

An infant came in, looking vaguely familiar, fetched a toffee out of the fridge.

'Is this good for your teeth?' I demanded, obediently unwrapping it for her.

'Ta.' The kiddie left to join six others milling about outside. Fairground children are always so businesslike.

'Yours, Francie?'

She didn't look up. 'Mmmmh. And you got off today from Tipper Noone's accident, Lovejoy. Two out of two.'

That explained the familiar feeling I'd got from looking at the little girl. Family likeness. 'Eh? Oh, aye. I'm a master of escapology.' She came and sat on the bunk seat, facing me so our eyeballs practically touched. Odd that I'd never seen her kiddie before, though I'd been to her caravan a few times. Shy, I suppose.

'Still trying to fit two days into one, Lovejoy? Still hopeless with women, with money?'

'Don't talk daft.' The kettle was whistling. She rose to see to it. Women are always narked when they find somebody who understands them better than they know themselves. And as for being useless, they should bloody well talk. 'You got much to divvie?'

'Maybe.'

These caravans are modern trailers, windows and bunks in tiers, a kitchen at one end. Francie's is small, but mirrors cunningly exaggerate the space she has. Tables fold out of walls, all that. She saw me looking.

'Fancy the life yet, Lovejoy?'

'Among the wraggle-taggle gipsies O? When the Mounties are after me, happen I will.'

She was bringing out the stuff while we spoke.

'Over there,' I told her, nodding at the table across from where I sat. A reasonable light falling semi-obliquely across my field of view. Francie knows the drill.

'Yes, love,' she said. 'I'll be quiet.'

Eyes closed, I relaxed and waited until she told me, 'Right, Lovejoy.' I faced the heap of items and began reaching, touching, stroking, listening, feeling.

It seems daft to say things actually speak, doesn't it, but they do, they do. Correction: antiques speak, and do it with a resonance that tremors through your very being. Gunge —and I do mean everything modern—is inert, lifeless. It deserves to remain so. The explanation is that you can't trick Nature. Humanity gets back exactly what it puts in. Passionate learning plus artistic creativity are what made little Tintoretto a bobby-dazzler instead of simply a paint-mixer for his dad. Look at a great oil painting, and then at the front cover of a magazine. Just as many colours, maybe the same size and even the same subject. But there's a difference.

The caravan's interior was hot. I lifted objects, peered, sniffed, fondled, laid them aside and went on to the next.

Feeling—I mean touch—is the great modern omission. People dance apart. Even old lovers merely wave hello. It was different when I was little. You got a thick ear for not remembering to kiss even your most wrinkled auntie. Folk embraced, patted, impinged. Human contact was in. Nowadays everybody intones catch-phrases proving we're hooked on togetherness, yet we run from contact. Talk loudly enough of love, and you conceal from yourself the terrible fact that you've forgotten the human act of loving. That wondrous joy of loving is everything, everything . . .

Headache. God, it was terrible. The interior was suffocating, the watery sun blinding. I felt old, drained, weary. There were three objects left on the table. The caravan's floor was littered with junk. Francie was sitting with her little girl watching me.

'You talk to yourself,' the little girl said.

'Shut your teeth and brew up.' I didn't need criticism from a neonate.

'Are those genuine, Lovejoy?' Francie asked.

'Yes.' Pulling myself together I priced them. 'This tatty watercolour's not much to look at, Francie, but it's worth a bit.' No known artist admittedly, and a crudely drawn row of Georgian shops. 'Mid-eighteenth century. He's painted the three balls on the pawnbroker's sign blue. They didn't change to brassy gold until modern times.'

The little girl said, 'Mam said you'll mend my doggie bell.'

I tried to sip the tea but it was scalding. Francie remembered, quickly rose to cool it by pouring it into a bowl.

The doggie bell was a bell-shaped silver fox's head. 'It's a cup, sweetheart. Posh people drink from them before, er, going riding.' Ritual drinks are still taken when the unspeakable pursue the inedible. These marvellously embellished cups are the best thing that ever came from fox-hunting. 'Don't let anybody stick a clapper in it, for Gawd's sake.' The AB and GB initials were probably the Burrows, a rare husband-and-wife team of silversmiths in old London. Francie would have the sense to look them up. The trouble is that nowadays people make them into 'nice' things. I've seen a silver beagle-head stirrup cup, 1780 or so, made—with great skill—into an eggtimer. Cleverdaft, my old granny used to call such folk. Leave beauty alone, I always say. Sometimes.

'Is the dolly's house yours too?' It was a white porcelain cottage, two storeys. Coloured porcelain flowers adorned it. Antique dealers the world over call them Rockingham, but you never see these little white cottages marked.

'No. Daddy found it. Mam'll sell it.'

Daddy is Dan, nice bloke if you like swarthy and tough. He does a motorbike act, Wall of Death.

'Tell Daddy to ask a lot of money, love. It's a pastille burner.' I showed her the recess which led to the cottage's hexagonal chimney. 'You put a perfume cone underneath, and the chimney smokes a lovely scent all day long. Mam will light it for you. People called them Staffordshire fumiers. This is a lovely one, 1830.'

'Is Staffordshire near Penrith, or Edinburgh?'

'Er, that way on, love.'

'We're going there.'

Those were the three. Betty and I chatted while Francie sorted the crud. A few good collectibles lay among the discards—fairly recent wooden household implements people call treen (cheap but soaring); a few Edwardian photos but none of the most highly-sought kind (military, industrial, fashion and streets); a recently made pair of miniature wainscot chairs six inches tall (very fashionable to collect these small repros).

'You did well, Francie. Got any grub?'

She made me some nosh, then walked me to the war memorial with Betty. She'd worked out ten per cent of my estimates and insisted on giving me a part of it.

'I'll post the rest, Lovejoy. Buy an overcoat.'

'Er, good idea.' It was coming on to rain. I left them there, crossing among the traffic. They stood side by side. Betty had a little yellow umbrella up. I acted the goat a bit, turning and waving umpteen times till she was laughing. It was fooling about that saved me.

The traffic had become a sullen and glistening queue like it always does in drizzle. I was moving across the traffic lights, on red, when I did another half-step back, turned to wave. It happened all in a second. The nearest car's engine boomed. Its side edged my calves and tipped me over. I heard Francie yelp. My trouser leg tore. Its tyres squealing, the bloody saloon streaked across against the red light and swung down East Hill.

'Here,' I yelled indignantly. 'See that silly sod?'

The lights changed to green. The traffic moved. Witnesses dispersed in the worsening weather. I grinned back at Francie. 'I'm all right, love,' I called cheerily. 'Lucky, eh?'

If I hadn't been fooling about to make Betty laugh I'd have been . . . Keeping up a brave smile for Francie's benefit, I made the opposite pavement and walked on before looking across the road to where Francie and Betty stood by the war memorial. I waved once, then the museum cut them off from sight. Only then did I start the shakes and lose my idiot grin. Luck's great stuff, but it's not stuff you can depend on.

CHAPTER 6

Everybody lusts, but differently. And it seems to me that lust's main function is the pursuit of what you haven't got. So nuns in their lonesome beds may not all crave similarly. Likewise, me and Jo were panting after different prey when we met at the Tudor Halt. I was super-consciously nervous about having luckily stayed alive. Tonight I'd be the perfect lady's man.

She was especially pretty, wearing a dark silk shawl

and a late Victorian Neapolitan mosaic brooch, neat and minute. Her hair was ringletty, her face oval. Her lovely eyes had dark lashes ten feet long. She glanced about, amused.

'You chose this place because of some antique, Lovejoy. I know you. And I've lost sleep achieving this Regency look.'

'It's not. Honest.'

We bickered all through supper. Lovely candlelit grub in the nooky old joint, with a beautiful woman shimmering opposite. You can't spend your time better, almost. I enjoyed her company even though I was sussing out the other diners, checking that Karl's waitresses hadn't transmuted into thinly-disguised mafiosi. Jo explained what the meal was—posh grub comes hidden under sauce—but knows me well enough to gloss over the grue. Finally I got Karl to bring me a cigar so they'd bring me one of the antique smoker's companions. Jo laughed and clapped her hands.

'I knew it, Lovejoy!'

Found out. My face was red. This restaurant has an entire dozen of these lovely creations. Tonight I'd drawn the silver figure of a frog leaning on a toadstool. Remove the frog's head and there's a spirit reservoir. Decorative holes sprout spills for lighting your cigar with a grand flourish. Antique dealers often advertise them as 'silver ornaments, incomplete', thinking they've bits missing. Wrong. Buy them even though they're little more than a century old, which isn't much. You can still talk them off a dealer for an average week's wage.

Jo and I left the nosh-house holding hands. Karl's an old Hanover man whose wry good night was as good as a body search. For six years he's refused to sell me the smokers' companions. But one day . . .

'You love those old things, Lovejoy, don't you?'

'Yes. Same reason as I love you older women.'

'Cheek.'

She came in for a coffee, and told me enough about her friend Shona. Enough for me to find her, I mean.

'You think it's worth phoning her, love?'

'It would only worry her, Lovejoy. And her bureau was probably insured . . .'

Shona McGunn, I listed mentally. Teacher. Near Dubneath, Caithness. Single. House owner, etcetera.

Jo stayed a long, long while. I was on my very best super-romantic behaviour, really gallant. As the fire died into embers and pitch night began I suffered fantasies about noises outside. Twice I got up to peer nervously into the darkness. Once, too, Jo laughed when something scratched in my thatched roof, probably a bat or some night creature. Jo's jokey question if my cottage was haunted didn't help either. I'm thankful my garden's an obstacle course of weeds and brambles.

Hiding my nervousness, I became frantically adoring and, I prayed, adorable. That night I really earned survival. I was the world's most ardent lover. I became a raconteur, the wittiest humourist, sensitive and worshipping. And, it turned out, the most wide-awake sleeper. Not a bloody wink all the dark hours from worry while Jo softly breathed. All right I'm a coward, but that car business . . . Anyway, cowards last longer, even if knackered.

'Lovejoy,' Jo whispered as the curtain gained its grey dawn rims. 'I must go. Will you see me tonight?'

'Anything you say, er, darling,' I said fervently. After all, maybe I owed her my life, having used her as a night shield against the predators. 'Er, sorry about those, er, marks.' Her arms wore bruised fingerprints.

'Silly. I'll come at nine,' she said mistily. 'We must talk seriously. About us. And Bob.'

This sounded bad news. 'Of course, love,' I said sincerely.

Cautiously I saw her off into the palish world. I waited until the milk float clattered along the lane, then, calming in the comparative safety of dawn, I fried some bread for breakfast.

That evening, ostentatiously carrying no suitcase, I caught Jacko's rickety lorry into town.

Once, I saw a famous comedian die—not meaning he got no laughs, but as in death—on the stage. The newspapers trumpeted that he'd 'gone as he would have wished'. Never.

Death is the worst option, and I was going to give it up for Lent. The police would only ballock me if I asked their help because they always do. Flight was the best policy, and where else but to pretty Shona McGunn? And the prospect of that treasure mine of antiques.

An hour of flitting from alleyway to ginnel in town, from doorway to cranny, and I left the place underneath a friendly driver's tarpaulin bucketing along the A604. He dropped me off at a Sudbury tavern where I stayed until closing time. I stole a white towel during my sojourn there, and was down on the bypass by midnight among the windblown rubbish cutting letters from the towel with a penknife. When held, a passing motorist could see the name FRANCIE quite clearly. Then, soaked to the skin, I crouched miserably in the shelter of the hedge and waited with my improvised sigh. God, I was tired.

The fairground cavalcade came through three hours after midnight. Clapped out, I creaked erect, and held up my sign against the driving rain. The seventh vehicle was Francie's. I was among friends.

'Fairs are creatures of habit,' Francie told me as she drove northward through worsening weather. Husband Dan was driving the big wagon which carried his Wall of Death sideshow. Little Betty was asleep in a specially-made bunk in Francie's vehicle. She handled it with reflex skill, towing her caravan. Unless there was a hold-up along the Great North Road somewhere, they'd be pitching in Penrith in time to catch the early-evening crowds. The fair did the same every year.

'Penrith's always worth two evenings,' she explained. 'We call pitches two-ers, fourers, sixers, according to how many days.' She'd put the heater full on to dry me out. 'I guessed you were in trouble, Lovejoy. Dan was all for seeking that saloon car that tried to run you down when I told him. He was mad at me, not taking its number.'

Not imagination, then. I cheered up. Even a murder risk becomes easier to cope with when you know it's really there.

'Look, sunshine. I can't exactly pay for the ride, but I'm good value. Any ideas how I can fund this excursion?'

She was a full minute replying. 'I'll think of a way, Lovejoy.'

I took a further minute. 'Ta, love,' I said.

That day I slogged harder than I'd ever done. Illusion's my main problem. In fact it's the one main problem for us all, because illusion does us down. It's true: blokes are narked that their bosses turn out to have feet of clay. Birds go sour realizing their lover isn't exactly the handsome film star they'd imagined. Sometimes an illusion becomes an essential part of life; I've told you about Lily loving Patrick. She pretends that his womanlike behaviour is just a passing phase. Illusion. It catches you out.

My own illusion in joining the fairground was multiple wronght. I'd assumed that a travelling fair is jolly, colourful, gay—wrong. It's a million laughs a minute—mistake. Being with Francie meant free journeying . . . Oh dear. Very wrong.

We hit the pitch mid-afternoon, a big grassy field rimmed by hedges. I was woken by Betty shaking me and saying to come and help. The fair had to be up by seven. After only a cup of tea I slogged with a gorilla called Big Chas and his mate Ern erecting broadwalks and canvases, hauling generators and winching struts and wooden walls. I fetched and carried. Francie wrapped my hands in oily cloths to keep me going. As the fairground took shape I began to peter out so they put me on netting the dodgem cars. God did great making mankind, but He was all thumbs when He came to antique dealers. I felt useless.

By seven o'clock parts of the fairground were in action. Customers were strolling among us. Lights came on as generators throbbed. The sideshows were first off, rifle stands, darts for goldfish, chestnuts, hot dogs, an eastern phantasy show with burning torches and seductively moving bellies, quoits for ringing mystery prizes, the whole gamut. Then children's carousels, opening hopefully to tinny organolium music nine-ish. Dodgems, the caterpillar, the Giant

Wheel, and the Great Cavalry Ride (wooden horses) began about eleven.

'By-laws make us close at midnight,' Big Chas rumbled when I scraped enough breath to ask if we ever packed in for slumber. He was grinning at me with poisonous good cheer, the moron. He and Ern were pestilentially happy, singing hymns while we worked. 'Quite a decent crowd, Lovejoy, eh?'

Meek with exhaustion and self-pity, I reeled obediently on, toting dat barge and liftin' dat bale among the fairground's bright pandemonium. Once Betty brought me a bowl of mushy peas when I was half way up a perilous wooden structure trying to bolt some huge planks to something else, God knows what, among a tangle of great wet ropes. The din of these music engines sounds positively melodious from a distance, but you try dangling among their pipes screwing bits together and you're deafened and blinded. That Big Chas and Ern were alongside happily warbling *Sankey's Sacred Songs and Solos* did little to ease my bitterness.

Oddly, you miss hell when it stops. I was spread on a rain-soaked canvas a million miles up in the night sky near Andromeda when silence struck so suddenly I nearly slid off from shock. Blearily I looked around. Our Zoom Star had stopped careering through its demented ellipse. Whole banks of bulbs plunged painfully into dark. Quietness returned to the land. Thank God for by-laws.

'Finish that rope and we're done, Lovejoy,' Ern called up, flashing a krypton lamp and warbling, '*Lead, kindly light, amid th'encircling gloom.*' Bloody maniac.

A few minutes later I clambered down. Betty was standing there, neat and prim under her frilly yellow umbrella. 'It's dinner-time. I came for you, Lovejoy.'

'Shouldn't you be in bed?'

She pulled my hand. I stumbled down the trampled lanes between the booths to Francie's caravan. It seemed full of steam. Dan was wolfing a Matterhorn of spaghetti, his elbows flying. Try as I might, I couldn't quite see how he managed his with that enormous moustache. We said hello.

Francie dished up for me, and a littler mound for Betty who prattled all during dinner, telling Dan and Francie how well I'd done.

'Lovejoy's trouble should soon be over, Dan,' Francie said. 'He'll sleep in the wagon.'

'What job'll you do, Lovejoy?' Dan managed between yards of spaghetti. I was narked. Had I been resting?

'I shouldn't put him selling tickets,' Betty said. 'He swears all the time.'

'Shut it, you,' I said coldly.

'Big Chas said he's not much use,' the little pest reported.

'I'm the world's greatest antique dealer,' I informed her.

'You're hiding from the bobbies. Daddy said.'

Dan thought all this was hilarious, the nut, and fell about laughing. 'Do the Wall of Death with me!' Another roll in the aisles. I quite like Dan, ever since he got me that tricycle for Three-Wheel, but you can go off people.

'Stop it all of you,' from Francie.

So, amid Death-Riders and Sky Bursters, I was relegated to collecting pennies rolled down a groove in a wooden peg.

Big Chas and Ern laughed themselves stuporose when they heard I was second string on the roll-a-penny. Dan kept guffawing as he did his bikes. Ashamed, trying to look like a gruff-voiced lumberjack, I helped with the boards on his Wall of Death.

At noon I thought, Sod it, slipped away and phoned Tinker at the White Hart, cascading coins into the greedy slot. Mercifully he'd managed to get only slightly paralytic in the first hour. His cough quivered the receiver. I held it a mile away till his voice recovered.

'Where the hell you been, Lovejoy? Everybody's asking.'

'Who?' I badly wanted to know. That was half the point of being with this wagon train to Utah or wherever.

'Helen. Margaret. That Customs bloke's bird with the big tits. Jill, the slag. Three-Wheel Archie. Liz Sandwell, wouldn't mind stuffin' her. That poofy bleeder's tart Lily.' He means Patrick. 'And yon Scotch bint, arse and legs.'

'Charmingly put, Tinker.' Very little wheat in all this chaff. 'What'd Archie want?'

'Dunno. Wouldn't say.' He waxed indignant. 'Interrupted our dominoes down the George, the burke.'

Archie dicing with death there. 'Dutchie back yet?'

'Nar. Don't like his neffie barker, that Dobson.'

'Yeh, yeh.' Tinker's likes and dislikes can get you down. I thought a minute, the delay costing another fortune in the coinbox. I heard a gust of renewed hubbub as the taproom door swung. Voices shouted hello, one falsetto. That'd be Patrick making his entrance.

'Tinker. Tell Archie I say to pass the message on. I'll ring the Spread Eagle after midnight.' I added with brutal calm, 'And get going or it's no beer money.'

That set him coughing from worry so I hung up. Leaving the phone, I had an idea. Why not look around for antiques where I was, treat it like an antiques sweep through the countryside? That at least might pay my way and rescue me from the dreaded roll-a-penny.

I walked back to the fairground whistling.

CHAPTER 7

I'm one of those whose mind is ablaze in the dawn. It fires again going on for midnight. In between, though, my intellect becomes a rubbishy zero. During the daytime I just walk among mankind for the sake of appearances. It is very necessary, because in our dark East Anglian villages they start sharpening up long oaken stakes if a neighbour seems too nocturnally inclined. This afternoon, however, I was a ball of fire.

Betty ran me an errand, three dozen large sheets of yellow paper and a box of crayons. Between customers I made strikingly inept posters. There were six arguments with folk convinced their coins had rolled to victory; I gave in and paid up, to the derision of the entire fairground. By five o'clock I'd done thirty posters. Francie took over with Betty while I literally ran about the town stapling my posters to telegraph poles and bus shelters. I got so carried away I even paid a baker's shop my last quid to put one in their window. It read:

AT THE FAIRGROUND NOW!!!
CHRISTYS AND SOTHEBIES
JOINT OFFICIAL GENUINE
ANTIQUE ROADSHOW!!!

Expert Free Appraisal of Household Objects,
Paintings, Pottery, Furniture, Jewellery, Other Items!
All Valuations Free
As Seen On TV.

Then underneath, in the neatest painting I could manage:

This Genuine Antique Roadshow is Guaranteed
By The Trade Descriptions Act
By Parliamentary Law.

By six-thirty I was breathlessly noshing Francie's fry-up in her caravan with Dan and Betty. They were curious and asking me what I was up to, which made me maddeningly evasive. Francie got quite irritated.

The posters were quite legal, in that fraudulent way Law permits. Near-skating, I'd carefully misspelled the names of the two great London auction houses. The correct name of the BBC's so-called spontaneous antiques sweep uses the plural: 'Antiques'. Copyright. Make it singular, and it becomes legal. The Trade Descriptions Act simply covers trade, and I'd do the valuations free. At least my own particular roadshow really would be spontaneous, not a put-up job like all the rest. It was basically the old saying about the Mountain and Mahomet. I'd have to move on with the fair, so I wouldn't have time to scout the area for junk. Now, the countryside would bring their junk to me.

And they did.

Funny, but that first night I was really nervous. Francie pressed my trousers and jacket, and gave me one of Dan's least gaudy shirts. A maroon silken scrap poking from my top pocket as an artistic touch. My hair got semi-straightened and painfully I scraped my nails with a borrowed emery. I was neat, an all-time first. Francie bought me some new modern sponge impregnated with shoe-polishing wax to do my shoes. I was delighted, because Cherry Blossom thought that ancient idea up long before the modern fairground was born. Nice to see old friends.

Dan found me a corner in the peas-and-spuds tent, and Big Chas and Ern erected a section of green canvas. To the sound of roaring generators and in the fug of black peas I set up my borrowed rickety trestle and switched on Francie's Anglepoise lamp. Dan's best cufflinks gleaming at my wrists, my frayed jacket cuffs inturned and my scrubbed face frowning with sincere honesty, I was ready for the world.

Dross, when it comes in a deluge, isn't really dross. It's really something else, like snow. Look at snow one way and it's a nuisance, blocking roads and flooding your socks. Look at it another, and it's brilliant crystals spun into magical mini-webs up there in the heavens. If nobody's looking I always try to catch a snowflake on my tongue, outer space's holy communion . . . Where was I?

In this tent, waiting. A whole hour.

Another hour. Eight o'clock.

And a half. I was tormented by the aroma of black peas but determined not to spoil my grand image of the London expert.

Nine-oh-five, and in she came, an old lady with the inevitable brooch. I drew breath. One thing I've learned in this mad game is that sinning with a smile somehow detoxifies the transgression enough to make people want to join in.

'Come in, love,' I said, with a smile. She was the first of the horde that came between then and the midnight closing.

For a start, they brought jars of buttons and boxes of foreign coins. Every house has a jamjar full. God knows why. They fetched christening clothes and mysteriously ornate lenses. They wheeled in complex wooden garden structures. They carried in rusting machinery too heavy to stand on my table. They brought tiny pieces of jewellery, rings, bits of pendants that made my heart weep for the loneliness of it, opera glasses, stair-rod fittings, scent bottles, glass inkwells, old umbrellas . . . Dross is snowflakes. I was in paradise. Until, that is, Francie took a hand. Women have very decided views on paradise, thinking it bad for morale. In days when I was a terrified believer, women saints never seemed up to much. They didn't deliver the goods.

'Ladies and gentlemen,' Francie announced suddenly, appearing brightly. 'Our resident antiques expert will be having his break now, for twenty minutes only. Until resumption, please avail yourself of the fairground's refreshments at reasonable prices . . .' The queue groaned.

'Wait, Francie,' I began, but she gripped my arm and said with that steel, 'This way, sir.' I was hauled out. 'My caravan,' she whispered as we left the tent for the light-starred fairground night.

'Look, Francie,' I said, peeved. 'Can't you wait? And hadn't you better check Dan's not around?'

She tutted angrily. 'Not *that*, Lovejoy.'

Abducted by a desirable bird, yet not for rape? Could this be?

There was quite a delegation in the caravan. Dan, Big Chas but for once not singing hymns, Sidoli, Calamity Sadie the black-rooted blonde from the Wild West Show, Big Jon the Eastern Slave Spectacular's eunuch with the bad teeth, and silent sexy lone Joan the Devil Rider who crewed the Ghost Train. And Sidoli's two unshaven henchmen.

I entered, smiling and pleased they'd gone to all this trouble to express their thanks for my efforts. Dan rose, jabbed furiously at me with a finger like a rail.

'What the frigging hell do you think you're frigging playing at, Lovejoy?'

My grin felt like biscuitware. This was no congratulation party. I'd been summoned before the Supreme Soviet.

'Lovejoy the crowd-puller,' I said, narked.

That made him worse. 'Explain, Francie.'

'Priced and advised on twenty-eight items,' Francie said.

'Grass,' I accused, quite pleasant.

'Sod the list, Dan,' Sidoli said. He had one of those stiletto-and-alcove accents: Sowed dee leest Dane.

'There was some very collectible stuff,' I defended, narked. 'One bird brought a near-undetectable Sisley copy. And a millefiore glass bowl, 1870. It'll fetch—'

'Fetch!' Dan barked. He was having a hard time not clouting me. He was still in his spangled waistcoat from his death ride, all hair and brawn. 'Fetch? Who for, Lovejoy?'

'For . . .' Ah. They were worried about the money. 'For the punters,' I admitted.

'Any ideas on making it pay us?' Big Chas asked, and sang a phrase, *'Each other's wants may we supply . . .'*

'Shut that row, Chas,' from Sidoli, obviously first pecker. I said, 'Is that what's bothering you?'

Sidoli's face darkened. 'Don't bait me, Lovejoy.'

Dan came between us, placating but clearly worried. I realized that to the fairground I was his and Francie's responsibility.

Francie spoke up. 'Sid. Lovejoy's quite serious. He doesn't think much to money. It's old things. Antiques.'

They all stared at me as though I'd just dropped from Saturn. Joan's eyes penetrated my anxiety. I'd never seen such grey eyes. Steady, still. Ethereal almost.

'Not care for money?' Sidoli said. 'He crazy? He's making it on the side.' Own eee say-ert, in his exotic syllables.

'Let Lovejoy talk. Please,' Francie pleaded.

'I feel on trial, Francie. What's the charge?'

Francie said, 'If some of the things you valued were so desirable, Lovejoy, say why you didn't buy them.'

There was silence. Then I said, ashamed, 'Because I'm broke, love.'

I'd gone red. Dan looked at Francie, who glared a typical female told-you-so. Sidoli drew breath for more threats, said nothing. Glances exchanged. Despairingly I decided to help.

'There was a silver Taureg ring I could have got for a

couple of quid,' I said. It's hard to suppress enthusiasm. I found myself rattling on, smiling at the memory. 'An original Waterman fountain pen, the very first sort—the bloke would have let us have it for a go on the rifles. A pair of silver-and-glass cosmetic powder cylinders, late Victorian. They come in pairs, one for powdering each glove, see? And . . .'

Sidoli raised a hand. 'Shtope, Luffyoy.' Lovejoy stopped.

In the painful silence that ensued we were all thinking, some of us thoughts quite different from the rest. Everybody shuffled, eyes avoiding mine. Except for that level pair belonging to Joan.

'How many items could you've made something on, Lovejoy?' Dan said eventually. The assembled company leaned forward.

'Sooner or later? Ten. Three if you mean at the next reasonable-sized town.' I spend my life being ashamed of myself. It's another of my unpaid full-time jobs.

Sidoli gave a low moan. Calamity Sadie uttered one grievous sob. The rest exhaled despair and gin fumes.

Francie spoke to the row of sombre faces. I swear three of them were in surgical shock. She said quietly, 'I told you he was honest, even if he is stupid. You wouldn't listen.'

'Here,' I began indignantly, but Sidoli's hand lifted to shtope me.

Big Chas had cheered up. '*So we must hymns of welcome sing In strains of holy joy.*'

'Are you sure that's right?' I asked Chas. 'Isn't it: *And we . . .*?'

Big Chas frowned. 'You sure, Lovejoy? It's the *Instantis adventum Deum*, isn't it, where—'

'Ask Ern,' I said helpfully. 'It's *Hymns Ancient and Modern.*'

'He's off his frigging head,' Sidoli screamed. 'Right! That does it! Francie, you pick a helper to put up the money and rig a punter system.'

Francie examined the faces. 'Big Chas,' she decided.

'No,' Sidoli ruled. 'Enough hymns in this fairground.' Eeen eess foyergron.

'I will,' Joan said quietly. Her first words all that session. Maybe all year.

'Right,' Sidoli said brokenly. He had his face in his hands. 'Now get him out.' Dan jerked his head, I left.

Within half an hour the new system was operating perfectly. By that is meant that the poor public were being robbed blind. Situation normal.

In case you ever take your Sheraton cabinet to one, here are the hallmarks of the Great Antique Roadshow Con Trick:

You are put into a queue and given a number ('to make sure of your place . . .'). The 'expert' values your great-grandad's Crimean War medals, and off you go. Maybe he'll even scribble the valuation on your number. As you leave, you'll be approached by somebody apparently from the public—in the queue, just arriving, just leaving—who will say that his uncle/brother/auntie/grandad just happens to collect medals. And he'll offer you about a quarter of the valuation marked on your number. 'Good heavens,' you cry, recoiling. 'Certainly not! They're worth four times that!' With great reluctance, the chap ups his offer, and finally in considerable distress offers you the sum named by the expert. You'd be a fool to refuse, right? Because the great London expert's just valued them, right? So you sell your grandad's medals and go on your way rejoicing, with the gelt.

And the passer-by takes the medals, grinning all over his crooked face. Why the grin? Because he's the so-called expert's partner. The 'expert' of course grossly undervalued your medals. To make it worth their while, the average mark-down (i.e. underestimate) must be what crooks call 'thirties'. That is, they'll never pay more than thirty per cent of the current auctionable value, not for anything. Anything higher than that is going dangerously close to a fair market price, you see.

Francie used Betty, in a little coloured stumper's booth, to give out the numbered tickets. She herself scraped the punters, as the saying is, with two youngsters hastily borrowed from the electric generators. Joan, as she'd promised, put up the money, silently fetching the bundle of notes from her caravan in a grocery basket. She gave me her transfixing stare from those opal-grey eyes, and returned to her Devil Riding. I said thank-you, nodded to Betty on her perch and we were off.

Some things ruin pride. I told myself this crookery was all in a good cause, the preservation of Lovejoy Antiques, Inc. That and safely heading north to meet Shona McGunn. But I didn't feel pleased with myself and my progress any more. Like I said not long since, everybody lusts. I only wish we knew what for.

CHAPTER 8

I'm not the only fraud in and around antiques. Look at names, for instance.

'Dresden china' is really a descriptive term. The truth is there never was a porcelain factory at Dresden. The famed Royal Saxony porcelain factory started in 1709 was a distance away, at Meissen. The patron was King Augustus the Strong, whose domain took in Poland and Saxony, which is why the so-called 'Dresden' mark is actually his AR Augustus Rex monogram. There's a further truth, too: they weren't up to much at the beginning, mostly copying styles and adopting colours from the more sophisticated Chinese. This is why the early stuff looks eastern—robes on the figures, stiff-looking mandarins and clumsy attendants. Artistically they're dud, not a patch on the later stuff. But it goes big among collectors and dealers because it's rare. The modern dementia for rarity's a pathetic revelation of how little we know. I mean, this pen's rare because I made it myself from hawthorn, not another like it in the world, but it's still not worth a bent groat. Cynics say 'Dresden china firstly copied Chinese, secondly Venetian, and after that anybody,' but it's harsh criticism because once Joachim Kändler arrived about 1730 they really took off. His figures are lively original objects you never tire of: pretty ladies in fardingales and yellow-lined cloaks, hussars, dancers.

The night we left Penrith I sat mesmerized long after the

fairground closed and the folk had all gone. I'd bought a broken porcelain figure of a Harlequin. He was seated on a white stump in his chequered costume and grinning mask. Black cap in one hand, the other to hold what had once been a jug, now broken off and lost. A junk bloke had lugged in a great wooden box of assorted porcelains and slammed it on the table.

'Fifty quid the lot, mister,' he said. 'Good and bad.'

'For a flyer, yes.'

Without looking, I'd humped the box to the floor, got Francie to pay him. My chest was clamouring like Easter Sunday. Something pure and thrillingly antique lurked down among the clag. It was the Harlequin, when I looked. Harlequins are the most vigorous of Kändler's porcelains, these and dancing ladies and waistcoated gentlemen. They were often in pairs, but one swallow does make a summer.

'The show's pulling up, Lovejoy.' Carol and Mike ran the peas-and-mash booth, a noisy homely couple with their six spherical children. Carol had an idea it might advertise her grub if the antiques expert was seen dining off her elegant edibles. 'There's a bowl and a brew-up for you.'

'Oh. Right. Ta.'

As the crews fell on the fairground and began dismantling it, I had the pasty and peas while evaluating the haul. A piteously worn slender wedding-ring with the thick broad gold band that Victorians called the Keeper Ring, to be worn distal to the wedding-ring and prevent its loss. There was an old love-letter some young woman had told me was her granny's, and that she needed money for her baby . . . Her boyfriend, a flashy nerk with gold teeth and a giant motorbike, had waited outside. I'd paid up without a second thought.

'Lovejoy.' Francie was there, with Joan. And Sidoli, and his two stalwart lads off the electric generators. They still hadn't shaved. 'Sid wants to know what the take is.'

'Take?' I said blankly. 'You mean gelt? Nowt.'

'No money?' Sidoli's lads seethed, leaned in.

'Let him tell you, Sid,' Francie said. 'I've seen Lovejoy work before.'

'What you pay for this?' Sidoli pointed to the letter.

I shrugged. 'Fiver. Can't remember.'

Sidoli paled. 'Can't even remember?'

'He's been had,' the slinkiest lad said. He held a length of metal rod. 'It was a bird, crying poverty. She was dressed to the nines. With a bike bloke in leather. Stank of booze, both of them. She told Lovejoy the tale. He paid her, not a word. They went off laughing.'

'You're a trusting sod, Mr Sidoli.' I'm not keen on sarcasm, but it has its uses. This time it stopped him signalling his two nephews to annihilate me. 'No need to read the letter. Just glance. It's in two alphabets. Called "messenger writing"— a letter within a letter. Sort of secret code. The young couple who brought it had made the story up, granny's love-letter and all that. Messenger writing of that style was popular during the Great Civil War—sieges, politics, family conflicts, elopements, heaven-knows-what. The subject will determine the price. But 1642, or I'm not me.'

'How much about?' Sidoli asked.

'Twenty quid, maybe more.'

'The percentage'll reduce the loss, Sid,' Francie encouraged.

'Sooner or later,' Sidoli moaned. 'That's what this idiot said. His very words.' His voice rose to a scream. 'The loss is *tonight*! It rains two days people stay home and don't come to the fair! And he's got a box of old pots.'

'Francie told me about your loss rate,' I said, rising and stretching. 'You can forget it this pitch.' That stilled the galaxy. 'One of those "old pots" will cover you this stop.'

'Jesus,' Sidoli gasped. 'Is true?' Eeass threw?

'Yes, Sid,' Francie said. 'Lovejoy'll be right.'

Joan spoke. 'Profit or not, it's my stake, Sid,' she announced quietly. 'I have the say. Give him a week.'

Sidoli was staring into the box with awe. 'One of these is worth . . . ? Which?'

Big Chas came and shouted, 'Hey. Nobody striking the show or are you going to stand gossiping all night?' And he sang, '*Through the night of doubt and sorrow, Onward goes the pilgrim band . . .*'

'Coming,' I said, peering out at the rain past him. I felt all in, drew breath and stepped out to join the gang, leaving Sidoli to stew in his own explanations.

We finished bottling up, as they call it, about five in the morning. I spelled Dan and Francie alternately, one hour in three off for a juddery slumber in Francie's wagon. Ern normally spelled Dan but this stop he and Big Chas were among the rear gang who would clear the generators and heavy machinery and haul on after us by eleven.

Our next pitch was near one of the Lancashire mill towns. I was relieved as we bowled in, because it meant grub and a kip before the rearguard arrived and we'd have to start erecting the fair all over again. After Francie's fry-up I went straight out and did my poster stint.

When I returned, the cauliflower sky mercifully clearing into a geographical blue, the camp was still. Everybody was kipping. I made my way over the heath to the wagon hoping my blanket hadn't got damp during the journey, when somebody called my name quietly. Joan was sitting on her caravan steps.

'Coffee, Lovejoy?'

I hesitated. 'Well, ta, but I was hoping to sleep my head.'

Joan's grey stare did not waver. 'There's room for that.' She rose and opened her door.

'Well, actually, Joan,' I began, but she'd already gone inside, so there was nothing else for it. It's churlish to refuse an offer that's kindly meant, isn't it? My old Gran used to say that. 'Well, if you're sure . . .' No answer again, so I stepped inside saying, 'Just a cup, then.'

All that month we zigzagged up the country, moving from industrial towns to moorland markets. It was a slog. One heaven-sent pitch was six whole days long, the rest only three or four. The distances were less tiring than striking and pitching, because once you're on the road that's it.

As fairs go, I learned, we were quite a respectable size. Some deal which Sidoli had pulled off meant we stuck to the eastern slice of the country except for parts of Lancashire and bits of the north. I did well and started sending stuff down to auction houses in the south. Of course I used the long-distance night hauliers in the road caffs, mentioning Antioch's name. Some items I sold locally practically the next day, sometimes in the same town. One I sold to a town museum. It was only a dented lid off an enamel needlecase, but the curators went mad when they saw it: a Louis XVI piece showing a sacrificing nymph. They immediately identified it as Degault from its *en grisaille* appearance (just think grey). It had chimed at me from inside a leather-covered snuff-box—some Victorian goon had ruined a valuable antique needlecase to make a dud. I ask you. God knows what they'd done with the case's body, but there's a fortune going begging near Preston if anybody's interested.

By the third stop, tenth day or so, the profit was trickling in. Antique dealers live in a kind of monetary para-world, always owing or being owed by others. It became nothing unusual for a dealer to wander in, ask around for me, and then shell out a bundle of notes in payment for some item a colleague had received in the south a couple of nights earlier. Often they'd take away one of my items just purchased from the never-ending queue of punters. I always took a quick sale, following the old maxim. First profit's best, so go for it.

Half way through the month the income became a stream, and Sidoli offered me a regular pitch. And more. His percentage was the standard fee from stallholders plus a tenth of the take. For this he did bookings, the pitches, argued shut-out arrangements with other fairmasters, dealt with the local councils and hotly denied liability when people blamed us for anything. Or, indeed, everything. He brought three old silent geezers in dark crumpled suits who only tippled the wine and listened, and his two menacing nephews.

We talked all one long cold night in Joan's caravan, them smoking cigars in my face and poisoning me with cheap red wine. His two nephews bent metal pipes in the background, nodding encouragingly. But I declined. I had a job on, I explained. This made everybody frown, which terrified me into useful lies.

'It's a matter of honour, you see.'

'Ah,' said Sidoli, interested. 'You kill someone, no?'

'No,' I explained. 'I've certain obligations . . .'

'Ah.' He beamed at this and to my alarm signalled for another bottle. He was desperately inquisitive but I tried to seem noble and up-tight and he went all understanding. 'But after you have shot this pig and all his brothers, and his father—assuming he had one . . . ?' The nephews chuckled, light-heartedly bent more pipes.

'After,' I promised, 'it'll be different.'

'Excellent!' He poured more wine. 'Lovejoy, I have heard of your police record. Very formidable.'

'Er, that's all lies.'

'*Certo*,' Sidoli agreed politely. 'Police. The Law. Judges. All are complete liars. Now.' He leaned forward. It was the Joseph Wright lamplit scene straight out of the Tate Gallery. 'My fair will pitch the Edinburgh Festival.'

I looked at him blankly. 'Are we allowed?' Francie'd told me the arrangement: our fair stopped short and our rival Bissolotti did the Festival.

'Ah,' Sidoli said, doing that slow shrugging chairbound wriggle Mediterranean folk manage to perfection. 'Well, yes. I did promise. But, Lovejoy, it's a question of money.'

This sounded like more bad news. 'Er, Mr Sidoli. Won't the other mob be, er, furious?'

He spread his hands in pious expiation. 'Is it my fault if Bissolotti lacks Christian charity?'

'No,' his nephews said. In the pause the three mute mourners shook their heads. We were absolved.

'Er, well, no,' I concurred obediently. 'But—'

'No buts, Lovejoy.' He patted my hand. 'I misjudged you. I thought you a man of no honesty, a man only interested in those pots. Woman's things. Now,' he smiled proudly, 'I hear you are a multiple killer, who fooled even Scotland Yard. You slew a lorry-driver. With your own hands in an ocean you drown an enemy. It is an honour to

56

have so great a murderer, when we fight Bissolotti. His people are animals.'

Some lunatic scientist once proved that headaches are actually useful. He should share mine.

'Eliminate Bissolotti,' a nephew prophesied.

'More wine, Lovejoy?' Sidoli invited. 'I say nothing about you in Joan's caravan.' He smiled fondly. 'And call me Sid.'

Cow-all meey Seed.

'Thanks, Seed,' I said. Out of the frigging frying-pan into Armageddon. Headache time.

CHAPTER 9

Better explain Sidoli's crack about Joan before going on.

Joan was the most reserved bird I've ever met. Even for a sensitive bloke like me she was a puzzle: thirty-two or so, smallish, hair permanently fading from mousey, face unremarkable in daylight and eyes that lovely grey. She'd be what other women call plain, except the first night I saw her by candle-light, and then I knew. Her beauty hit me like a physical blow.

We'd pitched that night after Joan gave me tea and a lie-down, me working with Big Chas and Ern. Joan had asked if I wanted to use one of the spare bunks in her caravan. I checked with Francie, who said it'd be fine. Betty asked if Joan would be my mummy now. Dan fell about and slapped his thighs. After the midnight dowsing I went over to Joan's caravan and knocked. She called me to come in.

For her devil-riding on the Ghost Train she wears a crash helmet with horns and a bone-and-spangle costume, bat wings and a forked tail. Sparks shoot from her head and her suit belches coloured smoke and radiates a green fluorescence. Because of this she always has her hair in a tight bun and flattened on her head. It was the only way I'd seen her.

The caravan was in darkness, except for slits of wavering

yellow light showing from behind a cross curtain. Hesitantly I called, 'Joan?' and she said to come through. Making plenty of noise in case—she might after all be shacking up with Big Chas or somebody—I coughed and pulled the curtain slowly aside. The sight caught at my breath. Her face was looking obliquely back at me from the dressing mirror. A single white candle in an old pewter candlestick, the only illumination, stood to one side. Her hair, enormously long, hung down her back to her narrow waist. It was now a lustrous brown, even russet. Her skin was smooth, her lashes long and dark. She wore an old lace nightdress —some would have said wrong by reason of its age, but not me. In the mirror's frame she was a living Gainsborough.

'Sorry about the light,' she said.

'Eh?' I thought: it spoke.

'My father was strong on the right light for make-up,' she said calmly, doing something to her face with folded tissues from a jar.

'You're beautiful,' I heard myself say, to my alarm.

Her so-grey gaze returned to the mirror for a quizzical second, then she nodded slightly. 'If the beholder says so, Lovejoy.'

That was the start of what Sidoli meant. From then on I, well, lived in Joan's caravan. Francie still scraped the queue from my Christys and Sothebies Great Official Genuine Antique Roadshow, and Joan still banked it. But henceforth Joan also banked me as well. I owned up to little Betty that, yes, Joan and me were family.

The night before we hit Edinburgh was the week working up to the Festival. The city was already bubbling, teeming with actors spilling over into street theatre. We pitched a mile or so south of the centre. All the world and his wife had turned up. Bands, orchestras, dancers, artists, poets, jugglers, the lot. You had to have your wits about you or you found yourself frantically hip-hopping among bedecked morris teams. Sidoli was beside himself with glee. 'Bissolotti is late!' he exulted, frantically exhorting us to greater speed as we threw the fair into one glittering noisy mass.

By now Sidoli's advance agent—a near-legendary figure called Romeo who got ballocked every time our cavalcade rested long enough for Sidoli to reach a telephone—had learned of my Roadshow, and was papering the towns for me two days before we hove in. This made life much easier.

Tinker did his part of the antiques scam, fixing sales, and organizing transport through Antioch. He was getting a regular screw through money drafts—essential, because he can't even remember his name when he sobers up. Get him sloshed and instantly he's the Memory Man. It was my plan to jump ship at Edinburgh, preferably before Bissolotti's 'animals' cruised in and wanted their rightful share of the Festival crowds. Also, Maslow would be very, very cross indeed if I blackened his district's reputation up here among the dour Provosts of jolly old Edinburgh. Sidoli had as good as admitted that he himself would take any blame, but from vast experience I knew only too well who'd carry the can.

So my plan was to do a moonlight as soon as I'd done one night's pitch, then head off north to net Shona McGunn. In any case, this was as far north as the fair would travel. For me it had outlived its usefulness.

I found a phone in a pub near the little green and reached Tinker contentedly imbibing his daily swill in the White Hart. He sounded mournful.

'Lovejoy? Here, where the bleedin' 'ell are you?'

'Mind your own business.' I was a bit sharp with him. The White Hart's never without a mob of dealers. All along I'd been ultra careful, not wanting neffie people following me with unkindness in their hearts. I wanted no baddies lurking to catch me when I leapt from the fairground. 'Ready? Here's the list of stuff I'm sending during the night. Most to Brum and London; a few bits and pieces to you.'

'Yeh, Lovejoy, but—'

'Shut it and listen.' Patiently I read him my list, adding which dealers to try and minimum prices to accept. 'Right?'

'No, Lovejoy.' The old burke sounded really down. 'It's Three-Wheel. Remember?'

For a second I had to rack my brains. Of course. I'd told

Tinker to phone me Archie's message. It seemed so long ago. Days, weeks even. I felt a hand close on my chest.

'They did his motor, Lovejoy.'

'Oh, Jesus.'

'Smashed it to smithereens. Windows, bodywork, set fire to the inside. Some boat geezer down the estuary saw the smoke and wirelessed the fire brigade.' Long pause, me mechanically feeding the slot coins. 'Lovejoy?'

'How's Archie?'

'Knocked down on his trike hurrying home. He wuz at the auction when they brung the news. But he's only a little bleeder. He rolled clear, scooted through the hedge. Says he saw nothing. Not bad hurt.'

'Did the Old Bill have any luck?'

He snorted. 'Them idle sods. Archie's trike's a write-off, Lovejoy. Sorry, like. Archie says now he never had any message for you at all.'

'Any chance of finding out what his news was?'

'You think I'm not trying?' He was very aggrieved. 'You're a grumpy swine, Lovejoy. I'm sweating my balls off while you're . . .'

We slang-matched abuse for another costly minute before going over the payment—part into Sidoli's numbered account, part into Joan's with my commission. I told him to pass the word to Jo somehow that I'd be trying to reach her during the early hours.

'She won't talk with you, Lovejoy,' he was warning me as I rang off. I'd had enough of people explaining why everybody else was even more narked than me. I felt it was time I began to be justifiably narked instead, and decided to work out a scheme.

My scheme was temporarily interrupted by World War III. The Bissolotti convoys arrived that night.

Joan's Ghost Train wasn't due to open until the following noon, as was usual with the bigger rides. They drank too much electricity, needed extravagant cabling up. And Joan, being nominally without a feller, so to speak, depended on the main fairground: she paid her percentage to the fairmaster and received help with striking and pitching from Sidoli's mob, hefty blokes. All except Big Chas, and Ern, his toothy walnut-faced mate, seemed to be Sidoli's nephews, and dined at Mrs Sidoli's tent.

After fixing the antiques shipments with Tinker I went to Joan's caravan. She had some stew thing frying or whatever it does. She was a good cook. Once, some days previously, I'd asked her what was worrying her. She'd smiled beatifically and said seriously, 'Would you hate lentil soup?' which made me realize you can be somebody's lover for a million years and never really know her.

'Wotcher, love,' I said, coming in. 'Sid's ordered no break tonight. We're to open at eight in the morning.'

'Big Chas and Ern will be on the Caterpillar in an hour, Lovejoy.'

'Eh? That's back to front.' We normally got the Little Giant Wheel and the generators centred first after the sideshows.

'Sid's ordered.' She placed an aromatic dish for me and sat watching as I made to dine. I waited a bit. She was alongside me, elbows on the table, grey eyes and soft skin shining in the candlelight, like the first time I'd . . .

'Here, love. Are you not having any?'

'Not yet.' She sprinkled pepper on my grub, watching me nosh. This was typical Joan, guessing condiments for you.

'And you're not in your working clothes,' I observed, mouth full. 'You seem . . .'

'Ready for bed,' she completed. She was smiling but not in a way I liked.

'What's up, chuck?' I said.

She gave that curt nod at my hands. It was a gesture I recognized and had come to love. It meant: Carry on, my reply will be along in a minute. Obediently I did, but sussing out the caravan. Joan's home. It was her place. Where the outside wheels had stopped for the night didn't matter. Inside, the candlelight, the soft furnishings, the old photos of her parents who'd started the Ghost Train, the romance books she read in quiet times . . . I stilled, waited. This feeling is one I mistrust. In antiques there are enough terrible risks without heartache.

'You're leaving tonight, Lovejoy, aren't you?'

How women do it beats me. I'd not said a word. 'Maybe, love. I've a job on.'

That abrupt nod. 'On the door mantel,' she said quietly. 'I've guessed how much you're due. Not wanting to ask Francie direct.'

There was an envelope on the shelf over the speer. 'Look, Joan, love,' I tried uncomfortably, but she shushed me with her other characteristic gesture, a tiny handshake with a blink.

'Don't, Lovejoy.' Her eyes climbed from the table to mine. 'I've no illusions. Life is a lone business, isn't it. Nobody's permanent. We're like places.'

Places? 'Will you tell Sidoli?' That'd stop my flight for certain.

'There's no way of keeping a . . . partner if he's going anyway. Even the best affair is only half a film. You get the movie up to the interval.'

I could have clouted her for making me feel bad. Women always blame me. Why should I be the one who ends up with this rotten bloody sense of being ashamed? She put her hand on mind gingerly.

'Don't feel like that, darling. It's nobody's fault.'

I pulled my hand away. 'I wasn't feeling like anything,' I said bluntly. 'Silly cow.'

She smiled properly then. Her eyes were wet. 'No, Lovejoy. Of course not.' She rose, took my hand, pulled me to the curtained alcove.

'Look, love,' I said weakly. 'There won't be time . . . '

She slipped a breast into my hand, then slowly raised her arms to shed her gown. 'Yes there is, Lovejoy,' she said quietly. 'It's tomorrow there won't be time.'

Past one o'clock on a cold frosty morning, fed, loved, and enriched in material ways, I left Joan's caravan and started work with Big Chas and Ern hauling the cables for the generators.

'You're late, Lovejoy,' Ern said, grinning. We worked by paraffin lamps until the electric's set. 'I worried you'd miss the scrap.'

'Scrap?' I ragged up my hands, took hold of the cable.

Big Chas sang piously astride the generator, *'Mighty are your enemies, Hard the battle ye must fight.'*

Over the other side of the green strange wagons were pulling in. Even the vehicles looked sullen, hateful, as their engines revved and their headlights swathed us.

'Bissolotti?' I croaked nervously, thinking: Hell fire. The new convoy was forming a crescent. The green was on a slope, and we were below them. Even as I paused to look, another set of headlights rummaged the darkness to our right. 'Hell, there's a lot of them.'

'Big mob, Bissolotti's,' Chas agreed cheerfully. 'What weapons do you usually use in a rumble, Lovejoy?'

My legs, mainly, I thought shakily. Or a Jaguar. I'm not proud.

'I heard he's a gun man,' Ern said.

Those lunatics were actually pleased at the notion of an all-out battle with Bissolotti's. I felt sick. This wasn't my scene. A peaceful fairground, yes. But a military column tearing to a private El Alamein, a thousand times no. Soon I'd go for say a pee, and vanish.

For about an hour we worked on. Every few minutes I sussed out the growing arc of lights about the green. Bissolotti's wagons began to pitch. We were only a hundred yards apart.

'They're pitching,' I said apprehensively to Ern.

'Aye, Lovejoy,' he called laconically.

'Will we share the pitch?' I was hopeful.

Big Chas roared with laughter from somewhere under the Caterpillar's railed wheels. 'Lovejoy's worried there'll be no rumble,' the idiot bellowed.

'Don't worry, Lovejoy,' Ern said consolingly and carolled, *'Ye that are men now serve him, Against unnumbered foes . . .'* Big Chas joined in the hymn. I worked on, sane in a world of lunatics.

They hadn't finished that particular hymn when negotiations began between the two fairmasters. Bissolotti with ten blokes met Sidoli near where we worked. Our fairmaster also had ten nephews. They stood in two cagey crescents, the bosses talking vehemently for quite a time before our lot returned, chatting animatedly.

'Ready, Lovejoy?' Sidoli called. Ray-dee, Luff-yoyee? He'd caught a glimpse of me on the Caterpillar bolting the hub's canopy roof. 'You get your wish!'

'Great,' I called back. That one wobbly word took three swallows.

'Come on, then,' Big Chas said. '*Fight the good fight.*'

Men were gathering into small groups from our wagons. The pitch was falling silent as the hammering and clattering ceased. Our people were talking. Groups formed. Tactics were being discussed. It was eerily happy, and here was I frightened out of my skin. Madness. Sidoli was among a cluster of paraffin lanterns lecturing strategy. Heads nodded. Some maniac was dishing out steel rods. I thought: For God's *sake*.

'Just finish this, Chas.'

'Won't let a scrap interrupt work, eh?'

He and Ern left to join the nearest group, laughing and shaking their heads. 'He's a cool bugger,' Ern said admiringly.

'Good night, lads,' I muttered. I checked the scene once more, then slid off the wood on the dark side, nearest the enemy camp. 'And good luck with the war.'

Across the damp grass the Bissolotti mob's lanterns were wavering as their men assembled. Behind, our own lamps showed where clusters of blokes were being positioned. I crouched indecisively near a pile of wooden façades from the Caterpillar. What were the rules for a rumble? From what little I'd learned, fairs were pretty orderly along time-honoured lines. Maybe they were as set in their ways when it came to all-out warfare. Apprehensively I darted a few yards towards the Bissolotti vehicles, then hesitated. Surely the thing was to avoid both gangs, never mind the wagons? Our own pitch was a circular lay-out on the green's down slope. Ahead and above stood the Bissolotti crescent, all flickering lamps and din. A wall, terraced houses and some sort of iron railing formed the perimeter where streets began. There were three exits for vehicles, but for an enterprising slum-trained coward spiked railings were hardly an obstacle.

Suddenly the lights in the Bissolotti camp vanished.

In ours, there arose a subdued murmur, then somebody called a nervous order and the glims dowsed here and there until Sidoli's pitch was black. I heard Sidoli yell. A hubble of voices responded, one panicky shout stilled by a threat. We'd been caught napping. Only a sort of air-pallor from the nearby street let you see a damned thing. I went clammy, cursing myself for not having escaped sooner. If it hadn't been for Joan's loving farewell I'd be miles away by now. Bloody women. No wonder I'm always in a mess.

Somebody shouted, 'Fan out, lads,' and somebody else shouted, 'No. Two lots. Over there . . .' Then a third, 'Bunch up. Get in line . . .' So much for Sidoli's confidence. His men were a shambles. I began to move instinctively to my right. I'd once been in a real army and recognized only too well the authentic hallmarks of disorder. Time Lovejoy was gone.

I froze in mid-slink. Nearby there was a steady touch of movement. The night air somehow pressed on my face. A hoary old sergeant—a survivor—once told me, 'Never effing mind what you frigging see,' he'd said. 'Survivors *feel*.' So I felt, lay down with my head towards the Bissolotti camp, and stayed still.

A line of men crept past and over me. One boot squelched an inch from my hand. I swear it. The guilty thought came that a true friend would behave like a Roman goose and cackle the alarm. Not me. As soon as the silent line of assaulters had passed I rose and moved tangentially right. No more than forty slunk paces and I came against a giant wagon. I felt my way along its flank. My heart was throbbing. I'd not breathed for a week.

The wagon's side seemed to go on forever and I cursed Sidoli for a lying swine. He'd represented Bissolotti's as a small vulgar outfit. If they could afford massive new transformer-generators like this supersize it was no cardboard cut-out job. And the chug of new Bissolotti arrivals in the next street showed that enemy reinforcements were at hand.

Smoke. Cigarette smoke. And nearby. Somebody was probably cupping the fag into his palm the way convicts and soldiers do. I'd nearly eeled into them in my fright. I edged beneath the enormous generator wagon and crawled out under the other side. Even then I nearly brained myself by standing up. My shoulder caught on the cab's open door.

'How much longer?' a man's voice muttered.

'Five minutes. Then we shout the rest up.'

Hell fire, I thought. There must have been thirty or so in that assault line. Plus those vehicles I'd heard nearby. Sidoli's fair—not to mention me—was caught between two aggressive mobs. A classic pincer movement. I almost moaned in terror. As soon as the rumble started Bissolotti's would switch on every light they possessed. I'd be spotlighted like a prisoner against a wall. That explained the Bissolotti tactic, of lining his wagons facing down the slope towards our pitch.

This wasn't for me. I lay down and wriggled under the vehicle's vast bulk. The next wagon was smaller, probably a slab carrier, to transport the wooden façades. I heard two more men muttering by the tailboards, found the driver's cab of the slabber, and lifted myself up. Somebody said, 'What's that?' as I slipped the gear lever into neutral and the handbrake off. I dropped and crept behind my transformer wagon's quadrupled rear wheels and wormed towards the front. The slab lorry creaked. Its bulk drifted past.

'Christ. It's moving.' Somebody ran past, grunting with exertion as he tried to swing into the cab. A man shouted for a torch. Two men cursed. 'Over here! Over here!'

I was up and into the transformer's cabin. A flashlight jumped the gloom. The slab lorry was trundling slowly down the slope, three blokes clinging to its sides and one man already in the cab struggling with the wheel.

Headlights sprang. The green showed brilliantly. I

snicked my wagon's gear and the handbrake, then saw there were no bloody keys. As my vast wagon began to glide down the slope I fumbled desperately with the dashboard, failed to find the wires, crouched and fiddled. The sodding vehicle went faster. I fiddled faster. Somebody yelled. Boots clashed on the door. I dived, clobbered a bloke's face and he fell off. Something clanged on the truck. Glass shattered. Men were yelling, running, throwing. I finally shorted the wires with my teeth as the giant vehicle juddered and careered down the slope. The engine boomed. I struggled up, cast the headlights and gave an appalled moan.

It was like a battlefield. The slab carrier had caught some of Bissolotti's assault men on the green. Two lay strewn. A third was pinned against the Caterpillar's gearing where the lorry's front had nuzzled itself to rest. Blokes were tearing about here, there, everywhere. I gunned the engine. Two strange faces appeared, one on the windscreen, I yelled at him in terror, drove crazily to shake him off. They vanished. I jolted round the field, slammed back through the Bissolotti convoy and glimpsed a street lamp in the distance.

Putting the big wagon at the narrow street took courage, or terror. I remember bawling in panic as the wagon thundered through and out into a brightly peaceful main road. A line of waiting fairground lorries to my right, so swing left to traffic lights, green so on through, to anywhere. Behind was death in that ludicrous war zone.

It's hard suddenly pretending everything is normal, but I did my best, stuck up in that tall cab and trying to look like I knew what I was driving, where I was going. It was an interminable cruise in a puzzled Edinburgh, until I found a road that finally promised north by following the arrows. I was forty miles away before I stopped shaking.

Telling myself I'd done it, I relaxed and let the road decide what happened next, meekly following the headlights to my fate.

Quiet old life, antiques.

CHAPTER 10

Before I invented sex, when the world was flat and weather constant, I had all sorts of ideas. Cycling round the entire country in a record-breaking week; going for gold in mountaineering; discovering uncharted continents; rescuing damosels. A lad does a lot of this daft imagining, never grows out of his dreams. Girls do, but don't ever realize that the male is often miles away in his silly head being anointed king of a lost tribe in the Andes or whatnot. Women never learn to see blokes as we actually are, namely incurable dream-spinning romantics, because early in what passes for development women trade perception for appearances. The bird learns that her bloke could only go for Olympic Gold in flower-arranging. She starts assuming he's only what he seems—a portly geezer wheezing when tying his shoe. The point I'm making is that people aren't merely things. Never mind what politicians say. You can gaze at stones and tarmac, rivers and fence-posts, with complete dispassion if you want. They're no big deal. But you have to *think* when you look at people. You have to. If you don't, you become a robot.

One of my old dreams was knowing every town in the Kingdom, so that if some stranger mentioned a tiny village in, say, the Shetlands, I would casually say, 'Ah, yes. Population eighty-one. Stands on the tributary of . . .' I failed geography at school. Dubneath was therefore a mystery.

The big transformer wagon's petrol ran dangerously low in Clackmannon, though when I got out and inspected its container drums they showed half full. Perhaps you had to switch to reserve? Anyhow I decided to ditch it, before daylight revealed me in all my glory as the non-secret thief of the known world's largest fairground transformer-generator. I entered Fife, and drove across Kinross in a stealthy manner in the least inconspicuous of vehicles, with gaudy on its side. I started admiring myself. After all, it takes skill to nick a thing this big.

Ten miles outside Perth my brain had another mega-rhythm. Mentally shelving a niggling reminder that my previous brainwave had nearly got me killed in a night riot, I knew I'd now got a winner. Find a reasonably-sized transport caff, park my giant wagon, and get a lift into Perth where trains and buses lived, and zoom to find the enigmatic Shona McGunn. No road map in my nicked wagon, of course. Typical.

By dawn I was noshing among the hunched leather shoulders of the night hauliers in a caff near Perth, rather sad at thoughts of leaving my monster.

A walk of three miles along the road when the lorry convoy had departed, and I became a poor motorist whose car had broken down. A kindly motorist gave me a lift to the Perth turn-off, and I got a bus into that lovely city just as the shops opened.

Pausing only to sell a Hudson's Bay Co. folding rusty penknife pistol that I'd kept back from Francie—flat horn sides, percussion, two blades—for a giveaway price which still rankles (these 1860–70 collectibles go for twice the average weekly wage nowadays), I phoned the police, anonymously reporting that a Sidoli wagon was ditched in the night caff. Then I got on the train and dozed. I'd got a cold pasty and some rotten crumbly cake I couldn't control. They fetch tea down the corridor just as you're on your last legs, so I eventually made it, though weakening fast.

Painful thoughts of Three-Wheel came to me while I nodded on the journey. And Joan's grey eyes and long-term philosophy—maybe she was the one bird whose perception had made it? And Jo. And Tinker would be bewildered, with a score of deals waving uncompleted in the breeze. And poor dead Tipper Noone under the coroner's hammer. And yon driver, poor bloke. Naturally, a twinge of fear came with the haze. I'd started the journey north towards Caithness with a whole fairground full of tough allies, and ended it with two fairs bulging with enemies: Sidoli's for leaving them in the lurch, and Bissolotti's for, er, borrowing their vehicle.

Not much of a social record, you might say. But I felt that all in all I was entitled to pride. So far I'd reached Sutherland. I was in one piece, and being alive is always a plus. I had money in my pocket, and was heading for a mine of antiques, those precious wonderments whose very existence is proof of something more than the brute Man. And good old Shona knew where they were.

•

The last part of the journey was by bus. Our little local trains have been abolished in the interest of greater efficiency, so now nobody can get anywhere except by public yak. Dubneath's version of the yak was a bus carrying smiley basket-toting women and distant-eyed men. Before we bowled into minuscule Dubneath I'd revealed all, grilled by the clever interrogation of a pally little rotund lady. I confided that I was a visiting writer. Not going anywhere in particular, just travelling. And I might look up some possible ancestors . . . Oh, my own name, yes. That's what I wrote my poetry under. What name would that be? 'Oh, sorry, love,' I said absently. 'McGunn's the name. Ian McGunn.' Cunning, no?

It was the last bus that day. I was put down in Dubneath. The sea was there in the late evening. It earned a word of praise from me, which pleased my companion, though the little town was poorly lit and somnolent. Bonny place in full day, I supposed. My plump pal was going on to Lybster further up the coast, but she said there was an inn in Dubneath. 'Where,' she added darkly, 'folk drink.' We both agreed, tut-tut, sin gets everywhere these days. She'd told me that McGunn was not an uncommon name hereabouts. I said fancy that, and waved the bus off into the night.

The tavern, replete with drinkers, instantly recognized me as a fellow sinner and agreed to put me up. I'd bought a cheap cardboardy case in Perth, plus a skimp of clean clothes, so I could portray respectability. I was so thrilled at myself I offered to pay in advance. A huge meal, and I tottered exhausted to bed in a long narrow room.

Came daylight, I saw that it was Sunday. In that part of the world they go big on the Sabbath. Nothing happens. By that I mean nil. Even the bloody seagulls didn't seem to fly, except a couple of backsliders that revelled unrepentantly in the clear air squawking their silly heads off. I walked down the quay, examined the sea. Yep, still there, all the way out to the skyline. Back to the tavern, two streets from the edge of the known world.

The surrounding countryside was uncomfortably close. As long as it stayed loomingly over there and didn't ride into town to take over I'd be happy. The shops were closed. The harbour boats looked at prayer. A few people emerged blinking into daylight, hurried away bowed as if under curfew.

I walked down the quay, Dubneath's vortex. Two old geezers were there, eyeing the sky. A lone kid fished off a wall. I bade the blokes good morning; they said good morning. A riot. I sat on the harbour wall. Got off after a minute, and walked the streets of the metropolis.

And back.

About eleven a saloon car of baffled tourists—French registration—whined miserably through. It was all happening today in Dubneath.

High noon, and a man strode out with a spyglass, notebook, knees showing above elasticated socks. God, I was overjoyed to see him. We spoke. He was disappointed that I wasn't a bird watcher. I was disappointed that he was. We parted, him off into the countryside, smiling in happy anticipation. You get these nutters in East Anglia too.

The tavern creaked awake. By that I mean they served up at dinner-time, after which Dubneath plunged back into the twilight zone. Of interest: a few badges glass-framed in the taproom, wartime memories now worth enough to redecorate the downstairs rooms; a brass racehorse doorstep of Crowley & Co, Manchester, about 1860—go for these if you're wanting cheap Victoriana with class—and by the bar mirrors a trio of little matchstrikers. Go for these too: many pubs have them left over from times when every smoker used unboxed matches. You can get them for a song because pubs hardly change, and people have forgotten what they're for. The most desirable are German porcelain figurines by Conte and Boehme. A good one, with a humorous inscription, will keep you in luxury for a week. Three should pay for a modest Continental holiday.

'You know about those?' I couldn't help explaining their value to the taverner, a husky bloke called George Mac-Neish.

'Is that a fact,' he said.

'They're highly sought-after, you see.'

'Aye, but I like the wee things.'

My heart warmed to him. I'm always pleased to hear this. I offered him a drink, but no. The Sabbath.

A few hours later as I was strolling somewhere, or back, merely waiting for the world to reopen, George called me from the inn steps.

'There's a body to meet you, Ian.' He waved towards the quay. I felt pleased. A kindness shown, a kindness sown. Swiftly remembering that I was temporarily Ian McGunn, I waved thanks and went down the stone harbour front. A youngish bloke was sitting on the wall. His pipe was unlit. The Sabbath again, I supposed knowingly.

'How do.' I stood a second. 'I'm Ian McGunn.'

'Hello,' he said, smiling. 'Jamie Innes.'

'Not angling,' I observed, glad.

'Not on Sunday.' He grinned, blue eyes from a tanned young leather face. 'You?'

'No. Fish never did me any harm.'

'Hunter? Deer? Nature-watcher?' He ran down a list of lethality, earning a constant headshake.

'Ah, well. Poetry. One slim volume, a few here and there in obscure journals.' How obscure only I knew.

'I'm not a very educated man,' he confessed. 'But at least I can tell Shona I met you first.'

Shona? 'Shona?' I said as blankly as I'm able.

'We're engaged. She's a McGunn. She'll be pleased to meet you, seeing you've possible relatives here.' He rose and invited me to accompany him by tilting his head. 'You were saying on the bus. Old May Grimmond from Lybster's a cousin to Mrs Ross who keeps the shop, who's related to George MacNeish at the inn, who . . .'

Until that moment I'd assumed that the Highlands were a large underpopulated expanse of differing counties. Illusions again. Now I could see a strain of blood ties ran strongly round somnolent old Dubneath. What worried me was that here I suddenly was, Ian McGunn, urgently needing an entire clan's genealogy, addresses and photographs.

We walked a few hundred yards before Jamie stopped outside a terraced cottage and pushed open a wooden gate. The cottage door was pulled, and a melodious voice said, 'Welcome, Ian McGunn! You'll stay for tea.'

'Shona,' Jamie introduced. 'That beast's Ranter.' A dog the size of a horse stared at me with less than ecstasy.

'Er, hello,' I said. The impression was swirling blue, gold, yellow, and a smile. The bird, not the dog. 'I, er, trust I'm not inconveniencing . . .'

'Come in, man. Us here waiting and you so long to call I've to send Jamie Innes combing the town seeking you out wandering all the county before setting foot in the house . . .'

Gasp. 'Erm, thanks, er, Shona . . .' I honestly believe that a woman meeting a man only takes him in piece by piece—eyes, height, age, smile, face. But a man's different. We take in the complete woman at one swallow. That's why particular points—remembering the colour of her eyes, for instance—aren't really important to a man. It's also why women get very narked, because they assume we use their scoring system. I couldn't keep my eyes off Shona, and struggled to keep from being too obvious. She was lovely.

The cottage was prepared for action. Linen tablecloth, plates just so. The most formal tea-table you ever did see, while Shona swung her long bright hair and spun herself fetching the teapot and piles of sandwiches. She told Ranter to wait outside. It left calmly, giving me a warning glance.

'And what's this about you in a common lodging like that MacNeish's tavern no more than a pub and you not even bothering to knock on a door—' etcetera.

'Give the man a chance, Shona,' Jamie pleaded.

'Aye, well, if he's come through the south he'll only be used to them Edinburgh folk . . .'

Jamie winked. 'We blame Edinburgh for giving us all a bad reputation. There's a joke. Edinburgh folk tell callers: Welcome—you'll have *had* your tea!'

'What did that MacNeish give you for your dinner, Ian?' Shona demanded from the kitchen.

And we were off into womanchat. By sheer skill I managed to keep off my relatives for the whole visit. Shona was lovely in that spectacular way some woman are. Jamie Innes obviously worshipped her, laughing appreciatively at her stories of the schoolchildren even though I'm sure he must have heard them all before.

Getting on for six Shona rose to shoo Jamie away and summoned me to walk her out.

'Time for chapel,' she commanded. 'The Innes clan being famous heathens, Jamie doesn't go so you'll walk me down, Ian.'

'Er, if you wish.'

'And while we do,' she said, bright with anticipation, 'I'll exchange tales of the McGunns with you.'

'Shouldn't I go with Jamie . . . ?' I tried desperately.

Jamie said, 'But I'm outnumbered, Ian. You McGunns use unfair tactics.'

We parted at the gate. Jamie turning up the road leaving me and Shona to start towards the chapel by the waterfront. She slipped her hand through my arm. There was a low rumble behind us, Ranter stalking. Its eyes were almost on a level with mine. A stair-carpet of a tongue.

'Take no notice of the beast, Ian,' she said happily. 'Now we can have a really good gossip.'

'Gossip?' That was it. My heart sank. I invented desperately. 'Well, er, I think my grandad came from Stirling . . .'

'Not that, silly.' She was laughing prettily at me. 'What I really want to know is, are you and Jo lovers, Lovejoy?'

CHAPTER 11

That stopped me. She was rolling in the aisles laughing.

'Your face!'

Women really nark me. 'You're sly.'

'Oh, whist, man! I guessed when I heard you'd been telling George MacNeish about his old things. And you couldn't take your eyes off my old father's mulls.'

These are peculiarly Scottish containers for snuff, made of horns, silver, sometimes bone or stone. It's easy to pay too much for these, because usually they've bits missing. The complete ones have a decorative chain holding tiny tools—a mallet, scoop, prong—also of silver, and of course it's these that have casually been nicked or lost. Mulls come in two sorts, the larger table mull with castors for use after posh dinners, or the personal mull. Antique dealers invent wrong names, being too thick to learn the right ones, and call the portable sort a 'baby' mull, it being small. I'd never even seen a matching pair of snuff mulls before. But Shona had such on her mantelpiece, lovely horn and silver shapes with all the accoutrements. I'd only given clandestine glances, but should have remembered that women can always recognize a drool.

She was enjoying herself. 'Handed down. Family.'

'From about 1800,' I said with a moan of craving.

She fell about. 'Well you can't have them,' she said at last, recovering. 'Jo said you're a terror for old things.'

'Jo said I was coming?'

'Yes. She's been ringing every couple of days.' Shona grimaced at me. 'That's why I suspect you and she of . . .'

'None of your nosey business.'

She hugged herself as they do. 'I like you, Lovejoy. Secretly, I'm glad you won't tell.'

'Only women gossip about lovers.'

She thought a bit before beginning an argument about

diarists. I was too impatient to listen. 'Where did you get the bureau from?'

'The one Jo said got lost? Oh, a place I know.'

'A place with antiques?' I asked evenly. I'm not devious like other people. I honestly say exactly what I mean practically always.

She gave me a look, women being of a suspicious nature. 'Very well,' she said at last, some decision made. 'You'll come up to Tachnadray with me tomorrow.'

Tachnadray? I said great, never having heard the name. For the sake of propriety off she went to kirk and I went to read Untracht's monograph on jewellery. Each to his own religion.

That evening I had a demure supper ritual in the hotel lounge served by Mrs MacNeish. It was like a barn. Dead fish and stag heads on wall-plaques and sepia photographs of ancient shooting parties proudly dangling dead birds. I'd have to send somebody up here to buy these exhibits on a commission job. Someone else. I'm not a queasy bloke; I just can't rejoice in extinction. Mary MacNeish laid up for major surgery. I'd never seen so much crockery and cutlery in my life. I told her cheerfully, 'Just met Shona.'

'Aye, I heard,' Mrs MacNeish said.

We bantered a bit while I tried to keep my knees together and hold off the slab cake till the starting gun. Politeness is a killer. Also, something wasn't quite right. In the woman's prattle a discordant note was sounding. You can always tell. The publican's wife was open-faced and friendly, but she was having her work cut out to stay so when Shona was mentioned. Yet Shona was pally and really something to see. I wondered if it was me, and like a fool put it out of my mind.

During the gluttony I had the sense not to mention Tachnadray, and eventually returned to reading Untracht's methods of inlaying silver strips in English boxwood bracelet carving.

Maybe for once I should have thought deeply instead.

Next day I consulted the Register of Electors. They're those cobwebbed, yellowing, string-hung pages of local names in every village post-office-cum-stores. Pretending idleness—nothing new—I found that Tachnadray listed umpteen McGunns, plus one ectopic: plain James Wheeler. Yet even here somebody had inked in the McGunn surname, coverting him to clan. Odd, that. Amending electoral rolls is illegal, even if you changed your name lawfully. I checked its date: printed twenty years previously, and that ink had faded. I wondered if Lovejoy McGunn sounded better than Ian, then decided to let ill alone.

Shona brought Jamie's van about ten o'clock. She drove as fitted her personality, with good-humoured extravagance, and asked if MacNeish's pub was comfortable.

'Grand parlour,' I said. 'Are those places only used for funerals? It felt like the dust covers were just off.'

Shona laughed. 'In the Highlands the best room's always kept for occasions, Lovejoy.'

'Tachnadray got one too?'

She sobered swiftly. 'How much do you know, Lovejoy?' We turned uphill inland.

'This Tachnadray's where the antique came from?'

'Yes.' She faced me defiantly. Odd. Defiance is for enemies. 'I arranged it.'

'But down in East Anglia we'd been told to expect a reproduction.' I cleared my throat, not wanting to seem a crook. 'You see, if a genuine antique had showed up we, er, might have only paid you for a repro.'

'And claimed that a reproduction had been delivered.' Shona nodded, getting the point quicker than I really wanted. 'And then, Lovejoy?'

'Then?' I said blankly. 'Well, I'd have flogged your genuine antique.'

She was so patient. 'And *then*, Lovejoy?'

'I'd have come here to . . .' I slowed, nodding.

'. . . To find who was stupid enough to sell off expensive antiques thinking them reproductions.' She gave me a satisfied smile. 'You've found her. It's me. It was bait, Lovejoy.'

Expensive bait. 'But why?' We'd gone half a mile and already the houses had vanished. We were on an upland moor and still climbing, the van labouring and coughing.

'Because I need a divvie. Jo had mentioned you. I'd heard of one in Carlisle, but it's so difficult to trust anyone in antiques, isn't it?'

'Sometimes, love,' I agreed piously. 'Why didn't you tell Jo to ask me up without all this?'

'It hadn't to be me that procured you, Lovejoy. You had to wander in on your own. You pretending to be a McGunn simply made it easier for me.'

Therefore she wanted ignorance, which meant I'd have to get a move on to suss her game out. Antiques were at stake. If I allowed her to distract me they'd slip through my fingers. It happens to me every time when women are around. 'I'm part of your plot?'

'A plot for survival. We McGunns are a lost tribe, Lovejoy.'

'Here. I thought you'd given up pretending—'

'Be quiet and listen!' she blazed it out fiercely.

For a few minutes she drove, winding us away from the coast into bleak countryside. Rocks, gullies, a little rivulet or two, heather and a few trees having a desperate time. There was even a big-bellied bird noshing some heather. Funny life for a pigeon, I thought, though whatever turns pigeons on in Caithness . . . Shona cooled enough for her sermon.

'You picked an august name, Lovejoy. We McGunns are Picts, inhabitants here long before the rest of these . . . people came.' She meant anybody else was a serf. 'Yet now we're dispossessed. The Highland clearances of two centuries gone, the clan rivalries, everything in history has been against us.'

The sky was grey, cloudy. A distant grey house glided along the horizon. Wuthering Heights. A small lorry drove past us towards Dubneath. Shona beeped her horn in reflex salutation. A few sheep watched us, hoping for a lift to civilization. I hid a yawn. Nice place if you were an elk.

'We were driven to the coastal villages,' she continued. 'People who've heard of Armenians, the Jews and Tasmanians would think you mad if you classed us with the likes of them.' She shot me a hard glance, waggling the wheel the way women do for nothing. 'Wouldn't they?'

I thought a bit. For all I knew she might be a nut. 'Well, yes,' I said. 'But it's life. Families come and go. Names peter out, get revived.'

'In 1821 we tried,' she said bitterly. 'The Clan McGunn formed a society—like those Gordons and Grants.' She spoke with hate. 'But our last clan chief died and we were finished.'

'And you'll reunite the clan and march on Rome.'

'No,' she said, choking down an impulse to chuck me through the windscreen. 'But the loyals among us must share some feeling of . . . pride.'

Odd word, I thought, I'll bet that sentence was surprised when it ended like that. 'By giving away what genuine antiques you've got left? Slinging them on the first lorry heading south?'

'You'll see, Lovejoy.'

For a while she drove us angrily on into ever bleaker countryside without speaking. Just as I was wondering if she'd brought any nosh she screeched us to a jolting stop above a chiselled glen. There was a muddy-looking lake off to the right, seemingly on a tilt. Can lakes actually slope like that? Trees, clearly unwelcome tourists, clustered around a large gable-and-turret building of grey stone. Ranked windows and disguised chimneys, a long drive with drystone walling, and a bare flagpole. It could have been uninhabited except that the main door stood open and somebody was standing waiting in shadow at the top of the steps. I thought it was a woman. A man with a wheelbarrow near outhouses stood peering up the hillside at our van.

'Tachnadray, Lovejoy. Isn't it beautiful?'

'The architect read *Jane Eyre*.'

'During your visit, Lovejoy,' Shona said after a moment with careful coolth, 'you'll refrain from sly digs. Understood?'

'Not really, love,' I said, opening the van door and sliding down to stretch my legs. It was time me and Cousin Shona got a few things straight before hitting the old homestead.

'I've gone to a lot of bother to get here. Right now I could be out of your hair, and home in peace. I sympathize with your diaspora, but we Lovejoys never had a posh dynasty.'

'So?'

'Explain why you're Pretty Miss Welcome down in Dubneath, and Boadicea as soon as we see that phoney Victorian castle. And,' I said on as she drew furious breath, 'why you think you have the right to ballock me as soon as we're out of Jamie's earshot.'

She said quietly, 'So it's money you want.'

'Or antiques. Or both.'

'Very well, Lovejoy. You'll be paid.' Pause. 'Enough.'

A minute's reflection, and I nodded. We rolled as I got in. She nearly took my toes off with the wheel. Our relationship was deteriorating fast.

'The . . . owner of Tachnadray agreed with my idea of having copies of the antiques made and selling them. We have two men doing it.' She turned us between two tall stone gateposts bearing carved coats-of-arms. 'I believe we —Tachnadray—are being defrauded.'

Such disloyalty, I thought, but didn't say. 'And I'm to prove your suspicions?'

'Much, much more, Lovejoy.' She'd recovered her smile. However daft her dreams, she really seemed to come alive again in Tachnadray. She'd recovered all her sparkling good humour as soon as we made the glen. 'You're to prove who's doing it.'

'Here, love,' I said uneasily. 'You're not wanting anybody buried at midnight in the crypt, are you? Because hunting's not my game—'

'Here we are, Lovejoy,' she said gaily, stopping the van below the steps. 'Tachnadray.'

The woman waiting in the shadows of the main door stepped forward into view. She walked with grave composure to the top step and stood to welcome us. I got out and went forward. For half a step I was a bit uncertain. After that there was no question. Between the two women the air had thickened with utter hatred. It's not fair that hunters last longest, or that prey wear out fastest. Somebody should change the rules. Quickly I stepped to one side, put on my most sincere smile and went bravely up the steps. This new woman couldn't give me a bigger pack of lies than Shona.

CHAPTER 12

Caithness is one of those places you think of as perfect, full of plain wisdom, isn't it. The simple life: dawn porridge, down to the trickling burn to brew up the day's malt whisky or whatever, then highland reels all evening. Idyllic. Instead, here I was ascending these wide steps, grinning hopefully at the elegant older woman smiling down at me, with a lovely bird like Shona smiling away at my side, and me wishing I was in battledress being fired at. It had felt safer.

''Morning,' I said pleasantly. 'I'm . . .' Who the hell was I?

'Ian McGunn, Michelle,' Shona introduced in her lovely brogue. 'We stopped to admire the klett.'

'Isn't it a lovely view, Ian? Welcome to Tachnadray.'

Klett? 'Thanks. Yes. Lovely, er, klett.'

'Do come in.'

'Ian's the one I spoke about, Michelle.' Shona walked ahead with her, ever so pally. Neither tried to stab the other, with visible restraint. 'A furniture craftsman. He trained at the London College.'

'Oh.' Michelle placed her dark eyes on me. 'You're going to be marvellously useful, Ian.'

French? Belgian? Her accent matched her dark hair, wavy and lusciously thick. She seemed about fifty. She wore that Continental dressiness which our women only manage on Derby Day. I blame those rotten hats the Royal Family keep wearing.

'Eh?' Somebody'd mentioned antiques.

'Duncan will show you later on. I'll arrange it.' Michelle

rotated those deep eyes. 'But we'll expect excellent output, Ian. We can't afford passengers.'

Shona drew breath. Evidently multo double meanings were hidden therein for somebody not me. Between the two women I felt as nervous as a Christmas nut.

The house was a giant of a place, with those lovely Victorian wooden panels nobody does properly any more, and even the glass bowls chained over each hanging ceiling light. They've become a fantastic source of profit—nowadays builders clearing old housing estates let you have them, five for a quid. They're collectors' items. Tip: look in 'redevelopments' (as our psychopathic town planners now term vandalism). I once got a small cast-iron staircase, circular, with the Darby Ironworks stamp on and everything, thrown in because I took sixty glass light bowls off a builder's hands while he battered a priceless 1695 building to smithereens in East Anglia for a car park. I'd dined in superb elegance for six months on the profit . . .

'Ian McGunn, darling,' Michelle announced, showing me into the tallest sitting-room on earth.

The girl paused a second—surely not for effect?—and spun her wheelchair. I honestly gasped. She was the loveliest creature I'd ever seen. About sixteen. Limpid eyes, pale skin with that translucency you instinctively want to chew. She was so slight in her lace blouse. A tartan blanket covered her legs. Pearl earrings, a beautiful black velvet choker with a central silver locket, probably late Victorian, and hair pale as her face. She honestly did seem lit from within.

'Come in, Ian McGunn,' she said. 'I'm Elaine.'

'Elaine's—' Shona started, but the girl silenced her with an abrupt gesture and propelled herself forward.

'Don't listen to Shona's old clan nonsense,' she instructed. 'Somebody get us coffee, to convince this refugee from East Anglia that we're civilized in the north. I'll show him the house.'

Lame people always disconcert me. I never know what to do—help? push the handles? let them get on with it? It's a problem. Not only that, but here was the boss all right. I began to long for this Duncan to crash the party.

'Don't worry, Ian,' Elaine said, spotting the difficulty. 'Trail somewhere I can get a good look at you.' She smiled mischievously. 'This leg thing is permanent, I'm afraid, but I manage most things. It's only temporary disableds need assistance.'

'Ta.'

'You're English,' she said, like giving absolution. I followed her from the room, heading down a panelled corridor. 'And you bought some of our reproductions?' The furniture we were passing was all reproduction. I listened to my chest, hoping for a dong of antique sincerity, but no. Not a genuine antique in sight, though some of the work was really quite skilled.

'Er, one. Through a friend.'

Michelle had disappeared. Shona was walking by Elaine. She caught my eye and nodded. I was doing all right so far. Unhappily I met Elaine's delectable eyes in a hanging mirror. She was smiling, a naughty girl enjoying interplay. I sighed. Even peaceful women are trouble enough. Bravely I followed on down the longest corridor in the world.

Once, I went into an Eastern Bloc capital city. It was in the dark hours. The opera house was perfection, all brilliance and glamour. At half time, I strolled out to clear my brain of all that recitative, and realized with a shock that the lovely old street was a giant façade. Literally, the house fronts were shored-up replicas with only rubble behind. Since then I've never believed in appearances. The same sense of shock overcame me as Elaine turned to me and asked, 'Well, Ian?' We'd finished the penny tour.

'Er, yes. Lovely house,' I said lamely. Apart from two ante-rooms and the sitting-room the entire place was bare. Not merely relatively bare, note, but completely empty. Some bygone gas-mantle fittings remained, but with new-fangled electricity points hung on. And it was only in the main hall and reception place that the great old house kept up the pretence of past grandeur with any conviction. Uneasily I got the point. An unexpected visitor could be welcomed, even entertained, and be sent on his way praising the manor house's majesty, without realizing he'd been deceived. No living face behind the death mask. I felt sick. All this way, all that fairground shambles, and not a sniff of antiques. What little furniture the house possessed was simply heavy Victorian.

Barren. A wilderness where I'd expected a harvest. She'd told me that upstairs the west wing still housed a considerable store of valuable antiques. 'That's why it's closed off,' she'd said. Odd, really, because I'd not felt a single chime. And upstairs was clearly one place she couldn't get to, not on her own in a wheelchair. How neat.

We returned to find Duncan waiting. I was glad. Elaine introduced us pleasantly enough. 'Duncan, meet Ian. No prizes for guessing surnames.' She looked at me while saying this, that mischief smile again.

'Wotcher, Duncan.'

'Welcome, Ian.' He was a chunky, elderly bloke, his compact form slow but full of that sedate dynamism the born worker possesses. I realized that he must be the man who produced the reproductions. So who was Michelle? Elaine chipped in.

'You'll be wondering who Michelle is, Ian.' She emitted that beautiful smile and said, 'Michelle is Mrs Duncan McGunn. And our voice of sanity.'

'Then there's two of us,' I said companionably.

'Indeed? A cup of welcome, and we'll let you start work. Duncan needs all the help he can get.' She lit Duncan with a glance. 'You've guessed right, man. Ian no has the Gaelic.'

The way she spoke the words made it a skit. Duncan managed a wry grin, though the beautiful lass's mockery obviously stung.

'I'll give the man a wee dram, then. It's our own malt.' He meant whisky.

'Er, ta, Duncan, but coffee'll do.'

That halted the gaiety, except that Elaine fell about. In fact she laughed so much that tears rolled down her cheeks and she had to be helped to a hankie. Mentioning coffee had never seemed hilarious to me before, but each to his own giggle. I waited patiently for the girl to recover. Michelle was taking all this in her stride, Elaine merely a mischievous child. It was Shona whose cheeks showed bright red spots of suppressed fury. Our hostess was getting to her, and delighting in her success.

'Er, what's the joke, love?' I asked to clear the air.

'A Scot, Ian! One of the clan. One of us. Preferring coffee to our own malt! Isn't that an absolute scream, Shona?'

'Well, no,' I said to save Shona. There were clues here if only I could spot them. 'I'm not big on spirits.'

'Sure you'll not prefer tea?' Elaine gasped.

'Please,' I said politely. 'If it's no bother.'

Another winner. During the ensuing paroxysms Michelle gave Duncan the bent eye for us to withdraw to let the three of them get on with it.

Duncan's genteel exit line was, 'I'll show Ian the workshop. We'll be a minute or two.' I followed, really quite happy.

We walked out by the front steps towards the outbuildings near where the red-haired man with the wheelbarrow had stood peering. Nobody else about now, though.

'What was so funny, Duncan?'

For a little he said nothing. We passed between two silent stone buildings, leaving left the carefully tended forecourt.

'Well y'see, Ian,' he said finally, 'it pleases Miss Elaine to needle Shona about Scottishness.'

'And everybody else about their own particular fancy, eh?'

'Maybe,' he said drily. 'Yon's my wee factory.' We paused outside a low stone barn, slate roof tethered by large flat slabs against winter storms.

'Is that what Elaine needles you about?' I asked.

'O' course.' His honesty was disarming. I began to like Duncan McGunn. 'And my Michelle about being Belgian.'

'The question is why,' I prompted.

'Not so, Ian.' He did things to a padlock to let us in. 'The question is what will Miss Elaine find irks you, isn't it?' I didn't think much to what he said. I wish now I had, honest to God.

The place's interior was a hundred feet by forty, give or take, and daylit from a couple of long slender windows running much of the length. Its scent was exquisite to a born faker—oils, varnishes, sawn woods, glues, sweat. Duncan's current opus stood on a low metal bench.

'Sheraton copy,' I said. I could tell I was grinning from the sound in my voice. 'Where'd you get it?'

Cagey silence. I didn't blame him. No trader gives his sources away. It was a battered Victorian chest of drawers imitating Sheraton. Three big drawers below two 'half' drawers, with slightly curved short legs. Some nerk had given each drawer wooden bulb handles. The Bramah locks were a giveaway because that locksmithing genius wasn't around in 1786, the pretended age of this poor relic. I walked around it, pleased to be back in the real world.

'You'll reduce it, of course?'

He filled a pipe slowly. 'How?'

'It looks pretty well made.' I pulled a drawer and inverted it to check the wear and patination of age. Some wicked modern fakers add these small convincing details. It's terrible to buy a piece like this, only to find once you've got it home that it's phoney. We have a saying in this rottenest game, that you can never make anything good from a bad fake. But this was some skilled Victorian carpenter's forged 'Sheraton'. It had once glowed, been really quite stylish.

'Any ideas?' Duncan asked.

All right. He'd a right to expect proof I knew what I was on about. 'Only one,' I said, and tapped its top. 'Lose the two smaller drawers. Settle for the bottom three. They'll need cutting down in size, of course. Replace the handles with brass reproductions. Leave the Bramah locks; when you advertise it admit quite openly that they're later additions.'

'Aye, but if a buyer looks at the base he'll see where the curved front's been cut through the middle.'

'Then don't sell it to a sceptic, Duncan.' I'd given him the best recipe and he knew it.

'Fancy your chances?' he said. A challenge.

'Yes.' We got chatting then about some good 'reproductions', as I politely termed them, which I'd seen fetched through East Anglia. It turned out that he'd forged a

Hepplewhite pot-cupboard I'd bought and sold on to Dort-mund (think of a box with tall straight unadorned tapering legs).

'So you made that torchère I bought last autumn?'

'Aye.'

'God. Was it worth it? It must have cost the earth.'

He sighed, nodding. 'It did, Ian. Days and days of work. But it convinced reluctant buyers that somebody up here could do the job as well as most.'

'Well done.' I love a craftsman. The tall torchère had had a tripod appearance—three elegant mahogany legs, with three slender central supports up to an everting triple for the six-sided tray, that would hold the household's oil lamp. Some antiques are too expensive to fake commercially. The decorative torchère is one, because there are plenty of cheap pole screens about—genuine antiques, too—which fakers can buy to make them out of. 'Pity you killed a Queen Anne pole screen to build it, though.'

'How'd you spot that?'

I checked myself in time. 'Oh, the mulling top and bottom ran different ways, I think.'

'Did they now,' he said evenly, faithless sod.

'Mmmh.' Quite honestly I couldn't remember. It had been the sad little bleat of the genuine mauled antique that had brought tears to my eyes.

'One thing, Duncan. I thought clans had lairds. Isn't a chieftainess unusual?'

'The Laird James passed away a few years since.'

Aha. I'd save that bit up. Had plain James Wheeler become The McGunn? Maybe he married into the position. Well, it happens in business empires. Why not?

A bell clonked on the wall. I was glad to see it was an original spring-suspended clapperbell and not some shrill electric foolishness.

'Time to join the ladies,' he said, making for the door. He added scathingly, 'For tea.'

'I've nowt against your whisky, Duncan.' I went with him.

I felt three goals down.

*

Before Shona drove me back to Dubneath for my things, we settled my job amicably. This means I listened to Elaine and agreed with whatever she said. My terms were a fraction of the profit and all found—free nosh and bed in a stableman's loft among the outbuildings. They showed me a bare cube with a single bed, a cupboard, and one uncurtained window with a view of the barren fells. Great if you're Heathcliff waiting for Cathy, but I played along. Duncan was there too, ruefully swigging what he conveyed was his first and last non-alcoholic drink.

'We're assuming Ian proves capable, Miss Elaine,' he put in gently. That caffeine was getting to his brain.

'*Are* you capable, Ian?' Elaine asked innocently, looking across at Shona, a tease. Shona turned aside, busied herself with the sugar for Duncan.

'Your bills for plastic wood will take a turn for the better, Elaine,' I said. Duncan had the grace to laugh at the jibe. Plastic wood's the poor forger's friend.

They came out to see us off, talking casually. I turned to admire the house's clinging splendour, and saw the big ginger-headed bloke among the outbuildings. He was kilted, strong and stridey. Just as long as he was on our side.

'I can trust Robert,' Elaine said to answer my thought.

'Thank God for that.' I climbed into the van. 'Back before evening, then?'

'Ian.' Michelle came to my window as Shona hung back saying so-long to Elaine. Duncan was aleady off, anxious to be at work. His wife spoke softly, perfume wafting in. 'I'm so relieved you're here. It's time all was ... resolved.' Her fingers, probably accidentally, rested on mine. But the pressure and that faint scratch of her nails down my hand was communication. I swallowed, too near her large eyes to think straight. What was she saying?

'Oh, er, ta. I'll do what I can.'

'We'll make sure you *exceed* your potential, Ian,' Elaine called. She rippled her fingers in a child's wave. She must have hearing like a bat.

Shona marched up, flung in and revved noisily. She hadn't liked seeing Michelle speaking to me in confidence. She reversed at speed with a crash of gears, but Michelle anticipated the manœuvre and glided away in time.

We made Dubneath at a record run with Shona not speaking a word. Disembarking, I was jubilant at how things had gone. I was in. My thin disguise was holding. I was blood cousin umpteen times removed to this barmy load of clannites. Very soon I'd have the lion's share of a sound antique fakery scheme, at least. Stupidly overconfident, I decided to buy some curtain material before phoning Tinker.

Now the bad news, as they say.

CHAPTER 13

The best about little towns is that most things are crammed into a few shops. I found the drapery/general/household stores by spotting the only building in Dubneath with more than two parked cars. Women are the trouble, though. They immediately sensed I was curtain-hunting and started eyeing the swatches. The stores lady, Mrs Innes, hung about itching to decide for me.

'A pastel,' I hazarded, playing it close.

'You'll be Ian McGunn,' she said, smiling. 'That converted loft's a draughty old place.'

So much for secrecy. How the hell did they do it? 'You shouldn't know that. Naughty girl.'

She laughed, colouring. 'I meant, Joseph was always complaining. No wonder the poor man drank.'

'Joseph?'

Instantly she changed tack. 'And that pokey little window. You'll only get one pattern if you choose a large floral.'

'Boss me about and I'll go elsewhere.'

'You can't. The Wick bus left an hour gone.'

Her brass measuring rod was screwed to the counter. She fell about when I offered her eight quid for it and laughingly told other customers how I'd started to buy her out. I settled on a bright oriental print, bamboos and japonicas, and ballocked Mis Innco for not knowing the window's dimensions. We parted friends. I crossed to the tavern.

Joseph? Who had been my predecessor at Tachnadray. Something had driven the 'poor man' to drink. Not the draught, that's for sure. I didn't like the sound of all this.

I told Mary MacNeish I'd be leaving. By purest coincidence she already happened to have me booked out.

'You guessed,' I said drily. If they introduce gossip at the next Olympics we're a cert. Dubneath'll get the Gold.

'Eat your fill before you go, Ian.' It was the mildest of mild cautions, a very natural expression. So why the Mayday hint? 'Tachnadray's bonnie but can chill a man's marrow.'

'I'll be slinking back for your pasties, Mary.'

'I'll be pleased.'

On the spur of the moment I tried a flyer. 'Don't suppose it'll be easy taking good old Joseph's place. Is he around? Like a word with him.'

She was shocked that I knew, and the cake-stand just made it to the table. Her face suddenly went abstract, as women's do for concealment. 'Now what did I do with that butterdish . . . ?' she said vaguely, and that was as far as I got.

Margaret finally landed Tinker for me in Fat Bert's nooky shop in the Arcade. I'd wasted a fortune trying different pubs. Absurdly, I was really pleased to hear his long rasp.

'Where the bleedin' hell you got to, Lovejoy?' he gravelled out, wheezing. ''Ere, mate. We in trouble?'

'Shut it, Tinker.' Maybe he was only three-quarters sloshed, I thought hopefully. I hate to chuck money away on incoherence. 'You sober?'

''And on me 'eart, Lovejoy. Not a drop all bleedin' day.'

'Listen. That driver who got topped. His name Joseph Something?'

'Dunno, Lovejoy.'

'Find out from Antioch. I'll ring tomorrow. Any news?'

'Nar, Lovejoy. That bleeder's still round the Hook.' He meant Dutchie hadn't returned on the Hook of Holland ferryboat. 'But there's some Eyties hangin' round.'

'Italians?' My soul dampened.

'Aye. Millie's youngster Terry reckons they wuz circus rousters or summert. Two big buggers. They come soon after that tart.' Millie's a barmaid. Terry runs pub messages, bets for the two-thirty at Epsom and that. Terry'd know, if anybody would.

'Tinker.' I'd not had a headache all day. 'Which tart?'

'The one you used to shag down Friday Wood before—'

'Tinker.'

'—before that little blondie you had went for that shoe-shop manageress you fancied in the White Hart—'

That's what I need, I thought bitterly, hearing Fat Bert roaring laughing in the background while Margaret lectured the stupid pair of them. Friends. 'Clear them out, Tinker.'

Mutter, mutter. 'They've pissed orf, Lovejoy.' Tinker's drunken idea of subtlety. 'You remember her, lovely arse—'

'What did she want?' I'd already identified Francie.

'She come in hell of a hurry, after midnight. Said nothing, only asked where you'd got to. Her nipper told me it'd been in bed on a train.'

All children are 'it' to Tinker. Betty Blabbermouth, my erstwhile helper at the Great Antique Road Show. Francie must have hoofed into East Anglia on a night express, and reached Tinker a few millisecs before Sidoli's killer squad came a-hunting. I swallowed. In spite of Joan, Francie still felt something for me and had rushed to warn.

Well, I didn't have to be Sherlock Holmes to reason that various folk were cross, simply because I'd injured a few blokes, damaged a wagon or two, shambled a fairground's livelihood and nicked their vastly expensive generator. And now they wanted repayment in notes of the realm, my blood or other equivalent currency. I quavered, cleared my throat.

'Sure there was no message?'

'Only she'd be at the Edinburgh Tattoo.' A long pause. 'It's north of Selkirk,' he added helpfully.

Francie's way of saying steer clear of Edinburgh until that vast military Tattoo closed the Festival? Well, I was already in Edinburgh's black books, and there must be enough guns in two fairgrounds to make a jury think that one accidental shooting of a no-good scruff like me was a permissible average ... No. Francie's message was a very, very useful hint indeed.

'News from Jo?'

'That teacher bint? She visits Three-Wheel Archie.'

A glass clinked, Tinker finding Fat Bert's reserve bottle.

'And, Lovejoy. There's money from your sweep. We made a killin'. Margaret says as she'll send your slice to a post office if you'll say where the bleedin' 'ell you—'

Click and burr. I didn't want anybody knowing my address after that lot. Escape's like murder, a private business. I stood indecisively, then walked out of the tavern into Dubneath's cool watery day for a deep ponder. Life's got so many risks, you're lucky to get out of this world alive. Wherever I looked, enemies lurked. Back home in East Anglia fairground heavies dangled ominously in the trees. The long roads between Caithness and my village were filled with irritated night drivers whose colleague had got done in. I strolled down Dubneath's empty wharf to examine the vacant harbour.

Hell is people, somebody once said. He forgot to add that so's Heaven. The more I thought about it, the safer Tachnadray's claustrophobic solitude seemed.

Two hours I walked about the somnolent town. For ten minutes I stood with Dubneath's one layabout and watched the traffic lights change, really heady excitement. A tiny school loosed about four o'clock, pretty children much tidier than East Anglia's, with twisty curling accents. I thought longingly of Jo, a lump in my throat. And of Joan. And Francie. And Ellen. And, a startling pang, little Betty. I felt deprived of all life. Maybe it wouldn't be too long.

Dubneath was static. Not even a shrimp-boat a-coming. The wind was rising, wetting my eyes. I tried the obstinate child's trick of staring into the breeze until your eyelids give up of their own accord. Of course, I'd have to lie low. That much was plain. I didn't relish this on-the-run bit, even though it's the only rational course for a coward. It tends to throw you willynilly into weird folks' company. Like that lot up in Tachnadray.

Six o'clock I went for my last meal—no blindfold or cigarette—at the MacNeish pub.

Providentially, the television was on in the snug, a pleasant girl giving out the news. I caught the last of it: '. . . the theft of a vehicle from an Edinburgh fairground. Six men are in hospital, two of them critical. A police spokesman today deplored the increasing violence . . .'

The surface of my beer trembled. The glass rim chattered on my teeth and I saw George MacNeish glance slowly along the bar from where he was wiping up. I tried to make my momentary quake resemble thirst.

'Nice drop, George.'

'. . . search moved north. The vehicle was found abandoned but undamaged at a roadside halt frequented by long-distance . . .' She read it so chirpily, holiday camp bingo. I went to do the best I could with Mary's calories.

Seven o'clock Jamie brought his van. Shona, he said, was tired. I left the tavern clutching my curtain material, a hermit to the wilderness. It could always make bandages.

'Can we stop at the, er, klett, Jamie?' I said as we trundled inland. 'Lovely view.'

'You're keen on our bonnie countryside?' Jamie waxed enthusiastic, changing gears. 'There's grand scenery beyond that wee loch . . .'

Ten points on the creep chart, Lovejoy. The trouble was I'd painted myself into a corner. Crooks in East Anglia trying to do me in. Maslow would put two and two together when the Police Report stimulated his aggressive mini-brain, and hasten into Edinburgh to help his neffie brother peelers. All the travelling folk on the bloody island were out. And here I was at the very tip. Hardly possible to run any further. That's the trouble with being innocent. You get hunted by cops *and* robbers. Even the worst crooks on earth only get chased by one lot. No wonder people turn to crime.

CHAPTER 14

Houses are fascinating, aren't they? The house at Tachna-dray was superbly positioned for light, setting and appearance. Grudgingly, during the first few days of labour on Duncan's Sheraton lookalike, I came to admire the place. Catch it any angle and you get an eyeful. The old architect might have had delusions of grandeur, but he'd got it exactly right. Pretty as a picture, was Tachnadray. It brings a lump to my throat just to remember how it all was, in my serene encounter with the clan-and-county set. The surrounding moorland somehow seemed arranged for the purpose of setting off the great mansion's style. Hardly 'antique' in the truest sense of the word, pre-1836, but lovely all the same. The creation of an artist.

Very quickly I learned that routines were almost Teutonic in Tachnadray. The first afternoon I wandered across the grand forecourt to chuck some crumbs into the stone fountain. Goldfish sailed in its depths. I'm always sorry for fish because they have a hard life, no entertainment or anything and scared of every shadow. I'd saved a bit of russell roll and was busy shredding it into the water livening up their wet world when my own dry world was suddenly inverted. I do mean this. It honestly spun a hundred and eighty degrees and I was crumbing the atmosphere.

'What the fuck you doin'?' a cavern rumbled in my ear. Giant hands had clutched my shoulder and spine and tipped me upside down.

'Feeding the fish,' I yelped. 'Please.'

'Who the fuck said you could?' the cavern boomed.

'Down, Robert.' Elaine to my rescue. Wheels crunched gravel. '*Down!*' Like you say to a dog. Then something in a language I didn't understand, slidey smooth.

The world clouted my left knee. He'd simply dropped me.

Groggily I clambered upright. My trouser leg was ripped.

The big kilted man stood skywards over me. Another McGunn, I supposed wearily, making yet more instantaneous assumptions about good old Cousin Ian. He marched off on his great hairy legs. A knife hilt protruded from his stocking.

'You came just in time, love.' I was wheezing. 'I'd have put him in hospital.'

She laughed, applauding. Robert turned his maned head, but kept going.

'Don't mind Robert, Ian. He's big for the cause.' She wrinkled her face at the scudding clouds. 'Rain soon. The anglers'll be out as far as Yarrow Water.'

A distant clanking tapped the air, Duncan calling work on the iron rod which hung by the workshop door.

'My free hour's up, Elaine,' I said, but hesitated before sprinting back to the treadmill.

'Another time, Ian,' she said. 'Not on your first day. Turn me round, please.'

'Chieftainesses of distinguished clans shouldn't have to ask.'

She glared up at me. 'Oh yes we should!'

Some women have a terrifying knack of seeming to move their faces suddenly nearer you without stirring a muscle. They do it in love or in fury. I've noticed that. Elaine was the best at it I'd ever encountered. The images of physical love and the poor paralysed girl juxtaposed in my mind.

'Penny for your thoughts, Ian,' Elaine said slyly as I obediently set off along the drive to Duncan's workshop.

'Just how fascinating people's faces are,' I lied. 'I'm good at faces.'

'Women's especially?'

'Mind your own business.'

She was back to laughing then, swaying in her wheelchair. It was one of those oddish moments when the environment conspires. She was there beside the fountain. The sky behind her had darkened. Thunder rumbled. Yet a watery sun picked up the grey-yellow gravel, her white blouse, the colours of the old tartan. Lovely enough to mesmerize. Lucky I'm not easy to manipulate, or a girl this lovely could have me eating out of her hand. A terrible desire rose within me. My body's a hostage to hormones, but with a lass who couldn't walk—

'Actually,' she said, as we parted, 'we cripples have different ways of making . . . music, Lovejoy.' Another super-correct guess what I'd really been thinking about.

She left me so preoccupied that I hardly noticed Duncan playing hell with me for skiving instead of getting the bureau's drawers undone. Elaine was disturbing. Weirdly swift to guess what you were thinking—far too swift for my liking. Only supposition of course. I don't believe in telepathy or whatever it's called. But I didn't like this idea of not being alone in my own head.

Duncan put me at the old piece. He watched me like a hawk as I tapped and listened and set about marking the wood components. I'd got some self-adhesive labels from the Innes stores in Dubneath.

'A waste of money, Ian,' Duncan disapproved.

'Oh?' I cracked back sardonically. 'So you're the daft faker who pencils his illegal intentions all over the finished product, eh?'

He surrendered with a chuckle and lit his pipe to watch. He'd had to concede. Simplest tip on earth: when you're thinking of buying antique furniture take a glance at its inner surfaces. There you might see measurements indicating the faker's reduction factor—inches cut off, even types of wood to be used.

'One goon I know in Newcastle even writes it on in felt-tip,' I told Duncan. 'I ask you.'

'You know a lot, for a wandering cousin.'

Caught. 'Ah,' I stammered. 'We had to learn all that. At the London College.'

'Very thorough. Have you a family, Ian?'

'No. Except now you lot. My erstwhile spouse found my transparent honesty too much to cope with.'

Duncan helped me to up-end the bureau. The base was in a better state than I'd hoped.

'You should use Newcastle, Duncan,' I panted, struggling

to tilt it on a block support. 'Handy for Liverpool, without being too direct.'

'Aye, we tried . . .' He ahemed and reamed his pipe. I'd caught him, but absently worked on. *Aye, we tried and failed,* is what he'd been about to say. He'd discovered, like many antiques fakers, that there are folk pathways in dirty deals. New dirt's distrusted. Old schemes have a kind of inbuilt security. That's why a woman chooses a particular colour, fancies a special perfume: it swept Cecil off his feet, so why not Paul? It's the reason crooks stick to a particular *modus operandi* even when they know it hallmarks their particular chain of robberies. And a painter faking Cotman's genius, like Big Frank's mate Johnnie does in Suffolk, would rather polish off a dozen *Greta Bridge* phonies and sell them to that same fence in Hamburg than paint different ones every time.

Clue: Tachnadray's fakes had only one outlet, and that was through my own stamping-ground, East Anglia. Which meant also I could easily find out how much Duncan's replicas had made lately. I whistled, irritably searching for tools on the bench.

'No wonder you got rid of Joseph,' I grumbled. 'Messy sod. I'll rearrange this lot when I've a minute.'

Duncan stilled. 'Joseph?'

Unconcerned, I began rearranging the tools into some sort of order. 'I knew a bloke once was so bloody untidy that—'

'As long as you do better than he did, Lovejoy.' Duncan went down to the other end of the workshop to mix varnish. An unpleasant reprimand, that, with its hint of threat.

Come to think of it, where *was* this Joseph? I decided I'd better find out. Tactfully as ever, of course. That's my way.

It was three days before I had a chance of talking to Elaine without being up-ended by Robert the Brute. Which doesn't mean they had passed uneventfully. Duncan and me'd argued non-stop about our next opus. I favoured faking a series of small Georgian tables from scratch; Duncan stuck out for modifying—'putting back' in the antique-fakery slang—some tired Victorian bureau, very much as we were doing now. It was evidently his thing. And we had burden-some mealtimes with Elaine teasing us all, over Michelle's table. Her grub was Frenchified, by which I mean tangy of taste but ethereal. We had supper-time visits from Shona, and a couple of flying visits from Jamie who dropped us some materials in his van. This, plus a shepherd bringing two sheepdogs to prove they were topnotchers, was it. I quickly got the hang of life at Tachnadray, or thought I had.

But getting the hang of a scene doesn't mean tranquillity. It can mean just the opposite. There were just enough worry points to disturb my beauty sleep. Like, Michelle and Shona smiling their hundred-per-cent hatred smiles. Like, every-body knowing about Joseph but nobody saying. Like, Tach-nadray's pose as a glamorous laird's mansion complete with loyal retainers yet having barely enough furniture to dress out two rooms, a stage-set in a ghost palace. Like, Duncan's lone wilting attempts to provide the crumbling estate with an income. When at my noon break Elaine called me over to meet the shepherd's wriggly black-and-white dogs I thought: Here's quite an opportunity.

'Er, great,' I said, trying to sound full of admiration.

The shepherd grinned, said something in Gaelic. The dogs gave each other a sardonic glance as if saying, Here's another idiot townie who hasn't a clue.

'They like you, Ian,' the shepherd said. 'But they think you'll no be a countryman. I'm Hector.'

We nodded. Another cousin. Were I the genuine article I'd feel safe up here, even from Sidoli's vengeance-seeking mob of circus hands prowling the Lowlands.

'They're right, Hector,' I said. 'What do they do?'

'Best working pair north of Glasgow.' He waited, then explained, 'Sheep, Ian. Tessie's four, Joey two.'

'You bullies.' The dogs grinned and waggled round me, noses pointing up.

We talked about dogs for a minute while Elaine did one of her prolonged smiling stares at me. I felt her attention like a sunlamp, and listened while Hector listed his dogs' excellences. Dogs are all right but doggy folk are real bores, aren't they? Hector was confident about some sheepdog trials.

'How do you train them?' I asked. 'And what do you feed them on?' Much I cared, but Hector was loving all this in his grim Presbyterian way.

'You must come over and see them do an out-run or two,' he said. 'It's but a short step. Mornings I walk to check the cottage—'

Elaine interrupted brightly, 'Och away, Hector. Can't you see Cousin Ian's not really interested in your ould dogs?'

'True,' I said, maybe a little too quickly.

We all parted friends, me patting the dogs and seeing them off but thinking, The cottage, eh? Immediately Hector was out of earshot, Elaine said, spinning her wheelchair to accompany me back towards the house, 'The cottage is an empty crofter's place on the fells. We use it for winter shelter. There's quite a few about.'

It's that sort of nimble guesswork that makes you give up trying to out-think a female. I plodded along pushing her until she told me to walk beside her.

'Tachnadray must have been a lovely estate once, Elaine.'

'But . . . ?' she prompted.

'It could be developed. Tourists. Fishing. Build huts for nature cranks. Camp sites. Tours round the baronial hall.'

She halted. Thinking I'd struck oil, I enthused, 'Have your own Highland Gathering. Tents, pipers, dances, folk song evenings, original tartan kilts, Ye Olde Clan McGunn whisky-making kits. McGunn brand genuine Scottish bagpipes—'

'And breed hordes of McGunns? Repopulate the Highlands?'

She spoke with such quiet sibilance you had to strive to hear the venom. We'd stopped, her luminescent face white with anger.

'Well, er, not all of it.'

The nervous quip failed. She motioned me to sit on the wall and listen.

'Fall off a horse and lose the power of your legs, Ian. Myths are never the same again. They stand out with a certain clarity.' She laughed, an ugly spitting ejaculation I wouldn't like to hear again. 'So we should join the great Folklore Industry? It's the road to insanity. A social mania.'

I said, narked, 'I was only trying to help. A little profit—'

She pointed a finger at me. 'Don't interrupt. Just pay heed. Original tartan? There's no such thing. Listen: three centuries ago The Grant ordered his entire clan into his standard tartan.' She put on a cruel brogue to mock the words. 'And his own family turned up wearing a dozen different. You see? It's all fraud.'

'But tartan's—'

'A French word, Ian. "Tartaine" is a material, nothing to do with patterns. But then the *Irish* were great cloth weavers. The bagpipes?—the only invention ever to come out of Egypt. Scotch poetry?—our earliest indigenous one is in Welsh, for God's sake. The kilt?—invented by Thomas Rawlanson, an English iron-smelter in 1730. All tartans indigenous to our Scotch clans?—nonsense; there's even an authentic Johore tartan. Didn't you know? With a royal imprimatur, too!'

'I wish I hadn't come to see your bloody dogs.'

'We rhapsodize about Robert the Bruce and his spider, conveniently forgetting that he was an Anglo-Norman whose favourite method of murder was a stab in the back while the victim was unarmed and at prayer. Ask John the Red, whom he killed in the Franciscan church at Dumfries. And our fantastic Bonnie Prince Charlie?—a drunken Pole who thieved every penny his loyal followers possessed. And our famous Rabbie Burns.' She rolled her r's cruelly to mock. 'Don't tell anyone—his famous dialect is pure Anglo-Saxon. Nothing wrong with that, of course, unless you pretend it's a pure something else. When adherents trump up clan loyalties and urge me to "develop my clan's potential", I begin to ask what they're *really* after. You understand?'

'You mean what I'd get out of it? Twenty per cent—'

'Twenty per cent's out of the question.' She'd actually said her first three words in time with my last. Did she guess every bloody thing I thought? 'Five.'

'You mean bugger.'

She laughed, clapping her hands, and that terrible vehemence was gone as suddenly as it had come. At an imperious wag of her finger I trundled her obediently towards the ramp. Michelle emerged to see Elaine back in.

'Duncan's sounding for you, Ian,' Michelle called.

'What else is new?' I said irritably.

Elaine laughed. 'I've been telling Ian that we owe our tartans to Lowland machinery makers,' she announced. 'I think he's really upset.' She called after me: 'Still, Ian. At least our patron saint is real. Your English one's pure imagination.'

'Sensible bloke,' I said with feeling. 'If I were him I'd stay that way.'

Her musical laughter followed like a hound on my heels.

CHAPTER 15

That evening I struck out of my mental cocoon. It was definitely becoming time to rock the boat. Over a frothy frozen thing which tasted of lemons, I asked about Robert. I badly wanted a phone but wasn't even sure if Tachnadray had one.

'It's a question of money, folks,' I announced, mostly to Elaine. 'We ought to get Robert in to help us.'

Shona looked up quickly but it was Michelle who countered. 'He's no furniture man, Ian.'

'He's a pair of hands, love,' I corrected, thinking: So Michelle wants Robert kept out of Duncan's hair. Does Shona?

'No,' said Elaine as Duncan drew breath to chip in. 'Robert's already got too much to do.'

Duncan subsided. Happily I clocked up another fact: Robert was busily occupied, on Elaine's orders.

'Money,' I said. 'There's a lesson here. Me and Duncan have laboured long and hard, and finished the "antique" piece this afternoon. It's good, but now we're stuck. We must start looking for wood, materials, decide on the next—'

'You can't start one till the first's finished, Ian,' Elaine said.

'Wrong. It's bad fakery, Elaine.' I leant forward on the mahogany, eager from certainty. 'Even genuine workshops work by overlapping. Sheraton, Chippendale, Ince, Mayhew, Lock. Do one at a time and you end in the workhouse.'

'It's dangerous, Elaine,' Michelle said. Shona gave her a look, normally not this quiet.

'Ian's inclined to be bull-at-a-gate,' Duncan added. I don't like being apologized for and said so.

'Let him speak.' Elaine was in a lace blouse with a blue velvet neck ribbon. Some pudgy lady serf was helping tonight. New to me, but she was clearly a Tachnadray veteran and called Elaine "pet", to Michelle's evident annoyance. 'I've already disappointed Ian once today. He wants to make us an olde worlde Disneyland.'

'How much does running the estate cost?' I asked, ignoring Duncan's warning frown to go easy. 'Say it's X, for rates, wages, food, heating, clothes. And what's the income? Say it's Y, from Duncan's reproductions, sheep, crops—do you grow crops?' I enthused into their silence, 'It's Mr Micawber's famous problem: happiness is where X is less than Y. What's wrong with not being broke?'

Duncan cleared his throat. 'Like you, Ian?'

'Touché,' I said, beaming. 'We hire a promotions man for plans to make the estate solvent.' I gazed round at them all. 'It'd take one single phone call.'

'I won't have Tachnadray a mere tourist stop.' Elaine had spoken. 'I couldn't have dinner ogled by tourists at so many dollars a head.'

'It's degrading for a noble house,' Shona said.

'Not even a Clan McGunn coat-of-arms on headscarves, wooden plaques?' I pleaded. 'Pride's expensive. Christ's sake, Elaine. Have you never seen a Manchester mill on the go? For a percentage they'd do thousands a bloody day— tea towels, travelling bags, all in McGunn tartan. Cups, mugs, silver brooches, Tachnadray deer. And Duncan's workshop'd turn out phoney shields—' I was in agony. 'Can't you see?'

'No.' Elaine calmly pronounced over my distress, and with utter serenity gestured the serf to pour coffee. 'I'm becoming rather tired of your schemes, Ian.'

One last try. 'Then it's your dreaded Tachnadray secret.' Everybody stilled, even the beverage-toting peasant.

'Secret?' Michelle made a too-casual search for sugar, which anyway was within easy reach.

'What secret?' It wasn't until Duncan demanded point blank, his voice harsh and his pipe like a clutched weapon that the penny dropped and I thought in sudden jubilation, God, there really *is* something.

'Wine,' I explained, cerebrating at speed.

'Establishing a vineyard,' from dear innocent Michelle, 'takes centuries.' She'd dressed in lovely harebell blue.

'So we don't,' I explained, thinking: Give me strength. 'We never even see the bloody wine, see? A vineyard simply bottles us up Tachnadray Special. Print new labels, ships it to a distributor.'

'Outsiders!' Shona spat.

'No, Ian.' Another royal imperative. 'Too longterm.'

'Then you don't need money,' I concluded with angry finality. For a second I thought I'd over-acted, but not for Michelle.

'You're wrong, Ian. We're in dire straits.' She really did say it, dire straits, straight out of her English lessons.

'Michelle,' Duncan warned, too late.

I said, acting driven to the brink, 'Then we sell up.'

Outrage. Horror. The lackey almost dropped the coffee-pot. Duncan almost swallowed his pipe. Michelle gave a Gallic squeal of turmoil-powered indignation. Shona paled. Even Elaine's smile wilted somewhat, a case of needle reversed. Robert would have inverted me in the nearest soufflé.

'At an auction. Here, in Tachnadray.' It was my turn to smile now. 'We sell every damned thing. Even,' I said, chosing my words carefully, 'even some things we haven't got.'

Well, what works for Sidoli's travelling fairground can work for Tachnadray's immobile gentility, right? Elaine looked and said nothing. The rest tried to argue me into the ground. They hadn't bothered to listen to a word I'd said, so I just noshed, nodded, muttered 'You've got a point there' sort of responses, and started working out the scale of the operation. Barefaced robbery, lies and immoral usury are the tools of the work world's greatest auction firms. They'd be just as useful in Tachnadray.

Because of Elaine's telepathic swiftness in mind-guessing, I carefully didn't think of my other scam, which was to find this oh-so-unimportant cottage and raid the damned thing.

Theft, I often say to myself, is often in a good cause. It's especially beneficial when it happens to somebody else. Oh, I don't mean the great Woburn Abbey silver haul, though even that netted mind-bending reward money when those two workers found the cache in that Bedfordshire water-pumping station. Somebody always does well out of it, even when theft goes wrong. One problem is Finance Law, the great rip-off of modern times. Those lucky enough to be in on it—police, lawyers, estate agents—are of course all for it and want us, the oppressed majority, to join in their hearty approval. We don't. Reason? Because the Law costs us a fortune. All we can do is try to exist in spite of it.

That evening, aware now of the strong differences of opinion around the table, we separated with Elaine saying she'd 'take advice' and that we'd have a conference about it all in a day or so. Money was obviously Tachnadray's old battleground where Shona and Michelle fought daily. Very serious stuff. Solvency's a perennial laugh, though a rather moaning sort of laugh, at Lovejoy Antiques, Inc. But I've always managed by having friends I can rely on, borrow from, or otherwise sponge off, and Tachnadray only had this gaggle of clan innocents.

Up in my converted garret I easily worked out the solution, how to hold an important auction sale of the many valuable antiques we hadn't got. The idea wasn't new, but the actual sin would have to be. In immorality freshness is always important, like in fruit. I shelved it, and settled down to examine the Ordnance Survey map I'd brought. This cottage Hector had mentioned was niggling.

Scattered thinly among the colours and contours of the uplands round Tachnadray were black rectangles which indicated buildings. The mansion was clearly marked. I'd work outwards, and start with the cottage on the valley road. I'd noticed it standing maybe a mile beyond the end of the drive.

Which is how I wasted a couple of hours that night, stumbling along the driveway in virtual pitch darkness and trudging the Dubneath track to find a miniature collapsed ruin. Some giant bird—at least, I hope it was only a bird —swished past my head and frightened me to death as I felt the fallen stones of the old crofter's cottage. Maybe the gatehouse, a retainer's place from the estate's grander days? Nothing there, anyway. The bird mooed and swished me again, so I cleared off. One bare porch light was always left burning, on Elaine's instruction, so returning was less problematic. I just followed that lovely civilized glimmer down below, and made it safely.

A cross mark on the map to show which building I'd investigated—leaving about a dozen isolated buildings within about a five-mile radius of Tachnadray—and I was ready for bed. Nobody had followed me, I thought. I was quite confident.

Some people have a politician's mind. They're always highly dangerous because politicians, remember, have a vested interest in doom. Robert was like that. I mean, just because I was up early next morning and strolling a couple of miles across the uplands he decided to follow, obviously longing for me to turn out to be a traitor. Me! I ask you.

There was a light drizzle on a long breeze. It was only when I turned to shake the water off my mac hood that I saw the suspicious swine. He was perhaps a mile off, but covering the ground at a hell of a lick, his enormous hairy red head topped by a bonnet and nodding like a horse does at each pace.

He saw my pause and stopped. Casually I went on, giving a glance back down the hillside. He started up after me again. I paused. He halted. I moved, and he came on.

No use continuing in these circumstances, so I made a curve along the hill's contour and fetched up on the Dubneath track about a mile from where I'd started. Robert, by then higher up the hill, realized my intention and stopped to watch me without any attempt at concealment. He simply held the skyline looking down. I gave the hearty wave of the dedicated dawn-rambler, and cheerily whistled my way back to the big house for breakfast.

The building I'd wanted to inspect was over the hill's shoulder, about two miles off. Robert was proving a nuisance, especially as it was his terrain, but I couldn't get it out of my mind that if I found that cottage I'd find Joseph. Predecessors are always a nuisance in any job. Predecessors who prove elusive and taboo are even more disturbing.

'Och, the poor wee thing,' Mrs Buchan said, noisily brewing up. She was the serf-factotum, red-faced, plump and breathless. I watched fascinated amid the din. All kitchens look like pandemonium to me, but Tachnadray's was special. It was a vast long hall, sort of Somersetshire-ninepin-bowling-alley shaped but with huge iron ranges along one side. Mrs Buchan rushed everywhere. I'd asked about Elaine.

'Can't the doctors do anything?'

'Don't ye think they've tried, you daft man?' Mrs Buchan sang, trotting her large mass from table to oven with raw bread. 'It was that horse. A stupid great lummock. I'm against horses, always was. But do people listen?'

'Why aren't you a McGunn, Buchan?'

The far door opened and Robert entered. He sat without a word. With me at one end of the long table and the red-bearded giant glowering at the other we were a gift for a passing jokester.

''Morning, Robert. Breakfast presently.' She sprinted to the copper porridge pan, panting, 'I am. Before Buchan wed me. My two bairns are away in London.'

'Sinners.'

The joke fell flat. 'Aye,' she wheezed over the frying bacon, 'I pray for them night and day.'

'I walked out this morning,' I said hopefully as the porridge came.

'Aye. You were seen.'

The laconic shut-out. I bent to my spoon. 'I thought I saw Hector walking Tessie and Joey.'

'No, man. He'd be away in the opposite direction, on the . . .' Mrs Buchan's voice trailed off as Robert's massive hulk emitted a warning rumble.

'Lovely dogs,' I said casually, reaching for hot new bread.

Eating always cheers me up. And happiness brings luck, though folk mistakenly assume it's the other way round. Nice knowing that the cottage Hector inspected every morning lay in the opposite direction to the place I'd just tried to reach. Progress in Tachnadray.

Duncan told me when I reported for work that Elaine had called a meeting tomorrow morning. I'd have to get a move on with Plan X.

CHAPTER 16

You must have played that imagination game where you can have any woman (or man, *mutatis mutandis*) on earth? And 'have' in any way you like? It used to be my big favourite until matters got out of hand, over this bird called Wilhelmina. She was a drama student and lived on Natural Earth-Friendly Pulses, which means beans. It ended in tragedy when, in the throes of orgasm, somebody (she claimed it was me) uttered a strange bird's name. She played merry hell and stormed out in a rage. Naturally I missed her almost until the pubs opened, and felt the chill wind of economics because she'd paid the mortgage. Still, I got used to food again. God, those bloody beans. But the point of mentioning that dream game of yippee is, Shona was beginning to figure in my imagination. Disloyal to Jamie, of course, to think hopefully of Shona rapturously savaging my defenceless body. Only a heel would lust like that. Her great dog Ranter was the deterrent.

Duncan gave me permission to go into Dubneath that morning, to see what was available in a small lumber yard. It sounds quick and easy. In fact I had to walk four miles on the track to a cairn of stones and wait there on the bare hillside for a lorry to come by at half past ten. It was on time, driven by a warped old geezer called Mac whose one utterance was, 'Aye,' in various tones of disbelief. Oddly, I was almost certain I'd seen Robert stalking the upland stones while I'd waited, but looking more intently only seemed to make him vanish actually on the hillside. Clever, that. I got the lorryman to drop me on the outskirts of the megalopolis and walked in.

The lumber yard was soporific. A neat rectangle of sloped planks, a barrow, a wooden shed with a corrugated roof. A few pieces of second-hand furniture were covered by a lean-to on the side opposite the double gate. I shouted a couple of times, wandered a bit. The only rescuable items were a heavy rosewood desk, eastern, and a Wellington chest whose top and side panels had split badly. Beggars can't be choosers. I scribbled a note, offering for the two, and wedged it in the shed door saying I'd call back.

It was too early to phone Tinker, or call on Shona—I wasn't going to risk that great silent dog without protection —so I went to see George MacNeish. He was doing out the saloon bar with Mary. They seemed honestly pleased to see me.

I pretended to stagger to a stool. 'I'm in hell. No houses anywhere, and all the grub's French.'

'That'll be Michelle,' Mary said, smiling. 'But Gladys Buchan'll start you off right each day.'

'She tries.' I closed the door because two old anglers in tweedy plus-fours were chatting in the parlour. 'Look, folks. Who and where is this Joseph?'

The smiles faded. After a moment of still-life I said, 'I can't go out and ask Mrs Innes. Everybody in Tachnadray shuts up if I mention him. It's getting on my nerves.'

George was about to say something when Mary put in

one breath ahead. 'It's no business of ours, Ian. Maybe you've been too long in the soft south. Up here family feelings are best not touched.'

'Seems daft to me. Okay, he drank. Is that enough to launch a bloke into oblivion? And where's the harm telling me?'

George deliberately chose his words. 'Joseph is a McGunn, so he's rightly your clan's responsibility, not ours. But to settle your mind: Joseph worked up at Tachnadray, yes. And left under a cloud. That's all. Now stop your asking, and stay mute like a canny man.'

'There!' I said with evident pleasure. 'Wasn't painful, was it? And look how relieved you've made me. Just for that I'll drag your wife down into her kitchen, bolt the door and force her to warm up some of her rotten old mouldy pasties.'

Their expressions lifted and amid smiling prattle Mary started for the kitchen. I don't know which of us was the more relieved as normality reasserted itself.

'Typical McGunn,' George mock-grumbled. 'Always thieving.'

'Shut your face, MacNeish. Or I'll take up golf and thrash you at your own game. Here, missus,' I said, slamming the kitchen door after me. 'What's this about the soft south? I'll have you know I work bloody hard down there . . .'

My heart felt sick, though I cleared Mary's grub quick enough and kept up the rabbiting. The MacNeishes had been generous enough to give me a warning when I'd left for Tachnadray, but now I needed to know something definite they'd handed me a load of codswallop. I didn't believe that about Joseph leaving under a cloud. He was still around, and I badly needed to find him.

By eleven o'clock I was at the great Innes emporium, smiling as I entered and hoping to find it empty of customers. It was, but a glance at Mrs Innes's closed face made it apparent there'd be no joy there. She'd been warned. I put on a show of buying a few things—staples, resin, electric torch, stout twine, wood stain—and asked about the lumber man.

'Why, ye stupid man!' she exclaimed, clearly glad to be

on safe ground. 'He's at the pier loading his uncle's boat.'

'Wrong, Innes. There's only Jamie there.' I'd looked towards the water as I'd left the tavern. He'd been loading a small motor ketch, the only activity.

'Aye. It's him.'

'Jamie owns the lumber yard?' The only supplier of obsolescent furniture, the antique faker's raw material, was Shona McGunn's Jamie. My brain sighed an exhausted sigh.

'Of course, Ian. Didn't Mary McGunn tell ye that?'

'Mary McGunn?' I only knew one Mary in Dubneath.

'Mary MacNeish.' Mrs Innes was bagging up black currants. Her eyes held mine. *It's the best I can do,* her careful gaze said, as she joked, 'You McGunns are all too wrapped up in your silly selves . . .'

'Will ye no be resenting that slur from an Innes, Ian?' Shona came in the shop doorway behind me, smiling, her great dog beside her. It was enormous with the light behind it. 'The Inneses are great misjudgers.'

'Glad you came, Beautiful,' I said, joining the spirit of the thing. 'While Jamie's busy have we got time to sneak off?'

Shona laughed. Ranter grinned. 'For coffee, Ian?'

'I've had nothing all morning.'

'Oooh, the lies in the man!' Mrs Innes exclaimed after us. 'He's full of Mary's cooking!'

My least favourite headache returned as I walked along the narrow pavement with Shona and her pooch. It comes from fear, which is generated by a terrible realization of ignorance. Mrs Innes had tried a second time to warn me, in her way. I'd just been too slow to appreciate it. There was only one ally left, and that was Shona. After all, I thought, glancing sideways at her lovely bright face, she was the one who'd brought me up here. She alone knew who I was, and kept the secret. She alone had promised me a fair share. And she alone was on my side, however erratic her personality. This clan-loyalty business could surely be safely forgotten, except among the elderly gossipmongers of Dubneath.

I'd only been allowed back into town when Shona was free. I must have accidentally slipped her by alighting on the outskirts instead of being fetched directly into Dubneath's centre. She must have gone hunting me after realizing I'd gone missing. Still, an ally is an ally. I wanted to get Tinker because I badly needed things done. In the meantime I'd have to rely on the one natural asset we all possess. Perfidy.

'Darling,' I said at her gate. 'Won't the neighbours talk?'

'No,' she said evenly, 'providing you're quiet.'

Ranter came in and watched me make myself at home, as the saying is. It was quite unnerving. As matters progressed from the possible to the inevitable, I had to ask Shona to send the dog out. Amused, Shona compromised by ordering it into the little front garden, and led me upstairs after latching the door. After that it was all smooth sailing. If my brain had been functioning, I'd have still talked myself into making love to Shona on the grounds that the worst I could expect was betrayal. After some of the women I've known it would be a small price. I'm fully trained in disaster. As it was, my intellect had hibernated at the first hint of forthcoming ecstasy. I don't know how sociologists manage all that dispassion they brag about. Women only make me think hooray. With my own brand of logic going full steam, the mere act of lying dazed and sweat-stuck to Shona afterwards was somehow proof that we were more fervent allies than ever.

'Who's the crook, love?' I said, drifting from oblivion to somnolence. Women are always awake when I come to. How do they do it?

'That's my question, Lovejoy.' She lay aside, somehow. The pillow had fluffed up between us making it hard to breathe.

'It's not Elaine, that's for sure. Nor Duncan. He's a naturally nice bloke.'

'Is he a good . . . antiques faker?'

'Not bad. Certainly not in the same league as some.'

'Michelle?' Her voice was in exact neutral, oho.

'Your pal?' I was unsure. Michelle was one of those lovely succulent women who should be eaten whole with mint.

I've always been vulnerable. 'Dunno. What's her motive? Money?'

'That. And Elaine.' Shona's hatred showed now. Her throat thickened. 'Michelle's an intruder. A spider. She'll take anything she can. Men are blind, Lovejoy.'

'Oh aye,' I said drily. Fascism gets everywhere, even into lovers' beds. 'So Michelle and Duncan are your guess. Not Robert?'

She still spoke muffled. 'Robert does as he's told.'

'Which leaves Hector, but he's too busy with his dogs and sheep. And Jamie. Lucky that he runs the woodyard, eh?'

'Essential.'

There are two sorts of pests: women who never leave you alone after loving, forever inspecting your morphology and asking questions, and women who mentally move out and lie there, eyes closed, disowning the nerk they've drained to exhaustion. Shona was clearly of the second category, hunched away in the bed, making me feel a right hitch-hiker.

'Look, Shona.' I pulled her over to face me. 'Michelle couldn't pull a scam on her own. Duncan knows so little about the antiques game that he doesn't even suss out alternative routes, different fences. He's a craftsman, but no crook.'

'What are you saying, Lovejoy?' she said towards the window.

'There's been no crime.'

Which raised her, bedclothes pulled modestly over her breasts. 'No crime? Of course there's been a crime! We've been selling furniture and paintings to keep Tachnadray together ever since I can remember. For less and less money!'

'You'd only a limited number to start with. You've simply run out of originals.'

'*We*'ve never relied on lies, Lovejoy! That's *your* trick!'

Well, she'd a right to be angry. She was the only person I'd ever met who'd passed a genuine antique as a fake. I spend my life doing the opposite.

'The point is, love,' I said along the pillow into her lovely furious eyes, 'there's no antiques worth mentioning left at

Tachnadray. It's empty. That genuine bureau you sent down was Tachnadray's swan song.'

'How do you know, Lovejoy?' It was a whisper.

'The house feels dry, all wrong. It's got a few sticks, and that's it.'

'You really can tell,' she said with wonder.

'Afraid so, love.' I watched her beautiful blues well up. 'The stuff left in Tachnadray isn't worth a dealer's petrol for the journey. You made the wrong assumption. You couldn't understand why so little money was coming in when one or two reproduction pieces were being sent off every month. And poor old Duncan is slogging his guts out to make enough copies, fakes, repros to keep Tachnadray fed. He and Michelle were too tender-hearted to tell Elaine the truth.'

I was up and dressing, keeping an eye out for that bloody great dog. If it ever learned I'd made Shona cry I'd be a chewed heap.

'Where are you going, Lovejoy?'

'Tachnadray. Elaine's called a gathering tomorrow. I've to speak the plan out.' A naked man looks grotesque, so I was glad to be covered. Shona lay there, eyes dulled, pretty. Nakedness looks good on a woman. 'I can offer a reasonable scam, Shona. Only one-off, but it'd bring in a hell of a lot of gelt. If Elaine accepts, I'll stay and do it. If not, there's nothing to keep me here.'

'You'd leave? Because there's no antiques?'

'I can knock up fakes anywhere, love. It doesn't have to be in Tachnadray.'

For a few moments I dithered. I never know what to say when leaving a woman's bedroom. You can't just give a sincere grin and a thanks, love, can you? And women are too distrusting to believe dud promises.

'Will Ranter let me pass?'

She smiled, cold, I thought. She uttered the slow words like a thumbs-down to an arena. 'This once, darling.'

I gave her a sincere grin. 'Thanks, love,' I said, and left.

CHAPTER 17

'Shut your gums, Tinker,' I said into the phone, frantic lest Mac's lorry left without me on the home run.

The gabby old sod was woozier than ever. He was in the Rose at Peldon, sloshed out of his mind. The Rose is a pub by the sea marshes, always heaving full of antique dealers.

'Eh, Lovejoy?' he bawled. The background noise was Grand National Day. 'I'm lissnin'.'

'A month from now I'm doing a paper job. A mansion.'

'Us? Paperin' a stately home?' Tinker yelled, coughing between syllables.

The distant pub's racket silenced as if by magic. Some lunatic talking football was instantly throttled.

'Start enrolling the dealers, Tinker. Pass their names on to Margaret.'

'Is it secret?' he howled to the universe. Jesus.

'Not any more,' I said wearily. 'Tell Margaret she can chit and chop for me. And get Antioch Dodd to collect the pots. Got that?' 'Pots' are lorries, from rhyming slang: pots and pans, vans. It'd be quite a convoy. Chits are IOUs and receipts, chops the stamps of approval. It meant I'd honour whatever deals Margaret decided for me. I might murder her afterwards if she guessed wrong, of course, but fair's fair.

'Right, Lovejoy. How much do we need?'

Tachnadray was say, sixty rooms of which two were still respectably furnished. The rest stood bare. A quarter of the rooms would have been servants' quarters, say about nine.

'About fifty rooms, Tinker, assorted, but I split half and half.' In its heyday half would have been bedrooms, retiring-rooms, and half reception rooms, libraries, smoking-rooms and that.

'Fifty? Bloody hell. Where is it?'

'Never you mind. I'll phone down every fourth day.'

'Wait, wait! Lovejoy! Who's to reff the stuff?' Reff as in

referee, to gain some slight assurance of authenticity for the antiques—real or fake'd hardly matter much—as they were loaded up.

'Who've you got there?' I could imagine two-score dealers frozen in the pub, listening breathless at this news of the biggest scam to hit East Anglia all year.

'Here? Well there's Harry Bateman, Liz Sandwell, Helen, Big Frank from Suffolk, Sven, Mannie, Jill . . .' His rubbled croak became inaudible in instantaneous pandemonium. The silly nerks had erupted, grabbed for the receiver to bawl their names and shouting offers, percentages, splits on the knock, part deals—

Click. Burr. I get fed up with other people's greed when I've enough of my own.

It was coming on to rain when finally Mac's lorry hove in. Somehow he'd heard, God knows how, of the furniture I'd left pencilled notes for at the lumber yard. They were on his wagon under a tarpaulin in the back.

Robert met us at the crossroads, pushing a handcart. Mute, he transferred the two pieces without my assistance. I called thanks to Mac and in the driving rain followed the giant's form along to Tachnadray. I felt a spare tool at a wedding.

This next bit's about crooked money, and how you—repeat, *you*—will sooner or later be robbed blind. There's no escape, so if you're of a nervous disposition I'd skip it.

A 'paper job', a.k.a. 'papering a house', is one of the commonest antiques tricks in the world. And make no mistake, everybody in the game tries it. Since the Great Antiques Boom, however, it has come to be a speciality of the world's poshest auction houses. It works thus:

A householder dies, alas. In the ten seconds which elapse between the crusty old colonel's last breath and his widow phoning the insurance company, several dealers will call offering to sell the colonel's personal effects. The widow sorts out what she wants to take to her daughter's and signs a contract with a respectable auctioneer.

Now an auctioneer can do two things. Either all the

auctionable stuff is vanned off by the auctioneer's respectable vannies (they will be called assistants in the written contract) to the respectable auctioneer's premises, or else the contents—furniture, cutlery, linen, carpets, the colonel's campaign medals, paintings, porcelain—will be left *in situ*, and the house opened for a grand auction.

You can imagine that the final printed catalogue might look a bit 'thin', as we say, if old colonel, R.I.P., didn't have much. But oh how nice it would be, thinks our respectable auctioneer wistfully, if the deceased had a couple of handsome almost-Chippendale tallboys, or an oil painting possibly almost nearly attributable to Turner or Vermeer. How sad a respectable auctioneer's life is, he sighs.

Happily, sin slithers in to help out. Within hours of that respectable auctioneer's naughty daydream, would you believe it but the house's contents begin to swell, multiply, increase, until finally on auction day the colonel's antiques overflow into the garden, where the respectable auctioneer has thoughtfully hired numerous elegant marquees for the purpose. Isn't life great? Soon it gets greater.

The cataloguer's erudition helps the thing along. She (cataloguers are normally female; more careful, you see) will say of some neffie portrait of a bog-eyed clergyman: '. . . once attributed to the immortal Gainsborough . . .' or some such. The fact that the daub was created in an alcoholic stupor by an incompetent forger now doing life on Dartmoor is regarded as a mere quibble, because the words *as written* are actually true. So Law condones the fraud: the portrait *was* once so attributed—by a crooked forger. See how it works?

Just as theatres are 'papered'—i.e. crammed by the actors' friends, who are given free tickets—so auctioneers swell their offerings at house auctions.

Innocent souls might ask: 'But what's the point? Who gains?' To answer this, best simply buy any item at such a sale, then try to sell it. An old Lowestoft jug, say. First, offer it just as it is. To your alarm antique shops don't want to know. Dealers spurn you and your jug. They see a dozen a day, so what's one more? Tomorrow, however, take along the auctioneer's lovely catalogue. You can now show the dealer your jug's handsome picture and precise printed description. He'll be over the moon. Of course he'll still haggle over the price. The point is *he'll want your jug*. You've made a sale. Good, eh?

The reason he now wants it is that magic thing called provenance. He can ascribe your jug, truthfully, as 'from the famous sale at Nijninovgorod House . . .' and show your catalogue as proof. Appearance, condition, and provenance —they're the three great selling points in horses, cattle, bloodstock. And, oddly enough, people. Why not in antiques too?

Paper jobs are highly popular in the antiques game, because everybody profits: dealers, public, buyers, cataloguers, auctioneers, the colonel's widow, the bloke who prints the catalogue . . . The only slight hiccough in it all is that it's fraudulent. It *has* to be. Why? Because if every house was ramjam packed full of delectable antiques there'd be no demand. It'd be like everybody suddenly being millionaires. So the 'sets' of dining chairs aren't sets at all; they're made up from here, there and everywhere. Vases reputedly brought back from Japan in 1890 were actually fired in Wapping last week. The delicate Chinese porcelain pillows weren't shipped home from Canton last century: they were a job lot in a Hong Kong package tour this Easter. The colonel's campaign medals will be sold—and sold, and sold, and sold, for entire sets will be put together by every dealer in the country and sold as the colonel's one genuine set. Which explains why the printed catalogues for important house auction sales are always sold out instantly—to market twenty sets of medals you need twenty catalogues, right? It's cast-iron profit. It's today's favourite crime. All you need is a posh address, and you can make a fortune. The customers get diddled, but so?

That's the paper job. All you need is care, skill, and a team.

After dinner I retired to formulate my paper job, promising Elaine to reveal it in all its glory at the morning gathering. Then, in the cascading rain, I went out for a sly walk. The death simply wasn't my fault. Honest.

The drive to the main gate was the only orthodox way off the Tachnadray estate. Stone walls rimmed the thirty or so acres of paddocks, outbuildings, lawns, with a few straggly hawthorn hedges infilling the tumbled drystone stretches. Behind the great house, vegetable gardens were busily reverting to weeds. Glass cloches sprawled higgledy-piggledy. Greenhouses shed panes. Huts flaked planks. Even the outbuildings had joined the disintegration wholesale and gone toothy by extruding stones. I'd asked Duncan why he didn't grow stuff, market some produce. He'd waxed sarcastic: 'I'll get a dozen retainers in on it immediately.' The poor bloke was doing his best.

Hell of a place to hide, I grumbled inwardly as I drifted through the dark garden. Soon after Mrs Buchan had blundered by admitting that Hector's dawn patrol was on the hillside opposite to the main gateway, I'd sussed out a cracked path between lines of old bleached canes. It made stealth clumsy and full of din, but what could I do? The map showed a fairly smooth slope, then a few upland folds. And, in grand solitude two miles off, a cottage marked *Shooters* in a narrow gully.

Climbing the wall was easy, and quieter. Torch in my pocket, I began the long slow climb up the fellside, walking bent and pressing my hands on my knees. The ground was soaked to squelching over my shoes. It made me slip on rocks projecting underfoot. Heather started kicking back at each pace, whipping my legs. There was no moon. How the hell had highwaymen managed? I did my best to follow the direction I'd planned, but within minutes I was using my torch to find the first gale-torn hawthorn and check its position against the faint glow of light from the house below. There were two leaning crags which would be my markers to aim off at a forty-degree angle to the right. The cottage was more or less a mile from there.

Common sense told that *Shooters* wasn't Hector's home. If it had been, why did he need to walk out there? The

118

shepherd had innocently assumed that, being a McGunn, I was in on the cottage thing. Maybe *Shooters*, I hoped with spirits rising, was in fact a great Victorian shooting lodge and it was there that Duncan/Robert/Michelle or whoever had salted away the missing antiques from Tachnadray, if any.

Maybe nine o'clock when I set out. That made it getting on for ten when I made the first leaning crag. Odd, but I was starting to understand how the nightwalkers had managed. It's quite easy, really. Once you get used to being away from civilization's buildings and lights, night resolves into distinct components. Ground underfoot stays pitch black, but the sky's dark intensity lessens somewhat. Tall stones and trees condense the sky's consistency, so that though you still can't actually see them as such, you can somehow perceive that they're there in your path. Tachnadray's light was more distant, but seemed almost blinding from the hilltop. I stopped looking at it because it lessened my night vision.

From the crags the ground descended and took me out of direct view of Tachnadray for the first time. Even so, I wasn't too worried. The faint sky shine from that direction was enough to show me the hilltop's sky interface. Ever so often I cricked over on the stones that littered the fells, so I developed a trick of walking with knees bent, using short steps, not putting my heels down first. It intrigued me. I'd adopted Robert's curious gait. A new way of looking, and a new way of walking, all in one go. I felt a real discoverer.

In fact I was so busy praising myself that I was stuck when a building thickened the darkness to my left. I'd actually come upon *Shooters*. A disappointingly small edifice. A pointless low wall ran from it for a short distance. Something to do with cattle? A snowbreak to halt fell drifts in blizzards? I felt my way along it, stepping carefully in case tins or bottles or other fellwalkers' debris lurked in wait.

Derelict? There was no sound. I halted, listened. In the distance a short deep bark sounded, curt and businesslike. I dismissed it. Hector's dogs probably wouldn't be out at this hour. I'd heard Duncan talk of red deer. Perhaps a stag calling its herd, maybe scenting me and resenting intrusion on its patch?

Risking, I took my flashlight and moved off a few silent yards. If somebody saw me I wanted a head start. I wasn't in good enough shape to sprint the two boulder-riddled miles to Tachnadray without breaking my neck, so I'd have to do a short dash and hide among the outcrops. Escape by subterfuge is really my thing, but it's easier in towns than out here in all this loneliness. I crouched.

Flash. The beam swept, hit buildings, dowsed into blackness again. In that instant of brilliance, my eyes beheld a child's drawing two-storey cottage, symmetrical and unadorned. The windows were wood-shuttered. Slate roof. Single chimney. A bare building on a barren hillside. What the hell was I doing out here, I asked myself irritably. One upper-floor shutter had stood slightly ajar, I'd noticed. I thought over the image in my mind. The obvious thing was to wait a minute in case my beam had disturbed an inhabitant, then creep up and simply try the door. For all I knew I might be stalking an empty house.

As I felt around me for a couple of decent-shaped stones I heard again that deer's bark. Closer, and only once, but now out beyond the cottage. I actually chuckled to myself. If only that apprehensive stag knew how little it had to fear from me it would get back between the sheets and nod off. God's creatures are gormless. No wonder. God was a beginner at creation.

It's a fallacy to assume that burglars can't climb a wall without a ladder. A burglar can climb anything, because even a blank wall offers ledges, pipes, rectifying studs, cistern overflows. You might say that such feeble supports might not support a burglar's full weight—and you'd be right. But they'd support a quarter of a burglar's weight, and that's all he needs because he can do the bolus trick, the town burglar's favourite.

This evolved from sailing ships, I've been told. Others say it's what Argentina's cowboys do to hobble bulls. The stones make the cord whiptangle anything hit. I've even seen it used to put a rope round untouchable scalding steam pipes along a mill ceiling. You take a piece of strong twine a yard long, and tie stones at the ends. This is the bolus. Then fasten a long length at the midpoint, and coil that length on the ground beside you. Take the midpoint of your bolus between finger and thumb of your left hand, and hold one tied stone in your right. Then start swinging the other dangling stone in a circle. Clockwise or anticlockwise doesn't matter. Once it's going, you simply fling the opposite stone in the opposite direction, and you'll find you are holding a piece of string by its middle with two stones whirling round in opposite directions. Naked tassle-dancers do it in night clubs from their breasts—er, I mean I've heard they do. To keep the bolus spinning, you simply move your hand up and down.

You lean, fling the bolus with a slow overarm cast. The best is that if you miss the chimney you simply reel it in again, or cut your cord and make another bolus. This actually happened. I missed the chimney stack twice. I tried pulling on the twine but the bolus must have caught on something on the far side of the cottage roof. It's usually the guttering or a cistern overflow pipe. I bit through the nylon, let its free end whip away into the night air, and chewed away another one-yard length. By feel, I'd still got enough to stretch from roof to ground, and I was in no haste.

Mostly, I (I really mean burglars who go in for this sort of thing) prefer elongated waisted stones because they hold the string better. City burglars use spark plugs, partly to assume innocence if they're caught. I only took a minute finding a decent heavy pair of stones out in all this horrible countryside, and I was in action, for another go. I reached for my coiled twine.

And stopped.

Almost beyond hearing, I could just make out a faint yell. 'Run! Run!' Quite like a yell heard through glass.

Baffled, I strained to hear. Run? Run where? And why? I actually got up and turned this way and that, head tilted to catch the gnat's whine of a shout, before it dawned. It was inside the cottage. Somebody was yelling for somebody to run. If I hadn't been thick I'd have guessed, but I've a zillion untrained neurones. I was quite unconcerned, merely puzzled.

My beam cut the night. And something moved, far over to my right beyond the low wall.

Robert stood there. He looked gigantic in the solid glare from my torch. With him on a leash stood Ranter, its eyes two brilliants against jet. That bark had been no deer. Dogs bark.

'Hello,' I called feebly. 'I was just out for . . .'

Robert fiddled with the huge animal's neck. Nervously I backed away a pace. Robert stepped aside, a whole dark space between him and the giant hound. He raised an arm and pointed at me. His kilt flapped once in the night breeze.

'Run! Run!' the little insect screamed inside the cottage.

Frightened, I backed off. Run? Somebody was warning me—me—to run. Christ. From what? From . . .

The giant figure held its biblical pose in my torchlight.

'*Kill*,' Robert said. He turned and walked away. I turned and ran like hell.

CHAPTER 18

For a second or two I thought the damned animal wasn't coming after me. I fled across the slope I'd climbed, my torchlight flickering ahead on shining angles of granite projecting from the heather. Maybe I even imagined I was going at a speed Ranter couldn't match.

Then I heard it, breathing like a train. It slobbered as it ran, a flopping sound as its feet landed. It didn't dash like a greyhound or scamper like a beagle. It simply loped. In that first terror-stricken moment when I'd seen it start, its apparently casual movement said it all. What's the hurry? its graceful mass announced as it hunched up to start the pursuit. It's not a race—it's a hunt. Sooner or later, it seemed to say, the quarry'll tire, weaken, flake out, and then . . . I was moaning as I ran. If I'd had breath enough I'd have whimpered, prayed, screamed, anything.

Ahead a roaring sound. I'd say I headed for it except that that expression makes my progress sound like a ramble. Reality was different. I was scrambling, stumbling, gasping, across the stony hillside slope, trying to hold my torch out ahead for sight, anything to keep ahead of that dreadful slapping which proved the bloody monster was gaining.

It could have been only a minute when a roar opened the ground ahead, and I tumbled over an edge. I fell maybe ten feet, more, found myself in swirling water and floundered forward, anything to keep going.

A waterfall. Some sort of gully, with a narrow freshet of water. I'd kept hold of my torch. I splashed across, climbed a tall projecting slabbed rock dividing the swirling course. Maybe I could get to the top, sit there and somehow stop it climbing up after me. A stone, a cobble. I realized I'd got my new untried bolus still in my hands, stuffed it in my jacket pocket and hauled a cobble up out of the onrush.

A flop, flop, behind. Here it came. With a slither Ranter appeared at the margin I'd fallen over and without a pause came bounding on. I saw him hit the water with a ploosh, force his way up to the base of my rock, and try to leap up. I flung my cobble and hit the bugger. He leaped to one side, and halted. I squatted up on my pinnacle, sick from breathlessness and fright.

He looked at me, transfixed in my beam. Ranter's appearance arrested me. He honestly appeared noble. The strain of chasing hardly showed. He'd cornered me. His teeth would be along in a minute to perform massacre. It was all so serene, this hunting business.

So that's what a hunter-killer looks like, I thought dementedly. His stance was one of attention, of cool certainty. His tongue lolled. His flanks shone. What I hated most was that he was *thinking*. I honestly mean it. The murderous beast was actually cerebrating, its great head swinging as it took in the geography of the gully and the pouring beck, calmly working out how to catch and kill the shivering bloke perched ludicrously up there.

Directly upwards from the water my angular granite

projected, its faces a mixture of smooth and rough, but on the whole vertical, thank God. The side I'd climbed up had barely a fingerhold. I'd done well to haul myself up. I prayed fervent gratitude that I had hands and Ranter hadn't any means of clutching.

Its head swung, marcasite eyes glittering. I whimpered. It took no notice and benignly continued inspecting my slab. Don't worry, its urbane manner informed me; this is only a job. I'll get you in a minute. Above all, be patient. I moaned. The bloody beast was a real pro.

We were maybe thirty feet apart. The animal—it wasn't good old Ranter any longer; executioners don't have names —backed, tried to get space for a run, changed its mind.

My torchlight couldn't be helping it. I kept the beam trained on its face. Not much of a dazzle, but what else could I do? I found a single loose stone flake, chucked it. The murderer leaned its head an inch and the stone flew by, clattered down the rock wall. It didn't even blink. For a daft second I thought of persuasion. I said, 'Ranter. Good dog.' It gave me a glance of withering scorn. In fact, so compelling was its thorough examination of the stream's narrow gully that I did it too. We were a weird partnership, quarry and hunter.

Downstream no hope that I could see, the spate frothing on a mincing-machine of large stones. The gully's sides slanted outwards from the granite bed. My beam flicked, returned to the dog, flicked away for a quick glance, back. I didn't want the beast doing anything sly while I was being conned into studying the terrain.

The monster moved, one of those sudden tensions as if about to leap sideways. I yelped in fright. It stayed, splay-footed. I followed its gaze, used my torch to see what it had worked out. The sides of my slab were ripped vertically by ancient geologic forces. A man could just about climb up there but no dog. So? I shone back at Ranter. And it was smiling, its stare fixed above me.

Above? I shone upwards and nearly peed myself in terror. There was an overhang. Barely seven yards above my head the gully's side leaned in to form a shelf. Ranter could get me. I'd had it. Any creature on earth could get up there, look down on me. Then leap and . . . and . . . I whimpered.

The hound gave one last calculating stare, gauged the distance from the ledge to me, then splashed off downstream bounding from rock to rock with that casual, lethal grace. A mad hope swept into me—suddenly Shona had missed him and whistled one of those dogwhistles to call him off.

But no. The overhang was from the side opposite. No way to cross upstream, so it was doing the sensible thing. Downstream where the gully flattened it could easily lope upslope to gain the plateau, then reach the projecting granite and leap . . . I've made it sound like miles. It was maybe a couple of hundred yards, at most. I wondered if there was time to make a run for it . . . But it had nearly caught me when I'd had a start. And now I was knackered. I'm not proud of what I did then. I blubbered and wailed, yelled for help. And did nothing.

Wearily I discarded my jacket, some lunatic notion of wrapping it round my forearm for a last futile aquatic wrestle. It rattled. I felt in my pocket. Two stones. I pulled them out, still tied at opposite ends of the strong twine.

My bolus. That gave me . . . well, one go. The flopping sounded. I set one stone swinging, set the other going, and stood upright with the thing humming vibrantly in my right grip. Up and down, faster. Eyes on the tip of the overhang, I shone the torch there. It was only when I saw his great head loom above the overhang that I realized my stupidity. Too close. My perch was maybe a square yard wide. Any hit would bring me down with him.

He looked. For a millisec I saw puzzlement in his eyes as I leaned away, the bolus whirring. His head nodded up and down in time with my oscillating hand. Perhaps he could hear the string thrumming even over the torrent's din. Then his brow cleared. That humming cord in the man's hand was irrelevant. Orders were orders. He was to hunt and kill, string or no strings. He gathered and leapt down on me.

My arm came from behind. I was already in mid-throw when he left the lip. The bolus met and tangled. The stones were still whipping round and round him as I flung myself forward to avoid his hurtling mass. Foam pressed into my mouth and I was tumbling over, over. Stones slammed my legs, bum, head, shoulder. Noise deafened me. I rolled, engulfed and retching, too dazed to struggle or wonder which way was up. I was drowning. I lashed out, flailed at everything else not me. I was dying.

Except the pandemonium was now somewhere else, with me no longer part of it. I retched. Air. I was in air, not in the water. I breathed, vomited half of the torrent back where it belonged, breathed and crawled. A vertical stone stopped my crawl. I lay there, done for and too terrified to struggle further in case that damned hound heard me and came for me again. I lay, half hiding, half resting. I must have dozed a few minutes I suppose, not much more.

Something pressed against my feet. Something floating, pushing. Perhaps a log? I withdrew my legs, shoved them out.

Still there. It was being moved by the onrush. It was therefore inert. I reached out, scrabbled a cobble up from beneath me and lobbed it at the nudging thing by my feet. Thud. Not a splash, or a sharp crack of stone on stone. A thick bump.

Laboriously I raised myself, extended a hand. Fur. I recoiled in panic, started away. But it hadn't growled. I felt. A huge paw. A great head. A metal-studded collar. And, tethering its forepaws to its neck in a stranglehold, twine. One of the stones seemed to have struck its eye. It was my hunter, my personal executioner.

You can only retch a few times, they say, then the body gives up. True.

Countryside is supposed to increase insight, make poets. That's a laugh. Countryside does nothing but dull your wits. My mind was so addled that I actually started towards where I imagined *Shooters* to be before I said hey, and sat down for a think. It had emitted none of those chiming vibes, so it was no antiques cache. Whoever was in there had warned me, 'Run, run!' An ally. And trapped. Could I spring them? Perhaps, but would I get him/her as far as

Dubneath before the clan caught up? Hardly, the state I was in and burdened by a possible ex-prisoner. And I already knew Hector checked the cottage each dawn.

No. The thing to do was turn up at tomorrow morning's gathering and suss out the reaction to my sudden reappearance. So, typically stupid, I started in the reverse direction, then got lost.

An hour wasted wearying myself even more. See what I mean about countryside? Finally I followed the tumbling water downhill, going slowly and feeling my way. I was perished. No jacket, no torch, wet through, exhausted. The Tachnadray track crossed a stone bridge over a wide fast stream, probably the same water, about a mile from the gateway. I must have been travelling a good hour before I walked into the bridge arch and almost knocked my silly head off. I'll never make a countryman if I live the rest of my life.

Which is why I had a fluke, coming at Tachnadray from that direction. Not as daft as all that, I was on the drive's verge for silence, and moved on the grass round the big house, to reach my pad. There was a light showing beneath the curtain. I thanked my inexpert needlework that had left a wide gap. I slid to the wall and waited.

Shona and Robert came downstairs. The light was off now, but I could hear them clearly. I almost stepped out to warn her.

'Nothing but the map,' Robert rumbled.

'That's proof enough,' Shona said. Her voice was teasing, provocative. 'Ranter should be here now, lazy beast. Doubtless enjoying himself chasing something.' They both laughed. She gave in. 'Come, then, man. Let's lay your head.'

They walked together past the end of the workshop, over to the far outbuilding near the perimeter wall. There was no risk of being overheard. Duncan and Michelle slept in the big house, as did Elaine. Hector was miles off. Mrs Buchan slept downstairs in the cook's flat.

A light showed briefly. Robert having his head laid, doubtless. I stood unmoving for quite some time. Shona was a busy, busy girl. Sex as a reward for complicity. The idea wasn't new. What worried me was its use as an assassin's weapon.

Feeling a hundred years old, I crossed quietly to my garret, went in and locked the door. I had a bath in the dark and lay thinking until dawn blew the fright from the eastern lift. I wish I'd told Shona I'd had a headache in her cottage.

CHAPTER 19

''Morning,' I said brightly to the gathering.

''Morning, Ian,' Duncan gave back affably, pipe ready to stink us out. Michelle was in powder blue, her neat skirt stencilling her waist. She wore a light necklet—not necklace —of a single silver band with a central amethyst, say 1900. Risky, but stunning. Oh, and she too replied an easy good morning. Robert was silent, glaring. Shona, already pale and worn, whitened even more. She knew what my arrival —indeed, my existence—meant. Old Mac was there, to my surprise. And Hector, waving a cheery greeting. Mary MacNeish sat beside Elaine, who today seemed excitable, less transparent than usual.

'Good morning, Ian,' the boss said. 'We were beginning to wonder where you were.'

'Stopped off for a quick snack, love.' Also, I'd actually been to check that my finished fake antique had already gone from Duncan's workshop. I was very pleased at discovering that.

'I've heard about your wee snacks,' Elaine reprimanded drily. 'Mrs Buchan calls you Dustbin.'

'Bloody nerve.' She always pretends she likes my appetite. 'I'll take my custom elsewhere if there's criticism. She's not the only pasty-maker in Caithness, is she, Mary?'

If Mary MacNeish expected me to be staggered at seeing her revealed as a McGunn she was disappointed.

Elaine began. 'Listen, all. Ian suggests we pretend to sell

up Tachnadray.' She held a fragile hand to shush the murmurs. 'I've summoned you to judge the merits. You all know our difficulties. Income's too little to keep the seat of our clan intact. At best we'll last a twelvemonth. Then it's the bailiffs and a boarding-house—'.

'Never!' Robert growled, fists clenched, glaring.

'Whist, man! We have some reserve antiques still—'

My cue. I rose, ahemming. We were arranged round the hall on a right mixture of chairs and benches. I had no notes, standing at my customary hands-in-pocket slouch. The cultural shock had been too much for us all. Truth time.

'Sorry, Elaine. There's no reserve antiques.' I spoke apologetically, but why? 'Not a groatsworth.'

'That's quite wrong.' Elaine held out her hand imperiously. 'The list, Duncan.'

Duncan's gaze was fixed on the floor. He made no move as I went on, 'The list is phoney, love. Duncan and the rest made it up, probably to reassure you. They gave you some cock-and-bull story about the upper west wing being exactly right for storing the remainder of your antiques.'

Everybody tried to talk at once. Elaine cut the babble with a quiet, 'Go on, Ian.'

'Tachnadray is broke *now*, not next year. So, with the last genuine antique gone—'

'Well I mind that day,' Mac suddenly reminisced through his stubble. 'Aye. Me and Cousin Peter from Thurso took it. Your father's grand four-poster, Miss Elaine—'

'Shut up, you old fool,' Duncan said. 'The past is past.'

'It's a familiar story,' I went on. 'Youngsters drift to the cities, a few adherents cling to the past. We've empty villages in East Anglia for the same reason. Tachnadray's marsupialized. It's a rock pool inhabited by crustaceans and sea-anemones—yourselves—after the tide's ebbed.'

'Is this true?' Elaine demanded quietly. Nobody answered. She gazed at each in turn, waiting calmly until heads raised to meet her penetrating stare. She even gave me one. Suddenly I was the only honest crook on the campus. 'Continue.'

'There's only one way out now. We pull a paper job.'

They listened, doubts to the fore, while I explained the rudiments. Duncan's pipe went out. Michelle was enthralled, leaning forward and clearly excited by the whole thing. Robert sank into deeper caverns of hatred. Shona was still getting used to my resurrection.

'We start the papering with a pawnbroker.' Murmurs began, thunder from Robert, but I was fed up with their criticism and raised my voice. 'Not to use. To buy from. Pawnbroking law changes, when items exceed fifty quid. The trick is to find a pawnbroker who'll value even the Crown Jewels at forty-nine ninety-nine. In other words, the meanest. We take his stock—rings, necklaces, clothes—'

'And pretend they are Tachnadray's heirlooms?' Elaine asked. 'Isn't that rather hard on the widows and orphans?'

'Yes.' My answer led into a vale of silence. I was a dicey Sherpa in treacherous mountains.

'Will that be sufficient?' Elaine must have been painfully aware of the outraged glances from the others.

'No. We'll need more. But pawnbroking's gone downhill these sixty years. There's only a couple of hundred left in the entire land, which narrows our choice. We'll want an entire convoy of antiques from somewhere, especially furniture. I've already started raising the dealers.'

'And told them *here*?' Shona was on her feet, furious.

'Don't be daft.'

She subsided. Twice she'd absently reached out a hand as if about to pat a loyal hound. Both times she'd looked about, distressed. More grief was on the way, poor lass.

'I've one problem, how to bring the antiques in. It'll be a sizeable convoy.'

They waited. Elaine waited. And so did I, examining their expectant faces.

'Well?' Elaine's telepathy trick had gone on the blink.

'Air, road, or sea?' I asked. 'Same as usual?'

And Old Mac, bless him, said, 'Och, yon sounds a terrible lot for a . . .' Hector shut him up by a double nudge.

130

'. . . For a wee ketch like Jamie's,' I finished for him, nodding. 'And your old lorry, Mac. I'd better organize a road convoy. The airport at Wick's too obvious.'

Elaine was smiling. 'Congratulations, Ian. We can't be blamed for trying to conceal our method of delivery. I hope you don't think us too immoral. The fewer people know, the better.'

'Is it agreed, then?'

'Yes.' Elaine's pronouncement gained no applause. The atmosphere smouldered with resentment. 'How long does this . . . papering take?'

'A month. First, we need a compliant printer.'

'Hamish in Wick is clan,' Elaine said.

'Next, I'll need a secure helper. Can I choose?'

'Of course,' said the young clan leader, and everybody looked expectantly at Shona.

Shona spoke first. 'I can start any time.' She gave me her special bedroom smile.

'Thanks,' I said, beaming most sincerely. 'But no, ta. Ready, Michelle?'

We were given an office in the empty west wing. Hector and a couple of men fetched some rough-and ready rubbish for us to use as furniture. Michelle was awarded a desk: a folding baize-topped card table. They found a lop-sided canvas chair from somewhere, and, unbelievably, for me a discarded car seat nailed to a stool. An elderly lady appeared from nowhere and contributed a brass oil lamp. Elaine ordered herself carried upstairs by Robert to inspect our progress.

'I'm ashamed this is the best Tachnadray can offer, Ian.' She directed Robert as an infant does its dad, by yanking on his nape hairs. She held a fistful of mane.

'I've done nowt yet, love. Got some carrier pigeons?'

'The phone was . . . discontinued. I'm sorry. Mrs Buchan will gong your mealtimes. I've sent for writing paper.'

Just then it arrived, two incomplete schoolbooks and half a letterpad, and a bottle with an ounce of ink dregs. Michelle was pink with embarrassment. Even Elaine, who was anti-prestige, looked uncomfortable. But to me rubbish is about par.

'One thing, Elaine. I'll want to ask questions occasionally. If Robert assaults me every time we'll get nowhere.'

'Robert,' promised our chieftainess, 'will not hurt you. Ask away.'

'Question one: nearest telephone?'

'Dubneath.'

'Two: nearest stores which'll give us credit?'

'Innes in Dubneath.'

'No, love. I've had to pay for everything there.'

'We never shop in Wick,' Elaine said, aloof but mortified.

Lucky old Wick, I thought. 'Then I'll break with tradition. Three: transport. Old Mac's lorry, I suppose?'

Elaine hesitated. 'There's the laird's car. It's old.'

Laird? Presumably her late dad. 'Tell Old Mac to siphon petrol out of his wagon, enough for a run to Wick. I'll manage after that. And four,' I added as Robert became fidgety at my peremptory manner, 'I must be given a free hand. Okay?'

An instant's thought, then Elaine's see-through gaze turned on Michelle. 'Very well. You, Michelle, will be responsible for his movements. Entirely. You do understand?'

'Yes, Miss Elaine.'

I didn't, though the threat was evident to all. Michelle and I stood and watched the redhaired giant clump down the corridor. I reached out and shook Michelle's hand. She was puzzled.

'Yes, Ian? What . . . ?'

'Welcome to the antiques game, love,' I said. 'It's murderous, packed with deceit, wonderful. We begin, you and I, by making a promise to each other. I tell you everything I'm doing, and you do the same for me. Deal?'

That took a minute to decide. She nodded at last, and smiled, but with that familiar despair hidden in her face. It occurred to me that she was as imprisoned as Joseph, in her way. Interesting thought, no? I laughed as she flapped her hand helplessly at the room.

132

'It's ridiculous,' she said. 'All we've done is put some scraps in a bare room, and you're grinning all over your face. Why?'

A window-pane had lost a corner. Putty flaked the sills. Patches of damp showed at two fungus-hung corners. Plaster had fragmented here and there, exposing laths and bricks, and powdered mortar lay in heaps ready for a dustpan, if we ever acquired one. An old wall cupboard had lost its doors, its wallpaper blebbing in the recess. Three cavities showed where somebody had wrenched out the gas fittings. How very thorough, I thought. Laird James Wheeler McGunn must have been harder up than me, even. The floor lino was reduced to a torn patch.

'Showbusiness time, Michelle,' I said. 'Start.'

'Start what? How?' She was lost.

'We pretend to drive to Wick, but finish up in the opposite direction.'

'But, Ian . . .' she said uncertainly.

'Sod Ian,' I told her. 'My nickname's Lovejoy. Ready, steady, go.'

CHAPTER 20

The laird's car was familiar. I'd last seen it on a foggy night a wagoneer had died. I said nothing. It was a Mawdslay 17 h.p., that collectors call The Sweet Seventeen.

We drove beside Dubneath Water, my least favourite river, to gain the coast road north from Dubneath towards Clyth Ness. Using the louring mass of Ben Cheilt for guide, we forked left and made the inn at Achavanish with the huge old motor clattering away. It seemed glad to be out for a run. Certainly it hadn't seemed to notice the road's pitch, and took steep hills with hardly a change of note. I phoned from the inn, and got Tinker at Margaret's nook in the Arcade.

Margaret was relieved. 'Oh, thank goodness you've phoned, Lovejoy. It's practically civil war here. The Eastern

Hundreds are a madhouse. Everybody wants to know per-centages—'

'Don't we all?' I said with feeling. 'Put Tinker on.' I covered the mouthpiece and told Michelle, poised with the inn's notepaper, 'List what I say.'

Tinker's cough vibrated Caithness. 'Wotcher, Lovejoy. Gawd, you started summink, mate—'

'Shut it. Get Tubby Turner, that pawnbroker. I'll accept maybe three dozen items well over the pawn limit as long as they're in period. Plus a hundred separates under limit, and half a dozen baskets.'

'Gawd, Tubby'll go mental. You know what he's like.' His cough bubbled and croaked.

Michelle had stopped writing. 'But you said that there's a legal limit to what pawnbrokers—'

My digit raised in warning. She wrote.

'Listen, Tinker. Tell Alan the printer that he's had four hundred sale catalogues nicked.'

'Whose?'

'Catalogues for this sale. Now give me names, Tinker.'

'Right, Lovejoy. Helen wants in. She says you owe her.'

Only I knew how much. Plus there was the money side. She'd have to come in. Why is it women are born with so many advantages in life? Nothing to do all day, and all known privileges. 'Right-oh. Helen in.'

'Them two poofs. Sandy or Mel.'

'*Or* Mel? Not both?' The exotic couple had never parted since they'd become, in Sandy's gushy phrase, a real Darby and Joan. Tinker hates them. They're fast aggressive antique dealers, though, and that's what I needed.

'They had a scrap over some menu.'

How can you fight over a menu? 'All right. Sandy or Mel.'

'Next's Big Frank from Suffolk.'

That meant I could safely forget Regency and William IV silverware, thank God. It can be a nightmare. If only the Yanks had worked out a proper five-character hallmarking system . . .

'Is he out of trouble, Tinker?'

'Him? Some hopes. His second ex-wife's come.' Bad news for the latest wife, currently seventh, because his bigamies started with Number Two. But that meant he'd accept a lower percentage. 'Big Frank in.'

'Sven.'

'Not Sven.' His stuff's always got a leg missing.

'Margaret, Lovejoy?' Tinker knows about me and Margaret.

'Margaret, in. She'll reff. Next?'

'Liz Sandwell from Dragonsdale?'

'In, but not with Harry Bateman.' Tinker cackled. There'd been sordid rumours.

'Then Hymie. Says you owes him, that pearl scam . . .'

'How come I owe everybody when it's me that's bloody broke?' Tinker cackled himself into a coughing fit. For the first time in his life the antique dealers would be falling over themselves to buy him beer.

Next Lily. And Mannie of caftan and cowbell fame, dealer in antique timepieces. And Jill for porcelain, as long as she didn't bring her poodle and wandering matelots. And Brad because I needed flintlocks. And Long Tom Church for musical instruments. And Janice who never smiles, for late antique jewellery . . .

While Michelle tidied her lists I telephoned a general stores in Thurso, and asked to speak to the manager. I decided to become a Cockney trying to talk posh, Harrods-on-Woolworth.

'This is Sinclair, sir,' I announced gravely, which arrested Michelle's flowing pen. 'Butler to the laird, who is come to stay at Tachan Water. Local purveyors are not to my required standard. I am consequently obliged to send the laird's motor with his man Barnthwaite and the house-keeper. They are empowered to purchase. An invoice note is necessary for each item, if you please. They will arrive two hours from now.'

Michelle was aghast as I rang off. 'You said you were somebody else!'

'So?'

'And you told Elaine's gathering we'd only have cheap

antiques. You've just ordered three dozen that could cost thousands. Don't deny it!'

'All right,' I concurred amiably. 'Got money for grub? Driving always makes me peckish.'

'But you've not long had breakfast—'

'Stop arguing, woman, and read me that list. Incidentally,' I said as we boarded the motor, 'do the mean buggers ever let you visit Joseph?'

That shut her. She took a long time to speak. 'What's going on, Ian?' she said.

'How the hell do I know?' I grumbled. I hate being famished on a journey.

'No,' Michelle finally answered, listlessly letting the wind buffet her hair as we lammed off north-west. 'I've asked. And Duncan tried to go on strike once. Hopeless.'

'The rotten sods. That'd annoy me, if he were my son.'

'There's nothing we can do. Not after he'd betrayed Tachnadray.'

The immense bonnet nudged the winding slope, with me trying to hold her below thirty m.p.h. 'Look, Michelle. Betrayal's too big a word. You betray countries and kings, not a bloody house with a few ageing retainers. Your Joseph tried to make a few quid on the side by selling Tachnadray's last antique bureau. It isn't the end of the world. I don't know anybody who hasn't had a go.' Feeling my way still, but not doing too badly. 'Never mind, love. We'll see what we can do for Joseph, eh?'

Her eyes filled. She looked away and rummaged for a hankie in her handbag. What on earth do women keep in them? It took a fortnight before she was snivelling right.

'There's no way out, Ian. We just had to protect Joseph after the incident. Robert saved him from being caught.'

'Check your list,' I said with a cheery smile. 'Take your mind off things.'

Thurso's a lovely old place. Ferries from the north wend to the islands. Its size and bustle surprised me; North Sea oil, I suppose, or innate vigour. Folk might say it's not up to much, but for me Thurso will always get a medal. It was there that the whole thing fell into place.

Mr McDuff was pleasantly young, very impressed by our motor. I'd parked it outside in full view, surreptitiously asking Michelle who I was supposed to be.

'You told him Barnthwaite.' She sat, clearly having none of it. I yanked her out, maintaining a charming smile and gripping her arm bloodless.

'Smile, love,' I said through my smile. 'You're Mrs Mac-Henry until I say otherwise, or it's gaol for the pair of us.'

I introduced myself to Mr McDuff while Mrs MacHenry made her selections. We were told that a separate invoice would have to be signed for every order. I sighed, said Mr Sinclair the butler was a stickler for inventories.

It was after we'd loaded up that light dawned. The stores lad carried out the victuals, groceries, wines and whatnot, while Michelle and I went to sign. Mr McDuff had the invoices all ready and offered me them. I frowned.

'No, sir,' I corrected. 'I'm never empowered to sign. The laird's housekeeper does it, Mrs MacHenry.'

He ahemed, hating being caught out in protocol. He'd rather have died. 'Of course,' he exclaimed, passing her the pen.

Now, one of the most surprising facts of life is that women make bad crooks. Which, when you think about it, is really weird. I mean, they're born deceivers. Right from birth they're talented fibbers and conwomen. And their entire lives are a testimony to pretence. Yet how often do you hear of a really dazzling robbery executed by a bird? No. Birds go for the drip-feed: a zillion minor transgressions, debts created wholesale because trillions of housewives skilfully delay paying today's electricity bill. Individually, nothing. Totalled, a genuine migraine for Lloyd's of London. It explains a lot about the structure of society. Which is the reason I'd warned Michelle every second breath that she wasn't to forget her true identity, Mrs MacHenry. And even as she took the manager's pen to sign I watched her, heart beating, in case she absently signed 'Michelle McGunn'. That was how I saw her face when I mentioned the laird. For that fleeting moment, she suffered anguish. But it all passed smoothly, and we left for Tarrant's.

This was a mine of stuff. Brass, woods, sheet metals, resins, glues, studs, tools. Aladdin's cave. I'd had the fore-thought to ask Mr McDuff's opinion of ship-chandlers in Thurso. A phone call from Mr Tarrant to McDuff estab-lished our credibility, which sadly nowadays means mere credit-worthiness. Sign of the times, that the word for trust-worthy now relates only to money.

'The laird doesn't hold with plastic cards,' I told Mr Tarrant. 'He settles in money, though it'd make it so much simpler for us, wouldn't it, Mrs MacHenry? He won't listen.'

'True,' Michelle sighed. By then, to my relief, she'd stopped that awful inner weeping which started at McDuff's stores when I'd called her the laird's.

We got a ton of invaluable materials, promised to call in four days for more stuff, and departed. Luckily Michelle had enough money for us to buy pasties from the market. I pulled in south-east on the A882 for us to nosh.

Michelle gave a rather hysterical giggle, gazing at the car's contents. We'd had to buy a roof-rack to load the stuff.

'We've committed a robbery,' she said, laughing.

'Scrub that plural, love,' I corrected. 'You signed, remem-ber? In fact, we've got to call in at Dubneath police station and tell all.'

She laughed so much that she finally started to cry. I'm not much use at consolation, so I had her pasty to save it going cold. We weren't so credit-worthy that we could afford to chuck good stuff to waste. It was faith we lacked. Anyway there was no time left now for any of this malarky. It was splashdown.

The first splash occurred at the police station, where I spoke to the one bobby in charge.

'It's rather a serious problem,' I said. 'We wish to report a theft.' Which widened Michelle's eyes even further. She was already frantic, thinking we'd come to surrender over the groceries.

Michelle groaned. I admonished her, 'Please, Mrs McGunn. Do keep calm. The police are here to help in these cases.'

The bobby swelled with understanding and eagle-eyed vigilance. We got Michelle a chair while I explained, in strictest confidence, about the secret auction at Tachnadray.

'Naturally,' I said, leaning anxiously over the constabulary desk, 'Miss Elaine wants this information kept confidential. I employed a printer in East Anglia. I've just heard that all four hundred printed catalogues were stolen in Suffolk.'

The sergeant put his pen down. 'Only catalogues?'

'*Only?*' I bleated, aghast. 'Advance notice to antique dealers is valuable information. We hope to restrict the sale to a limited number of trusted collectors.'

'And?' He resumed writing, without enthusiasm.

'So we want a twenty-four hour police guard, please.'

He stopped writing. 'A what?'

'Round-the-clock surveillance. Now—' I waxed enthusiastic—'the way I see it is a road block, and a helicopter—'

'Sir,' the sergeant said wearily, 'do you know the size of our area? And the number of officers with which we're expected to run it?'

'But surely you see the implications for the sale?'

He sighed. 'Consider a moment, sir. These booklets.'

'Catalogues,' I corrected, frosty.

'Catalogues. Where would they have gone to?'

'Well, I ordered them posted to collectors as far as Germany, America—'

'And the material in them . . .?'

'Descriptions of antiques for auction at Tachnadray.'

He put his pen away. 'Well, sir. Naturally we're only too anxious to assist Tachnadray Hall, but auctions are quite legal. And for people to come and buy's quite legal too. How they hear about it's their own business. The only problem is the loss—you say by theft—of your catalogues. That's a concern for the Suffolk division. Naturally, if you have any problems about admission on the day . . .'

Polite, but undoubtedly the sailor's elbow. Showing profound disappointment with Dubneath's constabulary, I extracted a promise of complete silence on the matter, then left huffily. Michelle was already bewildered into obedience, so my dragging her into the MacNeishes' tavern to use the phone produced no demur, not even when I feverishly phoned the local *Tachan Times and Argus*, the district's *Pravda*, to issue a denial.

'This is Ian McGunn,' I told the reporter sternly. 'There is absolutely *no* truth in rumours that we attach the slightest importance to the outrageous theft of sale catalogues on their way to Tachnadray.' The girl squealed to hold on please, evidently scrabbling to snap her Marconi Patent Office Wax-Cylinder Voice Recorder into action. 'Furthermore,' I went on, 'we deplore the inability of the police to respond to requests for total surveillance, and demand that you omit any mention of this . . .'

We did the same denial for six other newspapers, including the *Glasgow Herald*. Mary hadn't baked that day, having been up at the Hall, so no pasties. I had to make do with a batch of over-sweet Chorley cakes and a left-over cheese and onion pie before we hit the road to Tachnadray.

'Anybody in the clan a crooked auctioneer, love?' I said through a mouthful.

Michelle smiled, thinking I was joking. 'Ian. How do you remember everything we're doing? Including all your lies to Sergeant Kerr?'

I said piously, 'I didn't lie, love.'

She gasped a pure innocent gasp, her hair fluffing in the breeze. I was beginning to like Michelle. 'There really *was* a theft? Our catalogues really were stolen? How dreadful!'

'Well, it actually doesn't happen till tonight.'

'But how can that possibly—?'

'Shut it, love.' Liking her didn't mean all this explaining wasn't giving me a headache. 'And don't admit I know about Joseph. They already know I know, but still don't.'

She gave a heartfelt sigh. 'Hasn't it been a day?'

She didn't know it yet, but the poor lass should've saved her heartfelt sighs. She'd soon need every one she could get.

CHAPTER 21

Just as you can't outdo the Maltese for doorknockers or the Swiss for cuckoo clocks, so you can't beat Caithness for conviction. Once Tachnadray had declared for crime, it became Fighter Command in a 1940 film, furiously active yet meticulous. Maybe it was their first delicious taste of scamming that gingered everybody up. I don't know. Within three days it came alive.

At my seminary school they used to set us a perennial problem: given the choice, whether to disbelieve in God or His absence. I never knew how to answer. Similarly, I'm never quite sure whether it's crime or sanctity which offers the least painful compromise for the human race. I've experimented with both, and found little difference. Now, I think perhaps sin has the edge, because it at least provides a decent income. So maybe it was the hope of solvency which spurred Elaine's retainers on.

At my request Elaine had spread word. Any old objects relating to the clan, or to any McGunn, Tachnadray, Caithness or indeed the Highlands, were badly needed at Tachnadray. Anyone wanting to sell the same should communicate with Michelle McGunn at Tachnadray forthwith. They actually started coming in by that first afternoon. How the hell did news travel? I tried asking an old woman who came trogging up carrying an infantry officer's telescope —leather-cased, War Office stamp and arrows—and she merely smiled, 'Och, I heard,' which was as far as I got.

Our peaceful scene had a visit from a police car asking if everything was all right. I started my favourite spiel requesting road blocks, helicopters . . . They drove off in haste. A Glasgow paper'd run a spread showing Alan pointing to bits of broken windscreen on the Ipswich bypass—the result of my phoned instruction to Tinker. Decadent youth, exploited by international financiers, was apparently to blame. More coverage—as the media nowadays term falsehood—

was on the way. A TV crew was turned away. That sat sullenly on the hillside until Robert mustered a sortie to persuade.

And the letters came in.

That second day, Michelle was thrilled, rushing to find me in the workshop and holding all three. 'And one's from London!' she cried, beside herself. 'From a collector!'

'Get notepaper printed, love,' I said. I was busily engraving Elaine's coat-of-arms on a mid-nineteenth-century pipe box, silver. It's murder by hand, but more artistic than the modified dental drills most forgers use. I felt bad about it for the box's sake, but murder asserts priorities.

'Notepaper? Think of the expense, Ian!'

'All right, love.' I regoggled and resumed my engraving. 'Only don't come wailing I didn't warn you.'

'Michelle.' Duncan was fretting out some wood sections I'd marked. 'Do as Ian says. Get young Hamish along today.'

'Very well.' Michelle was still doubtful. 'But I can't see why we'd waste money printing grand notepaper when I can just as easily write our address longhand.'

Duncan didn't glance at me. 'We've never done anything like this before, and Ian has.'

Hamish McGunn, printer, came on a bicycle about teatime, fingers black and face pale. He looked subnourished, Charles Dickens in the blacking factory. Michelle brought him across, still in a huff from being told off. She fetched tea in mugs and a bowl of barm-cakes with margarine. No jam, and it served us right.

'Ian wants notepaper printed,' she said, angrily offering the nosh so fast you had to make a dive.

'Embossed,' I said, 'if you've got that thermal process. Tachnadray's coat-of-arms left, and address. Put Michelle as "Auction Secretary". And our phone number.'

'Tachnadray isn't on the phone,' Michelle said.

Hamish wrote on unheeding, squarish writing, hard pencil.

'And then do a flyer sheet. The colours are yours, but choose discreet posh.' I gave him a crumpled paper. 'That's

142

the wording. A thousand of each by tomorrow noon.' I grinned inside as his head raised. 'Ten days Michelle'll give you the full catalogue. Two thousand, about sixty pages. There'll be one score colour plates and three score black-and-white.'

'Ay, there's just the question, Ian,' Hamish said, embarrassed.

'The money in seven days. But—' I raised a handy maul in threat—'use Linotron Baskerville or Bembo and the deal's off. We've got educated folk coming. Okay?'

He left laughing, pedalling like the clappers.

Michelle stuck to her guns. 'Tachnadray's no longer on the phone.' Poor lass, it was all becoming too much.

'A Telecom van'll be here soon, love.' I gave her my most innocent gaze. 'Could you direct them to Dr Lamont's office please?'

'Dr Lamont?' She stood helplessly.

'Doctors get priority with phones.'

'But is there really a Dr Lamont—?'

A kilted man staggering under a bookcase from Mac's lorry shouted, 'Michelle. A telephone man's here asking . . .' She left at a stumbling run.

'Honestly,' I said to the silent Duncan as we resumed work. 'Women. Set them a hand's turn and they go to pieces. Notice there was no jam?'

The whole of Tachnadray was silent. It was ten-thirty, long past nightfall. Michelle, lustrous as a grisaille-glass Early English cathedral window at sunset, had met me as instructed in our lonely office. Our only light was candles and an oil lamp.

'Ready?' I asked huskily.

'Yes,' she said. Her face glowed, her eyes danced.

Cunning to the last, I dialled and passed the receiver. 'Our first phone call from Tachnadray.'

'This is the house auction secretary speaking,' she said. 'Could I please have, ah, Tinker?'

I egged her on. 'Don't forget the room.'

'Tinker? This is Mrs Michelle, auction secretary. You

will please transfer to a separate extension in a room away from noise.' An alarmed expression, her hand on the mouthpiece. 'He says he can't, Ian. It sounds like a . . .'

'It *is* a pub. Tell the boozy old devil to take his beer and Ted can shoot refills through the hatch.'

'He's going,' Michelle whispered. 'What a dreadful cough.'

'You're doing great.'

'He said where's Lovejoy. That's the name you—'

Tinker's cough ground out as I took the receiver. 'Tinker? 'Course the scam's on. Listen: make sure you remember this bird's voice, d'y'hear? She'll be doing the phoning every night. She's new so talk slow, understand? And a new pub every night. Treble Tile tomorrow, same time. Make sure she gets the number.'

'Bird indeed,' Michelle muttered.

'And Tinker. I've decided on the auctioneer. Tee up Trembler.'

'Bleedin' 'ell,' Tinker croaked. 'Asking for trouble?'

I lost my rag. 'Do as your bloody told,' I yelled. 'Everybody's flaming boss until it's time to pick up the tab—'

'Awreet, Lovejoy. I'll find him. But Aussie's free and Flintstone's out of clink—'

'*Trembler!*' I bawled, then, smiling, passed Michelle the receiver. 'Off you go, love. Good luck. Tell Tinker to glam Trembler up. And get a typewriter.'

'Glam? A typewriter? Where from?' she was asking, round-eyed, as I took my leave with a candle to light my way. I didn't reply. Where from, indeed. Did I have to think of everything? I went to see if there was blood on the laird's old car.

The monster motor was housed in a drystone coach-house behind Duncan's workshop. Before knocking off as night fell I'd trailed a cable from the window while Duncan had a final smoke at the door, his closing ritual safe from our volatile solvents. I'd left the switch down.

The cable stretched to the coach-house, explaining its length. Robert padlocked the double doors on the motor's return, always good for a laugh. I opened the door, trailed the cable in after me, pulled the leaf shut. A bulb from my pocket, and I started searching.

Say, forty minutes later, and defeat. No blood that I could see. Blood's russet after a few minutes, then brown, then black. It was a common enough art stain in its time, and you can tell the shade. Therefore, Joseph, who was Michelle and Duncan's son, who'd 'betrayed Tachnadray' and was now kept imprisoned at *Shooters*, had returned without being bludgeoned. Persuaded? Drugged? Gunpoint? I gave up. Lots of puzzles in clan country. Not a lot of explanations.

Two dozen letters next morning, proving my denials to the world's press were working a treat. Michelle drumming her fingers saying things like, 'Where's that Hamish got to?' Mrs Buchan gave me a three-plate breakfast and some scruffy young lass zoomed coffee to our office.

'I like your new nail varnish, Michelle. Women don't use enough make-up.'

'Thank you,' she said. She was narked because the coffee bird was talkative. 'Shouldn't we make a start? There's so much to do.'

And there was. I'd nicked a few old fruit boxes, into which she sorted the letters by postmark. I was pleased. I like evidence of suspicion. It means people are thinking.

'Haven't you got little feet?' I said. 'Has everybody got titchie plates in Belgium?'

'Tinker's list is completely erratic,' she began, ignoring this banter. 'I tried to make him dictate items according to the dealers. He was most abusive.'

'Tut-tut.' I apologized for Tinker, struggling for sobriety. 'You'll have to crossfile, love.'

'And he doesn't seem to know you as . . . as Ian McGunn, Ian. Only by that absurd nickname.' She wasn't looking up. We'd never been closer. I said nothing. She shrugged and began, 'First, then. A tortoiseshell—'

'No, love. Give everything a number starting at one zero zero zero, or you'll make mistakes. Documentary errors run at four per cent among auctioneers.'

'Number one thousand, then. A tortoiseshell armorial stencil, from Three Wheel Archie. Then a word: quatrefoil.'

I almost welled up. Putting him first was Tinker's way of saying everything was normal between me and Three-Wheel, that he was back on my side. I coughed, and covered up my embarrassment by explaining, 'Quatrefoil's the code you'll use for secretly pricing Archie's items. No letter recurs; ten letters, see? Q is one, U is two, so on to L which is nought. It's called steganography. You can use the letters to denote any amount of money.' Craftsmen serving noble houses cut coat-of-arms designs in tortoiseshell for ease of repainting armorials on coaches, chests, even furniture. Women used them for embroidery.

'Secret pricing? What a cheat!'

'You know anybody who doesn't cheat?' I asked drily. She reddened and read on.

'Number thousand and one. A nineteenth-century button die from Helen, eight sides; she thinks the Howard family crest. Sutherland. Another code?'

'Yes. Helen always uses "Sutherland" as her price code. But refuse it, love. Too many wrong crests'll reveal it's a papering job. Pity.'

A button die's valuable because you can strike genuine silver buttons on it till the cows come home. A bit of sewing then converts any period garment into Lord Howard of Effingham's, with great (but illicit) profit.

'One thousand and two. Fob seal, glass intaglio on gold, Chester 1867. Big Frank . . .'

Hamish came at nine-thirty, looking even younger still. He was hesitant, definitely guarded.

'Noticed something amiss, Hamish?' I joked.

'It's this: Sotheby's "Standard Conditions of Sale" Apply Throughout.' He showed me a copy. 'As long as it's in order.' I reassured him a mite, and he went down to unload. His bike pulled a tiny homemade cart, a packing case on pram wheels. I went to the window to watch him in the forecourt. What a lot of people.

'Michelle. How many McGunns are there?'

'Thirty-two, but very scattered.'

More than I'd supposed. Yet if you counted them all over the Kingdom . . .?

'I mean retainers, pensioners, employees at Tachnadray.' Hamish below was hanging a wooden tray round his neck to carry those obsessively neat brick-like parcels printers make. 'What *is* a retainer, love? Is Hamish one?'

'Somebody on a croft belonging, that sort of thing.'

'Tied to Tachnadray by loyalty and economics?'

Michelle hesitated, unhappy at the way my questions were heading. 'Yes. But nobody would express it in those terms. Not nowadays.'

''Course not, love.' I gave her a sincere smile.

Still looking down, as Michelle, with ill-disguised relief, recommenced her list checking, and Hamish clumped up the stairs with the stationery, I couldn't help thinking: thirty-two, probably, not counting infants. Say, twenty houses or so. Which is quite a lot of hidey-holes.

At noon I decided to drive into Thurso with Elaine, leaving Michelle replying to the letters and sending out flyers in envelopes. She still hadn't got a typewriter. I'd refused her baffled excuse that there simply wasn't one. 'Don't plead unavailability,' I commanded.

'But, Ian—'

'Look, Michelle,' I'd said kindly, tucking a Scotch plaid rug round Elaine's knees. 'We've reached the stage where talking's done. We need action.'

She blazed up at that. I think she really only wanted to come a ride. 'Action, is it! Then what about postage stamps? By tea-time we'll have scores of letters to post and no money—'

'A post office franking machine arrives today, love.'

The post office supplies a little printing gadget which marks your envelopes. It's the only postage you can get on tick. You pay only when the man comes to read its meter.

'And,' I concluded, 'two letters'll arrive, neither with enough postage. You'll have to pay a few coppers to the postie.'

Michelle listened, nodded, didn't wave us off. First time in her life she'd ever shut up. Swinging us out of the gate,

I asked Elaine to issue an order to the vestigial remnants of the clan.

'Not you too, Ian!' she exclaimed. 'I've noticed it creeping into your bones. You're careful to say "Scottish" instead of Scotch now, even when "Scotch" is correct. Soon you'll be fighting drunk at football matches. You'll believe our stupid tribal myths.' She was watching Tachnadray recede in the wing mirror. I said nothing, making my unresponsiveness an invitation. She began to speak on, quiet and intense. 'That lunacy killed my father. He drank himself to death. Failing to become the legend of the Scottish clan chief. You know something?' She gave me a woman's no-smile smile. 'He had a stroke the day after two immigrant Pakistanis registered a Clan MacKhan tartan. What could *that* possibly have mattered?'

'Shona thinks you're a heretic. Paradox, eh? Clan Chieftainess as iconoclast.' The giant Mawdslay's tyres made a crackling sound on the track. I could do with these vintage motors, but everything seems on the outside almost out of reach with you perched high as a pope in a palanquin.

'Wasn't William IV the best socialist of his time?' she shot back. 'Pride's for those with money to burn. Pomp and circumstance reduced Tachnadray to penury. The carriages —we had six, matched horses—went, the grooms, liveried servants. And Father entertaining, hosting the County Show, silver everywhere, guests by special trains we couldn't pay for. Shooting parties. Mother gave up early, passed away when I was two. I saw the whole film round, the dozen pipers on our battlements. One enormous sham. You know what? Father even had battlements built, because Tachnadray had none.'

Her bitterness was getting to me. I knew all about tribal ferocities, having seen Sidoli's war with Bissolotti.

'Why not simply take the gelt from whoever wants to pay you? Everybody else does. An ancient lairdship's marketable—'

'Because,' she said. The little girl's defiant silencer.

I wasn't having that. 'Because Shona's mob won't let you?' It was my pennyworth. I'd wrestled the great

Mawdslay as far as Dubneath Water before she answered.

'Whose side are you on, Ian? Tradition's?' The last word was spat out with hatred.

Well, I couldn't really say until I'd visited her mother's grave, but I gave her my best fill-in. 'The prettiest bird's.'

'Me?' She was smiling.

'Bullseye.' So far I'd counted two men watching on skylines, plus Robert.

'Then I've a problem for you.' A pulse beat, then, 'I'm still a virgin, Lovejoy. Which means I require information about sex techniques . . . Why're we stopping?'

'*What* did you say?'

'It's a golden opportunity. There's no one else I can ask. Tell me. Do women mostly make love on their sides sometimes, with their leg over the man? Only, with my handicap—'

The lumbering Mawdslay, slightly shocked, resumed its journey. 'Look, love,' I said anxiously.

'Don't go all coy, Ian.' She was quite reasonable. 'I read once that sexual intercourse . . .'

Shona's van caught us up by the first houses. She'd been following us, naughty girl. And Jamie was waiting in Dubneath's market square. All smiling friendliness, but very definitely there.

CHAPTER 22

Shona's presence in Dubneath put the kibosh on any further interrogation—me of Elaine about crookdom, Elaine of me about sex. Elaine had to visit the one bank, and Shona seemed determined to accompany her. Innocently I said I'd sightsee, happy to be squeezed out. Shona's furrowed brow cleared at that. Jamie went off down the harbour after we'd lifted Elaine's wheelchair to get her mobile. I walked to the chapel, slow and idle.

Reverend Ruthven was a pleasant balding man who told me, 'Two things, Ian. I'm a pastor, not a vicar. And secondly, I'm the exception that proves the rule.' He had to explain that Ruthvens were addicted to assassination over a long and bloody history. 'I'm probably the first peaceable Ruthven on earth!'

'Lineage seems a right pest.'

He sighed. 'It can be, Ian, heaven knows. Come. I expect you're here to see the McGunns. A fated clan, if I may say so.'

'Fated? Everybody's fated. Why McGunns especially?'

'Conflict dooms life. They say your very name is Norse, *gunnr*, meaning war. Etymological pilf, of course. But the war between those wretched Sinclairs and the Sutherland Gordons crushed the poor McGunn clan. It's a wonder there's any of you left. The Gordons are a rapacious breed.'

He took me among the chapel's gravestones, and pointed out Elaine's mother's. And the laird's headstone, coat-of-arms on marble, a little way off. James Wheeler McGunn.

'Elaine was telling me about her mother, Pastor. How very sad.' I shook my head sorrowfully as if I knew so much.

'Aye, Ian. Isn't that life all over? Unable to come to terms with The McGunn's fanaticism. Clan was everything to the poor man. Driven. It's often the way, with converts. Reasoning erodes. Jesuits call it a state of erroneous conscience.'

'I understand.' I was very knowing, and lied, 'My mother and she used to correspond, until matters . . .'

We both sighed. Pastor Ruthven determined to exonerate Elaine's mother. 'Then you'll know how hard The McGunn took it. Women tend to blame themselves in those circumstances.'

'And needlessly.' I was busy working out in what circumstances.

After that it was sundry graves, the chapel foundation stone, a list of former pastors, gold lettering on stained mahogany, before I decided it was time to go. 'You'll have had your bite, Ian . . .?' An Edinburgh man. He said to call again. I promised to, but wouldn't need. How come Ruthven likened James Wheeler McGunn to a 'convert', when he in fact was The McGunn?

Shona, Elaine and me sat down for a nosh at the Mac-Neish tavern. Mary told me that two letters had come addressed to me, care of Michelle, with only half the requisite postage. Elaine looked across. I went all innocent and said my friends were sometimes careless. My granny actually taught me the trick: registered letters hint at riskily valuable contents. But skimp the ordinary postage and the postman'll beat a path to your door to recover that outstanding penny. It's cheaper than registration and far more reliable.

'Just think, Mary,' I told her through a mouthful. 'Soon we McGunns'll be able to start paying for these tuppenny pasties of yours.'

She blazed up at that. 'Twopence? I'll have you know, Ian McGunn, that my cooking's worth more than—' etcetera, etcetera. A pleasant meal, with me prattling away and inspecting Elaine's and Shona's respective faces. Faces are fascinating, but I've already told you that.

Shona followed the Mawdslay back. I was determined to tell Elaine about attribution. Elaine was determined to ask about sex.

'When you buy a painting at auction,' I said firmly, 'you'll lose your life savings if you simply believe what's written in the catalogue. Never mind that it clearly states: "Giotto, *St Peter Blessing the Penitents*". That only means a work of the school of Giotto, by a student or merely some ninth-rate artist who painted in Giotto's style, and that the date's completely uncertain. In other words, it could be by the world's worst forger. Now,' I waxed enthusiastically, holding the booming engine in up the fell road, 'if the catalogue gives the artist's initials as well—'

'About sex,' Elaine interrupted.

'—then you're on safer ground. It means the painting is of the artist's period, though *only possibly* his work, in whole or in part—'

'Have you ever raped anyone, Ian?'

'What you look for,' I shouted desperately, 'is the artist's complete name. That means it's really by Giotto himself—'

'Who decides that sex will happen?' Elaine pondered. 'Does it hurt very much the first time?'

'Knock it off, love,' I begged, hot under the collar

'How does it end? I mean, do you both simply get tired?'

'You need your bum smacked, miss.' Me, with sternness my next failure.

'Spanking,' said this devil seriously. 'A sado-masochistic ritualization enjoyed by ninety-one per cent of women. A Salford survey—'

Good old Salford, still hard at it. See what I mean about women? If they find they've a problem, their inborn knack makes it yours. No wonder they live so much longer. One day, I promised myself, savagely bumping the Mawdslay along the stone track, I'll think up some privileges for myself. Then watch out, everybody.

'Why ask me, love?' I pleaded.

'You look lived-in, troublesome. You're sexually inclined. I can tell.' She was quite candid. 'Tell me. I'd like to know how it's actually *done*. I mean, a man's so heavy. Does the woman bear his weight? And how does a man's *thing* feel? I imagine something rubbery. Is this correct?'

'Please.' I was broken. 'I've one of my heads.'

'How did she know your address?' Michelle was in a high old rage, holding two letters out.

'Eh?' I'd come bolting upstairs for protection, leaving Robert to unload Elaine.

'A woman's writing. And you knew these letters were coming because you said—'

'Mmmmh,' I said absently. 'Is Elaine Aries?' I don't even know what Aries is.

'Libra. September.' Like Three-Wheel's motor.

Thanks, I said inwardly, and opened the letter. Margaret could be trusted not to give my location away. She'd sent me the list of Trembler's usual team, putting asterisks beside those who'd been in police trouble lately. That was all, and best wishes with one discreet cross. The other envelope, much thicker, held a mass of newspaper cuttings, notes, annotated catalogues and police notices. I'd told her to get them from my cottage.

Supper-time, the safety of numbers. I informed Elaine that our auctioneer would be arriving in a week's time, by air from Edinburgh to Wick's tiny airport, and could I have the car to meet him, please. She said of course, sweet and demure. Her grilling had really drained me. Still anxious about her telepathy trick, I didn't let it enter my mind that Trembler would of course come by road, and to Inverness, not Wick.

Late that night I pulled another sly trick, though I hated creeping back to our office in that draughty old deserted west wing. It was made for Draculas and spooks. I spent a long time on the phone talking to Doc. He's a genealogist, been one of my poorer customers, lace bobbins, some three years. He was delighted to be given a difficult problem, tracing a complex family tree. I dictated the dates from the gravestones, and what I knew about Elaine's family. I bribed him to secrecy. He demanded, and I promised, an Isle of Man lover's bobbin I hadn't yet got. See how friends take advantage?

Inspection time. We'd had a run of three days' warm clemency. Weather helps fakers, or, as I decided we should start labelling ourselves, reproducers and copyists. This meant that stains worked better. Sunshine is an excellent ageing factor. And we could move the McGunn clan's assembled items unafraid of drizzle. Elaine was nervous, for once keeping her thoughts above her umbilicus, as we trooped down to see the three days' worth.

'They've stopped coming in, Ian.' Her tone said therefore this was it, everything her retainers could raise. Pathetic.

It was unfortunate that Michelle had chosen the Great Hall. Our voices echoed. The long stained-glass windows accentuated the space. I'd nigh on thirty rooms and halls in a stately home to fill. This piteous heap was two journeys of Drummer's donkey-cart.

My dismay must have communicated itself to the others. I looked round, slowly, wanting faces. They were observing me in total silence. Hector, stoic and relaxed, with Tessie and Joey eeling round his feet. Robert's eyes gleamed hatred from that mass of red hair. Shona silent and dogless, whose heart must be beating faster because she more than anyone here realized it was crunch hour. Elaine, mortified in spite of herself. Duncan frankly ashamed. Mary MacNeish ticking off which neighbours'd contributed what. Mac patient, waiting orders. My annunciatory cough made us all shuffle.

'Not much, folks,' I said. 'Is it?'

Silence.

'Is it?' Still no answer. 'How many retainers, Elaine? Thirty or so? And they raise twelve mass-produced pieces of furniture, earliest date 1911.'

'You may have noticed,' Elaine said, pale, 'that my people are not well off. And Tachnadray is not Edinburgh Castle.' She had a right to anger, but insufficient reasons.

'True. But why not?'

Shona glanced at Robert. 'What does that mean?' she demanded.

'I mean that it was. Once.' I walked towards them, vaguely embarrassed by their being in a facing line, a barrister at somebody's trial. 'It's really quite simple. The clan centre, a great house. The laird tried to uphold . . . tradition. So debts mounted. The estate folded. Produce faltered, finally dwindled to a few flocks of sheep—'

'Here, mon,' Hector blurted. Sadly I waved him down.

'I know, Hector. Nobody could've done better, I'm sure. You must have slogged, winning cups at the Gatherings, doing what you could with damn-all help. Robert, too.' The man's head rose ominously. 'Probably the most loyal seneschal on the planet. You all tried. But people were paid off, and the laird finally passed the torch on to Miss Elaine.'

The end of the faces. I started a reverse stroll. Elaine in her wheelchair was the centre of the group. It was a Victorian clan tableau, proud before the magnesium flashlight struck their likenesses for the mantelpiece. All it needed was a dead tiger and bearers. And, in this case, a mantelpiece.

'So you hit on a scheme. I guessed wrong earlier, and none of you corrected me. Because there wasn't a bleep of

154

an antique in the west wing, I assumed there weren't any left. That they'd all been sold to pay Tachnadray's way. But they hadn't, had they?'

'What does he mean?' Elaine demanded of the world.

'That there's really quite a bit left. Right, everybody? Look,' I said, halting in the photographer's position. 'I needn't stay here. I can push off, leave you to it. You must at least help. Out with it, troops.'

Silence. Elaine's ferocity glowed, the radiance almost blinding. She was realizing she'd been had, completely, by this ultra-loyal mob of serfs.

'All right, I'll say it for you. You dispersed the remaining antiques among yourselves. When Elaine sent word for everybody to chip in any relevant saleables they had, you very carefully fetched only junk, and are keeping the authentic Tachnadray furniture, silver, God-knows-what, concealed.' I could have told how Shona, realizing I'd begun to suspect, bribed me with herself, failed, then sent Robert to hunt me to my death on the dark moor. I'd have been a fellwalker, carelessly falling down some crevasse. They'd have all told the police the same tale, and cocooned Elaine from the truth. Again.

'Bring it out, folks,' I said. 'Tachnadray needs you.'

'Duncan.' Elaine didn't even turn her head.

'It's true, Miss Elaine.' Duncan shuffled out of the line to address her, full face. He made to rummage for tobacco, put his pipe away, coughed uneasily. Nobody else spoke. 'We indeed did that.'

'I ordered everything sold!' Elaine said.

'You did, Miss Elaine. But it was selling out the McGunn heritage, despoiling your own—' he choked on the word— 'birthright.' Well he might, poor man.

'Permit me,' I interrupted. 'Bring the genuine stuff to the auction. You needn't lose it.'

Elaine rolled her wheelchair out, spun it with her back to me. 'All of you. Go now. Tell the others. Bring everything —every-thing!—back. Forthwith.' A sudden queen.

They dispersed slowly, looking back at the blazing girl. While they were still within earshot she pronounced loudly,

'And on behalf of us all, Ian, I apologize for your shabby treatment.'

'Then can I go places on my own?' I asked swiftly. 'Without being confined, or Robert skulking on some distant hill?'

'Granted,' she said regally. 'Wheel me outside. And get rid of that rubbish. It's defacing the Hall.'

'Ah, well.' I pushed. 'Old tat's useful in the workshop.'

That night I rang Tinker and told him to get Trembler up to the railway hotel in Inverness soonest. Antioch had nearly three dozen wagons ready, which news wobbled me. More would be loading up by dawn. It seemed only a few hours since I'd arrived at Tachnadray with all the time in the world. Now it seemed there wasn't sure any left at all.

CHAPTER 23

Trembler came down the stairs holding on to the banister like a beginner drunk. He's of a tallish lazaroid thinness, forever dabbing his trembling lips with a snuff-stained hankie. I like Trembler. Always tries to keep up appearances, wears a waistcoat, though stained with last night's excesses, and polishes his shoes. He tottered across the foyer from couch to armchair, from pillar to recliner, exactly as street children play stepping-stones. He knew I'd be in the hotel nosh bar. A porter helped him down the three steps.

'Wotcher, Trembler.'

'Lovejoy.' Shaking badly, he made the opposite chair and pulled my tea towards him. It slopped over the saucer as he sucked tremulously at the rim. His quivering upper lip was dyed snuff gold. Looking at this gaunt wreck, I wondered uneasily if Tinker was right. He looked a decrepit nonagenarian.

'Had a good night, Trembler?'

'Splendid.' His rheumy eyes closed as a server clattered cups. 'What day is it?' he whispered.

'You've a few days before the off, Trembler.'

'Right.' He opened his eyes, willpower alone.

'Grub's in front of you.'

Everything I could think of, including waffles, porridge, eggs in a slick fry-up, all on a hot plate. He focused and nearly keeled over. 'Jesus, Lovejoy.'

People began looking across to see where the noise was coming from as soon as he started. His cutlery fibrillated, his crockery clattered. He sounded like a foundry. Once he actually did tremble himself off his chair trying to pick up a fallen spoon. A kindly waitress came to ask if my father was all right.

'Yes, ta, love.' I gave her a soul-deep smile. 'He improves with the day.' I didn't tell her Trembler's age. He's thirty-one. Wine and women have transformed him. Trembler recovered enough to lust feebly after her. Luckily his vision peters out at ten paces, a spent arrow, so to speak.

'How much do I know, Lovejoy?'

Funny how glad hearing your own name makes you. 'It's a weird place, Trembler. Near derelict. They keep three rooms to impress visitors. The owner's a lady, seventeen, in a wheelchair. There's a few retainers still. All are suspect. So far I've a heap of rubbish which I'm transforming into saleables.'

Trembler nodded his understanding, as far as I could tell. He quakes so much normally it's difficult to distinguish a nod in his version of immobility.

'Where'll you get the stuff, Lovejoy?' he quavered.

'Tinker's organizing a convoy.' I hesitated, giving him time for the unpleasant bit. He managed to slop half a yolk-dripping egg into his mouth. I looked away, queasy. 'I want no whizzers who're in trouble, Trembler. Sorry.'

Normally an auctioneer, crooked or straight, has the final say on staff. Whizzers are those blokes—scoundrels to a man—who hump antiques about. An auctioneer's whizzers stay with him for life, part of his team, so I was asking for heresy.

'I heard it was special, Lovejoy.' He resumed his idea of eating, with distaste.

'Margaret sent me the list.' I passed it over. 'You've only

two who're holy enough for this, Trembler. Agreed?'

'A sad reflection on modern morality '

It's amazing what good grub and a job'll do for a man. Before my very eyes Trembler was filling out. His eyes were clearing, dawn mist from an estuary autumn. He drank another pint of tea. I gave him more, sent for another ton of toast, marmalade. Years were starting to fall from him with every mouthful. Even his voice, the querulous whine of an ancient, was becoming the measured and tuneful instrument of a Fellow of the Institute of Chartered Auctioneers. I watched admiringly. He only looked fifty now. A couple more breakfasts and he'd be down to a sprightly forty, maybe make thirty-five.

'So far, Lovejoy, you've told me nothing.' He dabbed his mouth with a napkin, rearranged the condiments, crockery. All really good signs. 'Are you bringing in valuers?'

My laugh made people smile across the tables. 'Who on earth can afford five guineas per cent, Trembler?' Valuing is robbery, money for jam—indeed, for not even jam. He's the bloke who comes to value your precious old table, guesses a guestimate (always wrong) and *you* pay *him* a huge percentage of that guess, for nothing. No, never let a stranger into your home, especially if he's a valuer. They are the antiques game's equivalent of politicians. 'There's some pinning to be done.'

He smiled. 'Thought as much. Who's the mark?'

'Are,' I corrected. 'Tell you nearer the day.'

'Pinning' is a noble art practised by auctioneers ever since time began. It means manipulating the bidding so as to land a particular lot on a poor unsuspecting member of the public who doesn't want it. When the Emperor Caligula auctioned off his dud antiques—he'd wasted a fortune buying forgeries —he ordered his auctioneer to pin Aponius Saturnimus. This rich Roman had nodded off during the bidding. He woke up poor.

'And I want a phone bank. Two.'

'Right-ho.' He knew I meant false ones, because otherwise I'd have asked the phone people. Big bidders phone live bids in as the auction progresses.

'About the money, Trembler.'

He shed another two years. 'I've put this hotel on my credit card, Lovejoy.' He carries only phoney credit cards, but he was trying to help me by deferring the cost of his stay.

'Good lad. You stay here and enjoy the . . . facilities. Now, Trembler, when I call, there's to be no delay. Get it? Ten minutes' notice, you move out. There's a code word. It's Lovejoy.'

'Your name's the codeword?' He was puzzled.

'That's because I'm under an alias; Ian McGunn.'

He repeated it to prove he was back among thinking men. 'One thing, Lovejoy. Can I bring my own tallyman?'

'No, Trembler. Sorry.' Trembler always picks some gorgeous tart without a brain in her head. I saw him once at an auction near Southwold where he'd hired a bird who actually couldn't count or write. Talk about a shambles. 'I've already got you a tally woman. She'll need training in, the day previous.'

He brightened. The deal done, we had another breakfast each to celebrate, seeing it was getting on for coffee-time. Then I rang Doc the genealogist and had my suspicions confirmed. Couple of good bookshops in Inverness. I got some paperback reprints for Duncan's benefit.

Michelle was working flat out now. Letters were coming in so fast the postie had graduated to a van. She was becoming conscious of the pressure. Each night we phoned up the list of antiques *et al* from Tinker. Next morning we sifted through them, and next night she'd tell Tinker which I'd accepted and which were refused. Tinker gave her nightmares: 'He doesn't seem to make any notes!' she complained. I'd go, 'Mmmh.'

There was a growing body of cards filed in old shoeboxes, a card for each collector writing in, and a spare list of antiques for which people, mostly genuine collectors, were writing urgently wanting special lists. These are almost always coins, medals, hand weapons, clothes or paintings. Then there was the catalogue file, the biggest. Michelle tried talking me out of one card per antique, thinking she'd discovered a quicker way. She tried the wheedle, even the vamp, to no avail. I made her stick to my scheme. I also made her keep an nth file, of those antiques which I'd told her to reject. She again played hell. 'What's the point of recording details of antiques we'll never see—?'

I clapped a hand over her mouth. This was the alluring lady who'd so joyously rushed to find me when the first letters came. Now we were inundated she was falling behind and inventing ever-dafter ways of ballsing up the documentation. A born administrator.

'You, Michelle, are attractive, desirable, and rapidly becoming a pest for other reasons, too. Get help if you like, but do as I say. And hurry up.' I let go. I had to sort the last of Tachnadray's genuine stuff out in the Great Hall. 'I've a job for you to do, later.'

This time the items arranged at the far end of the Great Hall were superb. Among them I recognized Shona's—well, Elaine's—double snuff mull. Some things make you smile. The silver wasn't plentiful. One triumph was a bullet-shaped teapot. Not a lot of people admire the shape ('bullet' meaning spherical as an old lead bullet), which is a ball with a straight spout. The lid completes the roundness, with a mundane finial topping the lid off. They were made from the late 1700s for sixty years. The engraved decoration of these characteristically Scottish teapots is one pattern carried round the join of lid and body. It sat among the rest glowing like, well, like Elaine smiling. Edward Lothian of Edinburgh, 1746, before the fluted spout came in. There was also a silver centrepiece. These so-called épergnes (it's posh to give things French names) usually weigh a lot, so you're safe buying one by weight alone, never mind the artistry. This was 1898, Edinburgh, a dreadful hotchpotch of thistles, tartan hatching, drooping highlanders, wounded stags. It was ghastly. It'd bring in a fortune.

The furniture was dominated by a genuine Thomas Chippendale library table. It was practically a cousin of the mahogany one at Coombe Abbey, mid-eighteenth century, solid and vast. I honestly laughed with delight and clapped. You see so many rubbishy copies that an original blows your mind. Five Hepplewhite-design chairs (where was the sixth?) with shield backs and an urn-pattern centre splat were showing their class. A few good Victorian copies of the lighter Sheraton-style chair were ranged along one wall. In the catalogue I'd call them something like 'Louis Seize à l'anglais', as Tom Sheraton designs were termed in Paris at the time. Only I'd be sure to put it in quotation marks, which would legalize my careful misattribution. It'd give Trembler a chuckle.

Predictably, the porcelain was anything. The retainers had clearly preserved what impressed them most. They'd gone for knobs and colours, hoarding with knobs on, so to speak. A few times they'd guessed right. A royal blue Doulton vase, marked 'FB 1884', indicated that factory's famous deaf creator whose wares Queen Victoria herself so admired. It might not bring much, but it'd 'thicken' the rest. A lone Chelsea red anchor plate in the Kakiemon style—here vaguely parrot-looking birds, brown and blue figures on white and flowers—would bring half the price of a car, properly auctioned. I loved it, and said hello, smiling at the thrilling little bong it made in my chest. The stilt-marks were there, and those pretty telltale speckles in the painting. The rest were mundane. Sadly, sober George the Fifth stuff. Not one Art Deco piece among them. That set me thinking.

The paintings were ridiculous recent portrait travesties, some modern body's really bad idea of what a gen-yoo-wine Highland chief would have been wearing. Talk about fancy dress. These daft-posh portraits are so toffee-nosed they beome pantomime. The one painting I did take note of was a little scene of Tachnadray, done with skill in, of all things, milk casein paint. These rarities give themselves away by their very matt foreground. (Be careful with them; they watersplash easily.) You let skim milk go sour, and dry the curd out to a powder. Then you make a paste of it with dilute ammonia (the eleventh-century monks used urine) and it's this which you mix with powder paint. 'Pity you're very new, though,' I told it. The painter had varnished it to make it resemble an oil painting. This is quite needless, because casein is tough old stuff. You can even polish the final work to give it a marvellous lightness. It's brittle, though, so you paint on rigid board ... I found myself frowning at the painting. Two figures were seated on the lawn, quite like statues. Modern dress, so there was no intent to antiquize.

A wheelchair's tyres whispered. 'What now, Ian?'

'I think some painters must have frigging good eyesight, love. This casein-painting's too minute for words.' Casually I replaced it. 'Pity it's practically new.'

'Is it any good?' She was oh so detached.

'High quality. The artist still about?'

'Me.'

I nodded, not surprised. Now I knew it all. 'You're a natural, love. Who taught you about casein paint?' No answer, so under her steady stare I decided to swim with the tide. 'Your dad? Or Michelle?'

'Yes. Michelle.'

'And egg tempera? You've a great career ahead of you, love. Copy a few mediæval manuscripts for me and—'

'Stop that!' Michelle came in. 'I'll not have you inveigling Miss Elaine into your deceitful ways!'

With Elaine laughing, really honestly falling about, I escaped into Duncan's workshop for my stint with the panelling. Michelle had come a fraction too late.

Later that day Mrs Buchan brought up two candidates to help Michelle in the office. One was a plump lass, fawnish hair, beneath a ton of trendy bangles and earrings, lovely eyes. The other was Mrs Moncreiffe, an elderly twig scented with lavender and mothballs.

Michelle chose the twig.

About ten o'clock I was working my way through a bottle of white wine in my garret, racking my two neurones to see if I'd forgotten anything, when the stairs creaked. Michelle came in with a woman's purposeful complicity, placing her back to the door edge and closing it with hands behind her. This manœuvre keeps the woman's face towards the occupant. They have these natural skills.

'Come in,' I said. 'Have a seat.'

'I . . . I just wanted to say that the catalogue's up to date.' She made to perch on the bed, rose quickly at the implications. I gave her my chair and flopped horizontal. 'We only have this evening's list to do. Mrs Moncreiffe has proved a godsend.'

'I'm glad. Out with it, love.'

'How many more days before . . . ?'

'Soon.' I didn't want to be tied. 'Michelle. Your son Joseph sent down an original antique, didn't he? Shona sent Robert after it in the Mawdslay, Tachnadray's one car.'

'Yes.' Her voice was a whisper.

'I don't know quite what happened, but Joseph was fetched back. He's hidden at *Shooters*, because he's supposed to have killed that driver. Dispute over the money, was it?'

Michelle nodded bravely. 'They . . . assumed so.' I watched admiringly. Women lie with such conviction.

'Tough for you, love. Torn loyalty and all that.'

'You're . . . you're really nothing to do with that London college, are you?'

'No.' I pretended anger. 'Have you been phoning people?'

'No, no. I just . . . surmise, that's all.' She regarded her twisting hands for a moment. 'You're not police. And you talk to things. You're a bit mad, yet . . . '

'Thank God for that "yet".' I gave her a sincere smile. 'Don't worry, love. I'm on Elaine's side. I'll honestly do the best I can when the time comes.'

She nodded and stood, watching me. 'I wish,' she got out eventually, 'we'd met in other circumstances. Better ones.'

'We practically did.' I shooed her out. 'I've got to think. Do Tinker's call on your own tonight, love.'

Eleven o'clock I went with a krypton handlamp and a small jeweller's loupe to look at the painting. It had gone. That told me as much as if I'd studied it for a fortnight in Agnew's viewing room. One of the two figures gazing so soulfully in the painting had been Michelle. The other had been a man slightly older, but not Duncan. He'd looked in charge, attired in chieftain's dress.

Which called for a long think to midnight. To one o'clock. To one-thirty. More deep thoughts for another hour.

Tinker was still swilling at the pub by the old flour mill. I told him to phone Trembler early tomorrow morning and just say, 'Lovejoy.'

'Right,' he croaked, anxious. 'Here, Lovejoy. When do we come? Antioch keeps asking. There's frigging trucks everywhere—'

'Now,' I said, throat dry. 'Roll it, Tinker.' I lowered the receiver on his relieved cackle.

CHAPTER 24

Economy's always scared me. Or do I mean economics? Maybe both, if they're not the same thing. I mean, when you hear that Brazil is a trillion zlotniks in the red the average bloke switches off. Mistakes which are beyond one man's own redemption simply go off the scale, as far as I'm concerned. Maybe that was why I'd run from Sidoli's rumble. Plus cowardice, of course.

The books I'd got from Inverness, paperback re-runs, showed Duncan a few more possibilities. He was hard to persuade.

'This pedestal sideboard from Loudon's *Encyclopædia* of 1833,' I told his disbelief. 'Plain as anything, simple. Never mind that architects call it cabinet-maker Gothic—'

'Make it? Out of new wood?'

'Out of that.' A wardrobe, slanted and damp-warped, leant tiredly in the workshop. 'By supper-time.'

'What about those great pedestals?'

'The design's only like a strut across two bricks,' I pointed out. 'So cut those old stairs Robert's trying to mend in the east wing. The wood's good. The pieces are almost the right size, for God's sake.'

We settled that after argument. Two new lads had come

to help Duncan, relatives of relatives. One was a motor mechanic, the other a school-leaver. That gave me the idea. Motors mean metal, which means brass rails, which with old stair wood means running sideboards.

'Make a pair of running sideboards. They're straight in period, Duncan. All it is, three shelves each with a brass rail surround, on a vertical support at each end. Put it on wooden feet instead of castors, French polish to show it's original, and it'll look straight 1830.'

Grumbling, I did a quick sketch. Sometimes I think it'd be quicker to do every frigging thing myself. 'Finish all three of these by sevenish, then I can age them sharpish.'

'All this haste's not my usual behaviour,' Duncan said.

'Times,' I said irritably, 'are changing at Tachnadray.'

Honestly. You sweat blood trying to rescue people, and what thanks do you get?

Michelle's first lesson in the perils of auctioneering. Explaining an auction's difficult enough. Explaining a crooked one to an unsullied soul like Michelle was nearly impossible. We were in the Great Hall.

'Auctioneers speak distinctly, slowly, in this country, love. It's in America they talk speedy gibberish.'

For the purpose I was the auctioneer, she the tally girl with piles of paper. She listened so solemnly I started smiling. Older women are such good company.

'There's a word we use: stream. Always keep a catalogue in front of you clipped open, no matter what. The cards from which you compiled the catalogue are in your desk. Those two, the catalogue and cards are your stream. Right?'

'Maybe I should have the cards on my desk,' she mused.

'You think so?' Casually I leant my elbow over so one card pile fell to the floor. 'See? A customer could accidentally do that, and steal a few cards while pretending to help as you picked them up. Then he'd know what we paid.'

'But that's unfair!' she flamed.

'Look, Michelle.' I knelt to recover the scattered cards. 'The people coming are all sorts. Some'll be ordinary folk who've struggled to get a day off from the factory. Others will come in private planes. But they'll all share one terrible, grim attribute: they will do anything for what we've got. They'll beg, bribe, steal.' God give me strength and protect me from innocence. I rose, dusted my knees. 'Cards,' I reminded her, 'in the desk. Catalogue on top.'

'Now I'm a customer.' I swaggered up. She got herself settled, pencilled a note. 'I ask, Where'll the stream be at twelve-thirty, missus?'

She thought. 'You're asking what lot number the auction will have reached by then?'

'Well done.'

'But how do we actually *sell* things?'

'Say I'm the auctioneer. Tally girl's on the left, always, except in Sotheby's book sales, where they know no better. Not real gentlemen, see.' I chuckled at the old trade slight. 'I call out, Lot Fifty-One, Nailsea-type Glass Handbell—'

'No. Fifty-One is a gentleman's Wedgwood 1790 stock pin, blue-dip jasper with a George Stubbs horse in white relief—'

'Michelle,' I said, broken. 'I'm *pretending*.'

'Oh. Sorry.'

'The auctioneer calls out the catalogue number, Lot Whatever, and then says, Who'll start me off? or something. The bids commence, and finally Trembler calls, Going, going, gone! or Once, twice, gone! depending on how he feels. Once he bangs a hammer, that's it. He'll also say a name—Smith of Birmingham, say. It's your job to instantly write out a call chit. It's the bill, really. Lot Fifty-One, two hundred quid, Smith. So you get that chit across to Mr Smith quick as a flash. That entitles Smith to pay Mrs Moncreiffe. Her only job is to accept payment, stamp the call chit Paid In Full, and tick her list.'

'Must I provide Mr Trembler with a hammer?'

'No, love. Auctioneers always have their own. Trembler's isn't a real gavel. It's only a decorated wooden reel his sister's lad made him.'

'How sweet.' She smiled, scribbling like the clappers.

Apologetically I cleared my throat for the difficult bit. 'Er, now, Michelle, love. There's a few rules.'

'Never issue a call chit unless I'm sure?' she offered knowingly.

'Eh? Oh yes. Good, good.' This was going to be more difficult than I'd supposed. 'Ahem, sometimes, love, you might not actually hear some of the bids. If so, you mustn't mention it. Trembler will see them, because . . .' I tried to find concealing words. Because he'd be making them up, 'taking bids off the wall'. 'Because, he's had special training, see? Bidders have secret signs arranged with Trembler beforehand. It's silly, but that's how they like doing it. They're all rivals.'

I ahemed again. 'And there's another thing. There'll be two telephones against the windows. People will be telephoning bids in for particular lots. The, er, assistants bidding from the phones are treated as genuine—er, sorry, I meant as if bidders were genuinely here.'

'Telephonists to receive call chits,' Michelle mouthed, pencil flying.

'I'll draft call chits with you when Trembler arrives. One last thing, love. Never, never contradict Trembler. Never look doubtful. Never interrupt.'

'What if I think he's made a mistake?'

I took her face in my hands. 'Especially not then, love.'

She moved back, looking. 'All this is honest, isn't it?'

'Michelle,' I said, offended. 'Trembler's a fellow of a Royal Institute. We've already certified that Sotheby's and Christie's rules govern every lot. We've certified compliance with Parliament's published statutes.' I gave a bitter laugh, almost overdoing it. 'If our auction isn't legal, it won't be for want of trying.'

Michelle stood to embrace me, misty. 'I didn't mean anything, really I didn't.'

'Am I interrupting?' Shona, silhouetted in the door light.

'Sealing a bargain.' I thought I was so smooth.

'A . . . gentleman's just arrived in Dubneath, calling himself Cheviot Yale. He told Mary he's for Tachnadray. He's just waiting, saying nothing.' She was still being accusing. 'His name sounds made up. Is it?'

'No.' I'd not felt so happy for a long time. 'That's the name he was born with. People call him Trembler.'

No way of stopping it now.

The Caithness National Bank manager was delighted with us. A big-eared man with a harf-harf laugh he made political use of during Trembler's curt exposition. Trembler was doing the con with his episcopalian voice, always a winner.

'In requesting a separate account,' he intoned, 'I don't wish to impute criticism of the Mistress of Tachnadray.'

'Of course not, sir.' On the desk lay Trembler's personal card and personal bank account number at the august Glyn Mills of Whitehall, London. Even when starving Trembler keeps that precious account in credit. It doesn't have much in it, but the reputation of an eight-year solvency in Whitehall is worth its weight in gold. Trembler gave a cadaverous smile straight out of midwinter.

'In my profession,' he said grimly, 'it falls to me sadly to participate in the demise of reputations of many noble families. Normally, it would be regarded as natural to use the lady's own account. But international collectors and dealers from London—' Trembler tutted; the banker shook his head at the notion of wicked money-grabbers—'are of a certain disposition. They demand,' Trembler chanted reproachfully, 'financial immediacy. The young Mistress's authority would carry little weight.'

'Sad. Very sad.' The banker's portly frame swelled, exhaled a sigh of sympathy.

'Mr McGunn here tried to persuade me to agree for the auction sale to be administered via the Tachnadray account in Dubneath.' Trembler paused for the manager to shoot me a glance of hatred. I smiled weakly. 'I insisted on coming here. Tomorrow morning, first thing, a number of small sums will be paid into the new account.'

'Very praiseworthy,' the banker smirked.

'One cheque will then be soon drawn on it. A small credit balance will remain. I will require a late-night teller on auction day to accept much larger sums.'

'Certainly, sir!' The man was positively beaming.

168

'I will require a special deposit rate of interest.'

The beam faded. 'Sir?'

'It will be a relatively vast sum.' Trembler didn't so much as get up as ascend, pulling on his gloves. 'Possibly the largest your . . . branch has ever handled. I would be throwing money away not to demand the interest. Have the cheque-book ready within the hour, please.'

We left, Trembler striding and using his walking cane so vigorously I had to trot beside the lanky nerk. You have to hand it to crooks like Trembler; always put on a great show.

'Here, Trembler,' I said. 'Notice that geezer's name? Only, I heard they were all assassins once.'

'Ruthven? Garn.'

'No, honest. Local vicar told me. Incidentally, Trembler. What do you think of openly cataloguing a couple of fakes in the sale? Reinforce confidence in the rest of the stuff . . .'

We went to celebrate. I promised Trembler his advance money and asked if he could manage until tomorrow. He said all right, which only shows how good friends help out. He really can't do without exotic women and drink. Same as the rest of us; he's just more honest. He orders the birds from a series of private Soho addresses. They're very discreet, but not cheap.

As we drank, me a lager, him a bathful of scotch, I stared out over Thurso harbour.

Antique dealers would now be booking the nightrider trains from King's Cross. The London boyos would have their cars serviced tomorrow for the long run north. Phones would be humming between paired antique businesses. Syndicates would be hunched over pub tables, testing the water. Auction rings would be forming, dissolving, reforming, illegal to a man.

And the convoy this very minute'd be rumbling on the great North Road, coming steady, a long line of weather-stained wagons carrying the beauty and greed of mankind. Soon they would swing left over the Pennines, then haul northwards for the motorway to Carlisle. Then they'd come Glasgow, Inverness . . . My mouth was suddenly dry. 'Have another,' I offered. 'Against the cold.'

CHAPTER 25

Nothing an antique dealer hates worse than fog and rain. Me and Michelle were for once agreed.

At three o'clock in the morning in a foggy rainy lay-by, it seemed to me that the wheel had come full circle. We were in the giant Mawdslay on the main A9 which runs northward from Bonar Bridge. Forty miles to Tachnadray. Not long since, it'd been Ellen and me in old Tom's hut, while a man had died bloodily outside. Then the disaster over Three-Wheel Archie, my escape with the travelling fair, my panicked flight from the fight between the rival fairground gangs . . . I've spent half my windswept life recently on night roads. I shivered. These old motors sieve the air. Michelle's breathing had evened. I nudged her awake.

'Watch for the lights.'

'Will they come? Only, Mr Tinker doesn't seem very reliable.'

I wiped the windscreen. Not a light out there. Nothing moved. 'He's the best barker in the business. Anyway, Antioch's running it.'

'Tell me about Antioch.'

'Eh?' I said suspiciously, but she was only trying to make up. 'Antioch and me's old mates. He was a Gurkha officer.'

'You know so many different sorts of people.'

'Everybody's into antiques, love.'

'Can't be.' She was smiling in the darkness. 'I'm not, for instance.'

'Aren't you?' I said evenly, which shut her up.

There came first a faint row of dot lights. Ten minutes later the convoy approached, a slow switching queue of lorries revving on the incline, the ground shaking as they came. Even in the night it was impressive. I heard Michelle gasp. I stood out, collar up against the drizzle, and held up the krypton lamp. Characteristically, the lead wagon merely flashed, slowed to a crawl. I smiled, recognizing Antioch's trademark. The double blink went down the whole convoy. The last lorry pulled out, overtook at a roar into the lay-by.

'There are so many!' Michelle was beside me, shoulder up to ward weather away.

'Love, if I could have done it by correspondence,' I said, going forward to greet Antioch in the din of the passing lorries. He saw me, waved at the column. It churned on past.

'Lovejoy.' We both had our backs against the roar.

'Wotcher, Antioch. Any trouble?'

He grinned. He enjoys all this, driving about in all weathers. He loves nothing better than a catastrophe, a breakdown, a flash flood washing a roadbridge. You feel you want to arrange an avalanche for the frigging lunatic.

'Police query near Carlisle, but I'd the consignment notes. A caff dust-up with some yobbos. Peaceful.'

'Antioch. About your drivers.'

'We'll unload, then can you feed them? I've compo rations but they'll need more before daylight.'

'Yes.' I'd already warned Mrs Buchan, who'd been delighted at my threat of dozens of voracious appetites. 'Then?'

'We'll run to Aberdeen, the oil terminals.'

'Your destination's a place called Tachnadray.' He likes directions military style, eastings and westings and that. I'd forgotten how, so I chucked in my own map with Tachnadray ringed. He shone his light, grinned and shook his head. His lorry's cabin door was open. Michelle was looking in.

'There's a tramp inside,' she said reprovingly to Antioch.

The ragged figure coughed, a long gravelly howl which silenced the roars of the last lorries passing us. Michelle clutched my arm. Recognition had struck.

It opened one bleary eye. 'Gawd, Lovejoy. Where the bleedin' 'ell?'

'Hiyer, Tinker. Go back to sleep. We're nearly there.'

Antioch climbed into the cabin, revved and joined the convoy's tail. I stood, smiling, watching the red lights wind into the fog.

Michelle got her voice back. 'He's . . . he's *horrible*!'

'Please don't criticize Tinker.' We made for the

Mawdslay 'He's the only bloke who trusts me. A lot depends on him. Me. Tachnadray. Joseph. And,' I added, 'maybe you.'

Ten o'clock on a cold wet morning. At eight we'd waved off the empty convoy, and I was just back from depositing a mixed bag of cheques, money orders and notes into the National Caithness. Me and Trembler had drawn Antioch's draft. He'd set off following the convoy. There'd been enough to give Antioch's drivers a bonus. Michelle had opposed this, exclaiming that it left hardly any. I didn't listen. You have to pay cash on the nail sometimes, and this was one of them. She was still at it when we found Tinker happily trying out Mrs Buchan's homebrewed hooch in the long kitchen.

'Giving away all that money!' Michelle was grumbling.

'Listen, love,' I said. Trembler strode past, discarding his gloves ready for his third breakfast. 'How many men would you say Antioch brought?'

'Forty-six,' Mrs Buchan called, in her element. The tubby lady had two crones and no fewer than four youngsters all milling obediently to her orders. 'Like the old days! You poor English, starving to death.' She wagged a spoon to threaten me. 'This poor auldie's never tasted a drop of homebrew in his life. The crime of it.'

Tinker raised suffering eyes long enough to wink.

'Forty-six,' I repeated. 'Look around.' The kitchen was like a battlefield. 'They aren't choirboys, love. What would have happened if they hadn't been paid? After loading, driving the convoy the length of the country? They'd have torn the place apart.'

Michelle shivered. 'It's all so violent. I mean . . .' She was bemused at the scale of things. 'Suddenly it seems, well, out of our hands.'

'It is, love. We're half way down the ski slope. No way of strolling back to the start, not now.' I patted her shoulder kindly. 'Have some nosh, love. We've a lot to do.'

She stared. 'But we haven't slept a wink. And everything is here. Isn't that the end of it?'

Tinker guffawed, his mouth open to show partly-noshed toast and beans. Trembler tutted and asked for more eggs, bacon, and perhaps just six more slices of fried liver, please. The women rushed, pleased.

A lass laid a place and poured tea as I said, 'It's the start, love.'

Michelle sank in the chair, pale.

''Ere, Lovejoy,' Tinker said. 'Notice yon Belfast geezer, tenth truck, fetched them frigging Brummy gasoliers?' The gaslight chandeliers had delighted me, genuine Ratcliffe and Tyler sets of three-lighters, 1874, with sundry wallbrackets for the extra singles. They are valuable collectibles now, especially pre-Victorian versions. Tinker was falling about, cackling. 'He got done at the sessions. Selling tourists *parking tickets*! Magistrate went berserk.'

Trembler joined in the reminiscing. 'Nice to see Antioch Dodd again,' he said. 'We last met when I auctioned that old mill down Stoke way. Antioch owffed it on canal barges. Even pulled a special police guard . . .'

Michelle was shaky, superwhelmed by all this criminology. Mrs Buchan on the other hand was oblivious, keeping her assorted team busy. Aren't women different? They're a funny lot. We talked on, preparing for the grind ahead.

By midday Trembler had made up his mind. All fixtures and fittings were to be assembled in the corridors for security, but I was downcast.

'What's the matter?' Michelle had left Mrs Moncreiffe in the office bombing out the checklist.

'It's not elegant.' I'd had visions of using the retainers— four more by now—to maybe redecorate the house. 'But Trembler's right. Bidders have sticky fingers.'

Trembler drew an outline plan on an improvised blackboard. He likes to talk to everybody at once. We were called to the Great Hall, crowded in among the furniture. Schooltime.

'This is where I'll hold the auction itself.' He pointed with his cane. 'There are all sorts of problems: security, money, catering, a bar, parking cars. But the most difficult is people. You'll all have a number. Anybody who hasn't memorized everybody's number by tomorrow must leave Tachnadray until the sale's over.'

People shuffled, looked askance, nodded. Tinker snored. He was on an early Georgian day bed, cane-backed. I guessed it was from Jake Endacot's shop in Frinton.

'Hector, you've got dogs. Patrol outside, and check cars in. One of you men will photograph, obviously as possible, every car arriving. One or two people might complain or turn away. Let them. Remember, these people are mostly townies. They don't know sheepdogs are harmless.'

Two of the girls nudged when Robert glared my way. More knew of Shona's missing dog than I'd thought. It still hadn't been mentioned openly.

'You will be in two groups.' Trembler notices everything, pretending not to. He'd have spotted those meaningful nudges. He'd ask me about it later. 'One group will help with the auction itself. The others will be stationed at a doorway, a corridor's end, wherever. *Stay there*. No matter what—a lady customer fainting, a man having a heart attack, a sudden shout for help, a customer telling you that Miss Elaine, me, or, er, Ian wants you urgently—*stay there*.' We all paused while Tinker coughed a majestic mansion-shaker of a cough. It faded like distant thunder. Trembler resumed. 'And nothing must be taken away. Suppose a bidder in fine clothes comes up to you with a receipt bearing my signature, saying they've got special permission to remove their lot an hour early. What do you do? You stop them. They'll be thieves, robbers, crooks who make a superb living.' He smiled his necrotizing smile. 'My rules never change: stay at your post. No exceptions. Everything, sold or unsold, stays until five o'clock. Then a bell sounds, and it's all over.'

'Sir,' one red-haired girl piped up. I liked her, our coffee lass. 'What if we need . . . ?'

'There'll be a floater. One of you circulates, takes the place of each of you in turn, for ten minutes at a time. Your

174

list will give the order in which you'll have a break. And when your break time comes, you *must* take it. No deviation.' He did his wintry smile. I watched it enviously. 'We have a rehearsal. It's called Viewing Day, which is Tuesday. Wednesday is Sale Day. Last point: take no bribes, accept no explanations, and *don't talk* to people. If they insist on talking, simply smile past them.'

Robert had been fidgeting. Now he rumbled. 'If you're so clever spotting the thieves, why not bar them? It's stupid, mon.'

'Then we'd bar all. They're all crooks.' Trembler looked down his nose at Robert, who flushed in fury. 'Rich Swiss, showy Yanks, suave Parisians, pedantic Germans, cool Londoners. The lot. Remember they work in groups. They'll lower jewellery, even furniture, out of a window to friends outside. They'll try all sorts.'

'But we know this place,' Duncan protested.

'Not you. Once, a lady carried an oil painting *in*. The guard let her pass. A minute later she left with her picture, saying it was the wrong room after all. They discovered she'd arrived with a worthless fake, and swapped it for an Impressionist painting worth a king's ransom. No. Do as you're told, and we'll profit. Do what you think is best, and we'll be rooked hook, line and sinker.'

Robert was still glowering, so I chipped in. 'Mr Yale is right. It's obvious you have no idea of the forces we're up against.' I hesitated, but Elaine nodded me to continue. 'The best experts in the country are on Tachnadray's side. They're me, Mr Yale, and Tinker there. Tachnadray's crammed with valuables. Your job is to contain them until the money's in. That's all there is to it.'

Trembler tapped the board. 'Those who will obey my orders without question, please rise.'

Slowly, in ones and twos, they stood. Elaine spoke once, sharply, when Robert rose. He remained standing determinedly. She nodded to Trembler.

'Very well,' Trembler said, smiling. 'Mrs Michelle will issue your numbers. From now you'll wear them. And remember one vital truth: it's Tachnadray versus all comers.

Everybody understand?' He had to insist on a reply before they sheepishly concurred He gave a warm smile as they shuffled out. 'The game starts now.'

I called, 'Mrs Buchan has coffee and baps for everybody downstairs.' She fled with a squawk, driving two girls before I hadn't warned her. 'Then back here for Mr Yale to allocate your groups.'

Tinker woke at the third rough shake. We were a tired quartet, but we started a quick tour of the house.

'It's not bad, Lovejoy,' Trembler said. The furniture was parcelled, as auctioneers say, meaning arranged in categories.

'It's bleedin' great,' Tinker corrected indignantly. They were both seeking my approval. I said nothing, though I sympathized. It's always a difficult time when the scammer, he who arranges the entire ploy, does the appraisal. 'We wus runnin' about like blue-arsed flies. I give more bleedin' scrip out than the friggin' Budget. Christ, in one afternoon—'

'Shut it, Tinker.' I walked quickly, the three of them in my wake.

Trembler had opted for the ground floor. Ropes were tied across each staircase and crude notices forbade entry. We'd have more imposing barriers by View Day. Heavy furniture stood along one wall of every corridor. Light stuff and assorted massive beds were in the larger drawing-rooms with musical instruments. The library was half full of books; books are most trouble when rigging an auction because booksellers want the highest mark-ups. That's why country house sales always lack books. It isn't because squires don't read.

'Frigging booksellers.' Tinker hawked phlegm. I raised a finger. He went to the window and spat out.

Porcelain, cutlery, decorative ceramics were in the east wing. We clumped, steps echoing, the length of the corridor and worked backwards to the Great Hall. Fireplaces, fire tigers, gasoliers, pole screens, in one room. Conservatory furniture and garden items in another. The big east drawing-room, once a light bath-house green, was now hung with sixty or more paintings.

'Thought that was in France,' I remarked in surprise. A Victorian lady in a pale lavender dress admiring a flower.

'Should've been,' Tinker grumbled. 'More frigging trouble than a square dick.' Barkers are addicted to pessimism for the same reasons as Opposition politicians: there's more mileage in it.

Farm implements, machinery, carts, outside in the bay between the densely overgrown rose-beds and the east windows. 'Good old Antioch,' I praised. They were arranged in a kind of Boer lager. The presence of a steam ploughing engine explained the bulky carrier in mid-convoy.

'Fair old lot, that, lads,' I said.

'Ta, Lovejoy.' Tinker smirking's a horrible sight, but the old soak deserved praise.

The jewellery was in one strip, a grotesque higgledy-piggledy array spread as it had arrived, in bags, trays, boxes, on wobbly trestle tables. Tinker grumbled at the trouble the roomful had caused him. He hates jewellery. 'Fiddly little buggers.'

'Shouldn't we be examining each piece?' Michelle exclaimed.

'Please, missus,' Trembler said.

'Aye,' Tinker added, 'gabby cow.'

The glass was in the east wing's smoking-room. The smaller withdrawing-room held the first miscellany.

'You described the laird as "that well-known collector",' Trembler said. 'So you'd want the collectibles separated?'

'Right.'

A room of bronzes, statuettes, sculptures. Two of silver. One of arms and armour. I left them chatting in the Great Hall as the retainers returned. Michelle seemed rather put out, par for the course, as I went outside and sat on the steps.

When preparing for a divvying job, I can never keep track of time. It must have been nearly an hour when Trembler emptied the whole house of people, Elaine and all. They came out in twos and threes, giving quizzing glances my way, one or two talking softly. Robert carried Elaine. She waved. Tinker stood waiting behind me, gruffly shutting Michelle up when she started to speak. Some things must be done in quiet. Women never learn. He knows this sort of thing can't be hurried. Trembler strolled past with a 'All yours, Tinker,' and got a wheezed, 'Fanks fer noffin'.' Silence. The great crammed house paused.

Afternoon moor light plays oddly on the rims of high fells. I'd often noticed it as a kid. For quite a while I'd been watching the hues discolour and blend. According to the map, some Pictish houses stood over to the south beyond the loch. I'd love a visit in peacetime. Miles north-westerly, Joseph languished alone. Behind me a bottle clinked. A gurgle, wheeze, a retching cough. Michelle tutted. A cloud slightly darkened the moor, fawns umbered, ochres into russet.

Maybe it was an omen. I rose and dusted my knees off for nothing. My big moment. Just me and antiques. Probably all I'm good for, showing off to nobody.

'Let's go,' I said.

CHAPTER 26

The tapestry was hung beside the stair foot. I'd heard Tinker say to Michelle, 'Shut it, missus. Just friggin' scribble,' but I was no longer listening.

Sometimes the best plan is its absence. Like, I never know how I'm going to divvy. Setting about examining an antique is as individual as making love. Even people who know a little (which excludes all known experts, museum curators, and antique dealers) approach the task differently. There's a geezer in Manchester who goes through a whole super-stitious ritual, knocking wood, hex signs, the lot. Another, a Kendal bird good with amber, always sits on the floor even if she's in public. Me, I just touch and listen. No particular order, no magic incantation.

Single antiques are easy, in a way, because meeting any one is like meeting a woman. The love quantum is immediately apparent. Encounter two together and immediately there's difficulty. They react on each other so a man's bemused. The only way he can recognize that inner essence is by concentrating on one, to the utter exclusion of the other. Society calls it rudeness. In divvying antiques it's essential. The trouble is the process is so seductively pleasing that it sucks time from the day. I mean, here was I with hundreds, maybe thousands, of alleged antiques to divvy, and I couldn't resist touching this tapestry, the first thing I'd clapped eyes on stepping through the porch.

'Hello, Jean,' I said to it, mist blurring the figures. Jean Bérain, Frenchman, once turned fashion upside down. He and his son struck eighteenth-century nerves by depicting naked courtesans reclining provocatively wearing the haunches and legs of a lion. You see Sèvres porcelain with similar figures. It became quite the thing for a famous beauty to have herself erotically depicted thus, like Peg Woffington the famous actress, for example. 'Long time no see.' I touched the lovely tapestry's texture. Warm. The feeling was heat, an exalting swirl of energy to the chime of melodious bells. I found myself starting to move, slowly at first, then quicker, quicker still, all else forgotten in a wondrous hedonistic spree. Distantly, Tinker's emphysematous croak was there, 'Hundred ern free, no; eight six nine, yeah,' but only for a while.

Battles do it. Orgies do it. Mysticism is said to do it. And women. Maybe it's true. The experience of beauty leads to a temporary death from recognizing its unattainability. I've never been in a trance as far as I know. I often wonder if it's the same as recovering from these other things. If so, I don't envy mediums. Certainly, coming out of one of these divvying sessions is appalling.

There was light intruding everywhere. My head was splitting. People talking in murmurs. A long leathery cough. A bottle, glugging. Somebody spluttered, murmured, 'Gawd.' A woman's voice thin as a reedpipe played out on the water. She was asking about something with numbers. I must have slept.

Headaches are a woman's best friend. They're not mine. The kitchen, shimmering. Mrs Buchan peeling something, one of her scullions doing mysteries on a cake's top. Another minion teasing about hair done different.

This end of the long table was fenced with beer and bottles. The talk was going on, that cough, her still counting. I drew breath.

'Help us up, Tinker.'

Hands hauled, propped. The place swam for a few seconds. I swigged the tea and stared at my hands until the world tidied itself up. Tinker scornfully refuted the women's suggested medications, clove inhalations, feet up, sal volatile. 'He needs a coupler pints, obstinate bleeder,' Tinker said.

'Shut it,' I got out, and winced at his cackling laugh.

'He's back. Wotcher, Lovejoy.'

'All right?'

'Aye, great. Missus, brew up. He'll be dry as a bone any mo.'

Michelle was there, weary. I told her she looked like I felt and got a wan smile. Trembler reached across to pat my shoulder.

'Beautiful, beautiful. A few questions when you're ready.'

That cheered me up. Auctioneers lust in percentages. Trembler was thinking ahead. As I recovered coherence, he began slowly introducing particular antiques into the conversation.

'That bronze cat, Lovejoy. What've you got, lady?'

'One Five Oh Seven.' Michelle's papers rustled as she worked her clipboard. 'It's one of six from Boy Tony, Winchester. Six reproduction metal sculptures, 1850, Birmingham.'

'As one's genuine Egyptian, we should delete it, Lovejoy.'

'And?' I prompted. Exquisite tea, strong enough to plough.

Trembler shrugged. 'I incline to Phillips, London.'

'No.' I'm never sad vetoing a deal between auctioneers. Once you've decided that money's the name of the game, all is clarity. 'No. Make out an addendum list. Have Hamish print it, free issue on the door. Say that One Five Oh Seven's now only five repro bronzes, that one's been withdrawn. Bronze cat, Egyptian, resembling Säite period 644–525 BC. And tell Boy we'll split the mark-up one to two.'

'But why take it out of the auction?' Michelle asked.

Trembler answered for me. 'If six cheap reproductions are listed, and one is specially withdrawn, it's as good as announcing that somebody's realized it is genuine. From ten quid it leaps to maybe ten, twenty thousand. Lovejoy says we ask for a third of that difference. The addendum sheet's the first thing dealers look at. Bronze collectors will pay on the nail.'

'Will Mr Boy, er, Tony agree to share?''

'Lady,' Trembler said gently. 'He sent off six grubby old doorstops hoping for a few quid. And gets a fortune. Wouldn't you agree to fork out the expenses?'

'Sod the explanations,' I interrupted. 'How far'd I get?'

'Did it all, mate.' Tinker was pouring himself another pint of beer. From the tomato sauce on his mittens he must have had a meal or two while waiting for me to rouse. 'Lady here hardly kept up.'

'I got all of it,' Michelle said, glaring at Tinker.

'Kiss, then,' I ordered. 'Chance of a bite, Mrs Buchan?'

'I beg your pardon!' Michelle exclaimed indignantly, then quietened when she saw Trembler and Tinker marking an X on each of her pages. I did the same. God, I felt stiff. Something happens to your muscles. I saw her staring and smiled.

'A St Andrew's cross used to be put at the bottom of legal documents as a sign of honesty. That's why it's still a valid mark from people who can't write. It degenerated over the centuries into a love kiss. We use it in its original sense.'

'Truth and honesty!' Tinker laughed so much one of the girls had to bang his back to stop him choking to death.

'The dolls, Lovejoy.'

'For heaven's sake split them into single lots, Trembler. Who the hell boxed them into one?'

'Bleedin' toys,' Tinker grumbled. My answer.

'That tall French bride doll's the one to milk on the day, Trembler, but there are some good German bisques. Incidentally, d'you reckon that mohair wig character doll's by Marque? One went at Theriault's for over twenty thousand . . .' We chatted as my grub came. Tinker was by then really enjoying himself. The girls pretended to refuse his request for another jug of Mrs Buchan's homebrew, liking the scruffy old devil. The divvying had been a real success for him, because the stuff was exactly what I'd asked for. By dusk he'd be justifiably drunk in celebration.

Trembler and me went on, Tinker spraying us all with mouthfuls as he put in an occasional word and Michelle making notes. The set of wooden decoy ducks, retain as likely in this area. The collection of twenty-six fans, accept. The sixty pieces of lace, retain but split into different-sized lots. And the William Morris furniture look-alikes, put into one motif room. The alleged early Viennese Meerschaum pipe was a fake, but leave in because some collector might be daft enough . . .

Late that same night Michelle came across me in the conservatory.

'What are you reading?'

'A real cliffhanger.' I held out the book. '*Dame Wiggins and her Seven Wonderful Cats*. I like Kate Greenaway. Can't help wondering if she had an affair with George Weatherby. Co-authors and all that.' She sat opposite me, composed, hands clasped.

'Yonks ago—' she used the slang self-consciously—'I'd have said you looked ridiculous sitting in that old bath-chair. Now it seems so natural, you reading an old book by candlelight when there are comfortable chairs, new books, electric light, television.'

'It's pleasanter, love.'

'Is it always like that?' She meant divvying.

'Not long back I divvied a few things for a fairground.

Took it in my stride. This was a bit of a marathon.'

'And payment, Lovejoy?' First time she'd used my name.

'Money? You fixed the percentage.' I shrugged. 'It never sticks to my fingers. A woman I knew says it's because deep down I hate the stuff. Pay me in Roman denarii, love.'

She showed no inclination to go. Well, in for a penny, in for a pound. I said, 'You must be very proud of Elaine. Sad that James Wheeler didn't live to see how she turned out.'

Women who delay a reply are usually opting for truth. It's unnerving, like all rarities. Michelle's face was pale when finally it lifted.

'I suspected you'd guessed, Lovejoy.' She looked away for the crunch. 'He took his . . . wife to the Continent. I went as a companion.'

'Because you were pregnant with Elaine.' Good planning. 'The wife condoned everything?'

'Of course.' She was faintly surprised at my astonishment. 'The importance of a clan heir overrode everything. Duncan didn't know. He stayed to help Robert run Tachnadray.'

'All these dark secrets put you in my power,' I threatened. 'Now I'll exploit you rotten.'

She smiled at that, really smiled. 'Anyone else, yes. But not you, Lovejoy.'

She rose, hesitated as if seeking something, then bent over and put her warm dry mouth to mine.

'Thank you, Lovejoy.'

'Don't say thanks yet, love,' I said sadly. 'Unless you know what's coming.'

Her eyes, so close to mine, showed doubt an instant before her woman's resolve abolished it. She decided I meant gain.

'Duncan won't expect me for an hour,' she said evenly. Her perfume was light and fresh. New to me, irritatingly. It's one of my vanities that I can guess scents. 'I was on my way to leave this list in your room.'

'See you there, then,' I said, just as evenly as her.

'Don't be too long, Lovejoy.' Her voice was a murmur.

I watched her recede from sight in the gold glow, then returned for a quick minute to Dame Wiggins. One of the Wonderful Cats would land in the gunge if it didn't watch out. Like Dutchie and Dobson. Except they'd only two lives between them. A cat's got nine. Right?

CHAPTER 27

One of the worst feelings in the world must be when you throw a party and nobody comes. I mean, that Bible character who dragged in the halt, lame and blind has my entire sympathy. I began to get cold feet, though all portents were for go. Letters were still arriving. We'd had three calls from Mr Ruthven, banker, ecstatic because nearly fifty firms or unknowns had transferred sums to the Caithness National out of the blue. Pastor Ruthven, notable non-assassin, blessed our enterprise. The phone was constantly trilling, bloody nuisance. Mrs Moncreiffe had her hair done.

Outside was like Highland Games day. Yellow ribbons on metal hooks fenced the tracks all the way from the bridge over Dubneath Water to Tachnadray. Robert and his men, now a staunch six, had put night-glitters on the ribbons, good thinking, and had laboriously mowed a spare field. Five hundred cars and eight coaches, he said. A man was sacked for blabbing in the MacNeishes' pub; drummed out of the Brownies, lost his badge, and got mysteriously convicted and clinked for a week's remand by magistrate Angus McGunn.

A trailer arrived from Thurso carrying a kind of collapsible canvas cloister. Mrs Buchan blew up, learning that Trembler was making inquiries among Inverness caterers, but I quashed her campaign when one caterer undertook to run a grub-and-tea tent and give us a flat fee. I agreed the same for a bar, plus a percentage. The catalogues were fetching in six times the printing costs. Hamish, maniacal by now, was doing a colour catalogue of fifty-one pages with a 'research index', meaning notes, by Mr Cheviot Yale, Auctioneer and Fellow of this and that. The coloured versions were for sale at the door, at astronomic cost to the buyer. Trembler prophesied they'd sell all right. A firm from Inverness brought a score of portable loos for an extortionate fee. They looked space-age, there on the grass, white and clinical. The local St John Ambulance undertook to send a couple of Medical Aid people, in case.

The estate had never seen days like it, not since the laird's spending sprees. Mrs Buchan's kitchen was going non-stop. Duncan finished his last piece, a pedestal case. This is the 1820 notion of a filing cabinet, with five hinged leather-covered cardboard boxes in a tier. It sounds rubbish but with its lockable mahogany frame it looked grand. I explained how to age it with dilute bleach and a warm stove. Duncan's products, a round dozen by now, would go into the auction as extra lots on the addendum.

It felt like a holiday. Trembler went off south for a well-earned, er, rest after ordering two of his exotic ladies from a Soho number. Tinker was paralytic, but messily filling out in the kitchen. It was there I roused him while Mrs Buchan's merry minions were screaming laughing over laundry in the adjoining wash-house. He came to blearily, hand crooked for a glass.

'Noisy bleeders,' he groused while I poured. Mrs Buchan's latest offering was like tar. He slurped, shook the foundations with a cough, focused. 'Yeah, Lovejoy.'

'Dutchie and Dobson.' I waited for his cortex to re-assemble in the alcohol fog. 'Dutchie back from the Continent?'

'Never.' He hawked, spat into the fire.

'You sure? Our local dealers say you can set your clock by Dutchie's reappearances.'

'Not this time, Lovejoy.'

'Tinker. I reckon Dobson did that driver, and Tipper Noone. Watch out for Dutchie and Dobson.'

'Fine chance, Lovejoy,' he croaked witheringly. 'Them bastards are too lurky.'

They'd both be here. I already knew that. The only question remaining was their attitude towards me. I was pretty confident Dutchie wouldn't—maybe couldn't— harm me. But that cunning silent knife-carrier Dobson . . . I hunched up and sipped Tinker's ale for warmth. What's

185

the explosion, an angel walking over your grave? I thought, some angel.

View Day's always a let-down, with added tension, same as any rehearsal. Everybody was keyed up. Trembler returned looking like nothing on earth but steadying as the day wore on. Tinker spent the morning 'seein' the bar's put proper', meaning sponging ale. Michelle checked the numbers, and fought Trembler over sticky labels on the oil paintings. I kept out of it. Robert and Duncan drilled the retainers twice. No hitches.

They came. First a group of three cars, hesitantly following the signs. They'd driven from Eastbourne. Then a minibus from George MacNeish's tavern with the six overnighters we already knew about. Duncan's men had erected signs everywhere. Nobody had an excuse for 'accidentally' getting themselves lost. Our people were on station in doorways, corridors and one on each of the seven staircases. Five hawkeyed men simply stood on the grass staring at the big house, Hector with Tessie and Joey spelling them in sequence every twenty minutes. One thing was plain to even the casual viewer: security was Tachnadray's thing.

Our viewing was timed for eleven a.m. to four in the afternoon. The trickle was a steady flow by noon. By one it was a crowd. Two o'clock and the nosh tent was crammed, the bar tent actually bulging at the seams. A coach arrived. The car park was half full, and filling. But throughout I kept a low profile. From the west wing's upstairs corridors I could see the main doorway. I had a pile of sandwiches against starvation and a trannie against boredom in case Dutchie and Dobson didn't show. I sat on the window-ledge watching.

There was only one way for them to enter the house, and that was up the balustraded steps. And one way out, the same. As people arrived, I counted with one of those electronic counters. Like watching an ants' nest in high summer. I recognized many, smiling or scowling as I remembered their individual propensities.

Lonely business. Twice Michelle sent a breathless girl—

we had two of these runners, not really enough—with some query, quite mundane. It occurred to me that maybe Michelle was checking on me, rather than proving she was on the ball. Once Tinker came coughing up, carrying me a pint of ale. At least, he nearly did. The beer slopped so much on the stairs he didn't think it worthwhile to finish the ascent, so he drank it and called up that he'd go back and get me another. 'Another?' I yelled down. 'I haven't had the bloody first yet.' He clumped off, muttering. That's friends for you. I mean, I thought from my perch by the leaded window, Michelle was really too attractive, but cuck-olding Duncan, whom I liked, hadn't been my fault. She'd realized how good and sincere I am deep down. That's what did it. Finer qualities always go over big with women . . .

Dobson walked from the covered way. He paused to scan the still kilted figures of Duncan's five watchers. Undecided, he strolled round the east wing. I smiled. Sure enough, he returned. Hamish's big cousin Charles, No 17, was posted there with his shepherd's crook and his noisy eight-year-old son. Dobson moved more purposefully, round the west wing. I waited while the viewers, now a teeming throng, poured about. And back he came, now surly and fuming. It was Hector's sister's lad Andy on that corner with his border collie. Dobson turned, shook his head slowly. No go, he was telling somebody.

My blood chilled. An overcoated man, bulky and still, was standing among the crowd. He raised his hand to his hat, and five—*five*, for Christ's sake; there's only one of me —others joined him. They came and ascended the steps with Dobson's lanky morose figure striding behind. I swallowed. Well, I tried to. These were hard nuts, Continentals from the Hook. Ferrymen, as Tinker calls them. Pros, the heavies with which our gentle occupation abounds.

They left after two hours, into the nosh tent. At four Duncan's bell started ringing. At four-thirty the last cars left, carrying the caterers. A lady dealer, one of the Brighton familiars, was winkled out of the loos by a dog. Five o'clock and Duncan's men raised an arm, Robert's numbers each holding a plaid flag from the windows. Michelle came out and signalled jubilantly up to me, smiling all over her face. I opened the window and yelled to stand down, everybody. One or two applauded, all delighted. Trembler had one small item missing, a fake Stuart drinking glass. Cheap at the price, but Trembler went mad. Tinker complained the beer tent hadn't allowed the statutory twelve minutes' drinking-up period, and went to fill the aching void with Mrs Buchan's brew. Other people haven't his bad chest. Elaine was thrilled and joined us all in the kitchen for a celebration.

'A perfect View Day!' she exclaimed, congratulating Trembler in the hubbub. 'Absolutely right!'

Nearly, I thought, as the retainers talked, grinning in the flush of success. Almost nearly. But I grinned yes, wasn't it great, well done. All there was left to do now was leave my promised panic message on Antioch Dodd's answer phone and wait for the dawn to bring Dobson's vicious army and the holocaust.

CHAPTER 28

Auction Day.

The Great Hall at Tachnadray was crowded. Seats were in rows, three hundred. Dealers, collectors, and even other auctioneers, plus a few stray human beings were cramming in. The talk was deafening. Michelle was lovely though pale on her podium with little Mrs Moncreiffe in place behind her neat blocks of forms. To the auctioneer's far left two solemn lasses waited at telephones. Retainers were stationed at the exit and by each window down the length of the hall. Trembler's two shopsoiled whizzers had arrived overnight. With the eidetic memory of their kind, they hastened once round the entire stock, then went to the beer tent to take on fuel, bored. I entered as Trembler checked the time, made for his podium. He looked great, really presentable posh.

''Morning, Lovejoy,' somebody said.

''Morning, Jodie.'

'How did a scruff like you get a commission like this?'

She was smiling as she jibed. Jodie Blane's a bottle-blonde who does business with those clandestine dealers who're forever in and out of Newcastle. She's genuine watercolours and Regency silver. She says.

'Me? Influential friend of the family.'

We laughed. I said I thought I'd just seen Dutchie. She said no, that I must be mistaken because she'd heard Dutchie was in Brussels. I asked from whom, and sure enough she replied Dobson. Surprise, surprise. Elaine wheeled in, emitting the ephemeral radiance of the love-child and smiling up at Trembler. Oho, I thought, moving on in the press. Trembler gavelled, and we were off. His two whizzers appeared from nowhere, one in each aisle.

'Good day, ladies and gentlemen. Welcome to Tachnadray. Please refer to the conditions of sale. No buyer's premium—' a few ironic handclaps met his wintriest smile —'but otherwise Sotheby's rules apply. Note that the auctioneers deny responsibility . . .' Jeers and catcalls, some laughter. In the buzz Trembler summarized all the other escape clauses, making sure we could get away with murder, and went straight in. It'd be a long sale. He begged for haste in the bidding.

'Lot One. De Wint: "Dovecot, Derbyshire", watercolour.'

'Showing here, sir!' cried a whizzer.

'Who'll start me off? Two hundred?' Trembler intoned, then in surprise responded to a nod from the furthest telephone girl. All phoney. Last Sunday he'd drilled her till she cried. He feigned a bid beyond me, also off the wall, and finally knocked the painting down to the telephone girl. She called the buyer's name: 'Gallery Four, sir.' The fourth private gallery registered incognito with the auction. It indicated big secretive buying interests. The audience's faces hardened, and settled down for blast-off. The phoney telephone wires dangled out of sight below the girls' desks, of course. It didn't matter, because the De Wint watercolour was also dud. Elaine had done it, under my guidance. But it had keyed the audience up to a spending mentality. Trembler's a real artist. I stepped into the corridor.

'Hector. All the men in position?'

'Aye. Why?'

The dogs panted, grinning up at me. 'One bloke yesterday tried sussing out the two wings. Ever seen him before?'

Hector tried to grin. 'No, Lovejoy. Should I have?'

'No. Any extra men we can use?'

'No variation,' he said. 'Your own rules, mon.' So no extra man guarding the cottage.

I bit my lip anxiously. 'Watch out for the blighter. Tall, thin. Looks sour.'

'Aye, I mind him. Dinna fash.' He laughed, thinking I believed him about Dobson.

Apologetically I grinned and left, hands in pockets and pausing for a last look at one of my favourites, a Joe Knibb bracket clock. Simple rectangular, 1720, and worth a fortune. 'Tara, darlin',' I said to its lovely face, and walked out just as I was. Tinker was in the beer tent as I'd instructed. I didn't glance his way, nor he mine. At the corner of the east wing Andy waited with his energetic collie. Why are dogs never still?

'Going well in there, is it?' he asked. Great how the retainers had committed themselves.

'Aye, Andy. Don't let yon dog nod off.' And I strolled on past, through the unkempt garden. Under a crumpled greenhouse's door stone lay the two-pound hammer and cold chisel. Heavy, but Joseph was probably bolted in and I'd need something for the door.

Then I trotted away from Tachnadray. I'd miss it.

Distances contract during daytime. I've often noticed that. Maybe it's because you know where you're putting your feet. I had the sense to follow Dubneath Water from the bridge, moving on the stones and eventually climbing up where I'd been baulked by Ranter. The guard was standing on the skyline a half mile off, facing the house in a patriarchal pose. From there he could see the cars and all the activity. No dog, thank God.

Somewhat muckily I climbed out of the watercourse and moved left, getting the cottage between us before I made a direct move towards it. The main door was on the side facing the distant guard, as was that unlatched shutter. The rear door my side was virtually rusted in place. Using the chisel, I levered off the bolt, and did the old lock with my belt buckle. A push on the Suffolk latch, and I was in. Must, rust, dust. Just to make sure, I peered into the two downstairs rooms, a parlour and a kitchen. Unused for years. Grime was trodden shiny on the middle of the stairs. A trannie played pop music above my head. I went up, a bit scared—well, not really scared as such. More worried. Maybe I'd got it wrong.

But I hadn't. Joseph was sitting in the upstairs room with that shutter ajar. They hadn't even allowed the poor bugger a light, perhaps in case he signalled. He stood, jaw dropping and stared at me in the doorway with my hammer and chisel. One hand was manacled to the wall, a long chain, and his ankles were chained to a granite cube. He could move, but he'd be noticed in company.

'Dear God,' he said faintly, his face drained.

'Wotcher, Dutchie.'

'I didn't kill the driver. Honest, Lovejoy. Please.'

'I know you didn't, silly burke.' I tested the wall chain. With that broken I could at least get him away.

'Lovejoy . . .' His voice broke. 'Is there a chance?'

'Let's make one,' I said, and started on the damned thing.

I was past caring by now. He had a towel which I used to muffle the blows. The cold chisel through the wall link with me banging the two-pounder on it in great sideways swings. When the wall insert did go it nearly took my eye out, whizzing past my forehead and pitting the wall opposite.

Dutchie carried his chains over his shoulder, me humping his granite cube. We left *Shooters* and crawled to the gully. We must have looked a sight by the time we reached the bridge. Dutchie was exhausted. I shoved him so he was in the dry under the arch, and heaved myself up to join him. He tried to gasp what the hell were we doing but I shut him and whispered that our own private express service would be along shortly.

Cars were still passing overhead heading towards Tachnadray, but only intermittently. One of them would be Dobson and his five sociopaths.

It was three o'clock in the afternoon before that ancient engine came thumping down the track and arrested humming on the bridge. Even then I didn't make a move until a gravelly cough temporarily muted the racket.

'Come on, Dutchie.' I tugged on his chain. We struggled up the bank. Tinker gaped from the Mawdslay.

'Bleedin' hell, Lovejoy. That Dutchie you got there?'

'Shut it.' I dumped the granite block in. 'Drive. South.'

He blasphemed at the gears. ''Ere, Lovejoy. Why's Dutchie in chains?' We slammed forward, skidding wheels spraying earth. 'Can we stop at a pub?'

CHAPTER 29

We ran into Dubneath, veered south and started the long run. In the first few miles we hardly spoke, except for me once.

'Give over hammering, Dutchie. The frigging floor'll fall out.'

'But I'm chained,' he bleated.

Aren't we all, I thought wearily. I'd lost all track of who I was being loyal to. The shyly elegant Michelle; the lovely Elaine inheriting the sins of her fathers, sic; teacher Jo; Shona the priestess-oracle of a McGunn renaissance; or this lout with whom I was now lumbered.

There hadn't been much choice of direction. North or east meant splash. West was back to Tachnadray. Within ten miles Tinker drove me mad, complaining about the signs.

'Kyle of what?' he grumbled. 'Strath of Kildonan? Here, Lovejoy. Funny bleedin' names up here.'

'Give us that wheel,' I said irritably. We changed places. Cackling joyously, he fetched out a bottle, the old devil.

'Give Dutchie a swallow,' I told him.

He coughed long and harsh, giving himself time to think

up an excuse. 'Dutchie shouldn't,' he wheezed, with rheumy old eyes streaming. 'On account of his chains.'

'*Tinker*.' For half a groat I'd have slung them both out. I was sick of the lot of them. Everybody was safe except me, heading back into danger.

Morosely Tinker passed his bottle to Dutchie, whose glugs made Tinker squirm in distress. He decided to get at me for enforcing charity at his ale's expense.

'There wuz only two of them burkes with Dobson,' he said.

'You sure?' I felt my nape prickle. I'd banked on all five, plus Dobson, turning up at the auction. Dobson must have guessed I'd make a sly run for it.

'I waited, Lovejoy. They went in. Eyes all round their heads.'

'Dobson's here?' Dutchie sounded pale in the rear seat.

'With five goons. Tough lot.'

Dutchie groaned. 'We've had it, then. They'll be on the road waiting for us, Lovejoy.'

'That's the spirit,' I said bitterly.

'Will . . . they all be safe at Tachnadray?' He sounded like a bloke on his deathbed.

'You mean your mother and dad? Certainly. I've got Trembler up. There's a big auction on the estate. Paper job.'

Tinker belched, hawked. 'Mam and dad?'

'Michelle and Duncan,' I explained.

'Dutchie's?' His eyes widened. 'You mean that bird you—?'

'Shut it.' Tinker always knows more about my affairs than I'd like. 'And your sister is fine.' Still nothing following in the rear mirror.

That took a minute to sink in, but he tried. 'You know about that, then, Lovejoy.'

'Only guessed. She did a painting, your mother Michelle and the laird. Pastor Ruthven gave part of the game away. The laird's wife couldn't conceive and he became obsessed with providing an heir for the crumbling clan. Dynasty delusion.'

'He was always like that. Ever since . . .'

'Ever since he arrived as plain James Wheeler.' I adjusted the mirror to watch Dutchie's face. 'Even had his name changed to McGunn, by deed poll. I had it checked. Which makes Elaine Michelle's daughter. You're Elaine's half-brother.'

'Elaine and me always got on, in spite of all.'

Tinker's brain buzzed. 'Then what she have you chained up for, Dutchie?'

I answered for him. 'Remember that bureau? The night of the fog, when the driver got topped? Dutchie was trying to nick it. You were hoping to make a killing of a different sort, eh, Dutchie?'

Tinker put his mouth near my ear to whisper hoarsely, 'Lovejoy. If Dutchie kilt the driver, what you give him that frigging hammer for?'

'Dobson clobbered the driver.' I kept checking my accuracy on Dutchie's face. 'When me and Ellen reached the wagon the bureau had been offloaded. Dobson organized the twinning job knowing its value. Maybe the driver also realized, so Dobson did him, poor sod. Dobson told Robert that Dutchie'd shared in the killing. With the fog lifting during the night, Robert drove Dutchie to Tachnadray. Dobson had to do in Tipper Noone, who'd done the twinning. He knew it was Dobson.'

Dutchie said, 'Robert came up just as Dobson clobbered me because I wouldn't go along with the driver's killing. I'd been unloading while he killed him.'

Tinker cackled. 'Bet Robert got an eyeful. Lovejoy was in Ben's hut shagging that Ellen. Biggest bristols you ever—'

'*Tinker*.' One day I'll replace the garrulous burke by a Cambridge MA. I'm always making these vows, never fulfil them.

'There was no hiding place except Tachnadray,' Dutchie said. He sounded really depressed.

'Because one of Dobson's goons is from Michelle's home town in Belgium. The Continental connection, eh?' I should have realized a million years ago, if only from Michelle's

194

accent. And Dutchie's nickname: anybody from the Low Countries is called that indiscriminately in East Anglia. Thick as ever.

Dutchie was telling Tinker. '. . . friend of my mother's side.'

The old drunk was delighted. 'Hey!' he exclaimed. 'I know it! Nice little place. I blew a bridge there. Up to me balls in water. Lovely little Norman arch it had—'

'One more word from you, Tinker,' I warned him. He shut up. 'Tell me if I'm right, Dutchie. Duncan and Michelle hid you at *Shooters*. You tried to escape, thinking you'd turn yourself in and tell the truth. Elaine supposed they were protecting you against yourself.'

'I tried telling them.'

I said, readjusting the mirror, 'Shona discovered my identity because I opened my big mouth about antiques. She claimed then to have deliberately sent a real antique to entice me to Tachnadray. Like a prat, I believed her. Here, Tinker, take a glance. Is that motor the one which Dobson and the goons had at Tachnadray?'

'Eh?' He screwed his eyes, peered. 'No.'

'It could have overtaken us twice, and hasn't.' I'd noticed it a mile since. 'It has the legs on us.'

Dutchie sounded almost in tears. 'There's no way out, Lovejoy.'

'Optimist.' The trouble with some people is they're not big enough cowards. Anyway, they didn't want Dutchie any more. They wanted me. 'There's nowt they can do until we pass Dingwall. We're going to double back north for a bit. The A890 to Achnashellach.'

'Funny frigging names round here.' Tinker started a prolonged cough, phlegm and spittle over the side. If his chest would mend we'd be ten miles faster.

The big blue Mercedes stayed on our tail. I took on petrol in Dingwall, as Antioch had told me to do, then left the Inverness Road and pretended to try to shake them off by over-desperate demonstration driving.

The day was fading. The road grew thinner and traffic lessened. An occasional car overtook us and a lorry or two passed going east, but that was about it. We left the security of towns as we hurried west. Countryside is rotten old stuff, lonely and ominous. The Government really should do something. I was as worried what was happening up ahead as much as by that bulky saloon dogging me, and kept staring into the mniddle distance on every rise. The skies abruptly lowered on us, and a drizzle started. The Mawdslay was a tough old thing, booming up each slope with ease, but steering it through the twisting dips was hell. It had a will of its own. Tinker started snoring.

As we ran on and the day ended there was nothing but hills, and woods and lakes to the left. Dutchie started some lunatic suggestion: drop him off and he would nip down an incline, granite block and all. 'I could reach the Strath Bran railway.'

'Ta, Dutchie, but don't be daft.' He was only trying to help. Bravery's more stupid than cowardice.

Tinker coughed himself awake and also made a contribution. 'Here, Dutchie. How'd you manage to go for a—?'

'The chain was long enough.' Dutchie rattled it as proof.

We were a couple of miles past the chapel near Bran when we saw the man mending a motorbike by a lantern, thank Christ. He didn't watch us drive past, made no move. I was beginning to worry I'd missed him.

'Hang on, lads,' I said, and cracked on speed. The old giant roared, fast as I could go in the darkening rain.

'Here, Dutchie,' Tinker was rabbiting on. 'What percentage d'you give that Dobson . . . ?'

Here I was sweating, grappling with the controls, and this pair sitting yapping like at a tea-party. The road curved, left to right. Down, then uphill. A slow bend, the Mercedes coming fast, its headlights on full beam. It'd be soon. I yelped, cornering too fast, wrestled up straight, cursing.

The tall lorry swept past in the opposite direction. I saw the Mercedes waver as its driver realized. A horn blared. The crash sounded actually in the Mawdslay and for one crazy instant I thought: Hell, it's us they've got in spite of everything, before sense reasserted itself. I was still driving, unimpeded. Something burst. Air rushed along over the

196

Mawdslay, blew on my ears. I slowed. Only the lorry's tail-lights in the rear-view mirror, nothing moving.

'Gawd Almighty,' Tinker croaked. 'See that?'

Head out of the window, I crawled in slow reverse to where the man was standing by his lorry. I disembarked and stood looking over the edge of the camber.

'Ta, Antioch. All right?'

He heaved a sigh, tutting. 'No gumption, some people. If he'd braked, he might have got out of it.'

A car was ablaze down below among a haircut of young trees. Even as I watched another bit of it woomphed. The air stank oil, rubber. A big bloke arrived on a motorbike, somehow folded it and lobbed it into Antioch's lorry's tailboard with ease. He nodded at the fire on the hillside below, as if acknowledging the inevitable. 'Well,' he said in a singy Ulster voice, 'they shouldn't go round killing drivers, should they?'

'Six in it, eh?' I asked Antioch.

'No. Three. They're using a band radio. They've a rover block on the A87.'

'What's best, Antioch?' Three from six leaves three.

'No smoking, O'Flaherty,' Antioch said absently. The man put away his cigarettes. He had the envious tranquillity of the professional. I'm only glad I'm not that tranquil. 'Look, Lovejoy. I can see you safe part way, say Glasgow?'

'I've a better idea, Antioch,' I said. Lovejoy Knowall. 'They'll suspect I won't touch Edinburgh.' I didn't give reasons. 'Will you put us that way on?'

'Right. I've things to do here, so O'Flaherty'll see you as far as Perth. Then it's motorway.'

The rain was worsening, but it made no difference to the fire below. A lorry chugged past. O'Flaherty waved.

With difficulty I turned the Mawdslay and followed O'Flaherty's lorry. Antioch gave a distant nod as we passed. Aren't people funny? He supports an orphanage in Affetside, then he goes and does a thing like that and stays cool. I kept having to clench my teeth to stop them chattering.

Dutchie's voice wasn't all that steady, either. 'Where to now, Lovejoy?'

'Down the middle, to Edinburgh.'

Past Balmoral. We could always pop in and check that the royal gardeners were growing enough flowers under the old Queen Mum's roses. She was murder on ground-cover plants.

CHAPTER 30

There's not a lot of northerly roads into Edinburgh. Unless you've a hang-glider, this means two accident-prone motorways. O'Flaherty pulled into a lay-by south of Perth, still not smoking as he shook my hand.

'Get them bastards, Lovejoy,' he said.

'Me?' I was amazed. 'I'm not like that. Honest.'

'To be sure. But the driver they topped was my mate.' He was so wistful as he said, 'I wanted Antioch to let me drive the pusher. Good luck.' I waved him off.

Assassins are pretty cool, and often misunderstood. I've often noticed that. I was trying to evade the blighters, not find them. Which worried me, thinking about Mr Sidoli and the travelling funfair. Except Edinburgh's Festival was still in mid-orgy. Which meant Sidoli and Bissolotti would presumably still be hurdy-gurdying grimly on that green. But, my hope-glands flicked into my mind, where can you hide a Lovejoy best, but in a lovely throng? I shelved the terrible fact that any solution would be only temporary. Dobson & Co. had my home territory sewn up. The north was done for, now I'd sprung Dutchie. Edinburgh was limbo, but a satisfactorily crowded one.

'We'll leave you in the motor, Dutchie,' I decided. 'A cutting file and you'll be free as air.'

'We're splitting up?' he asked.

'About Tipper Noone,' I said, concentrating hard on the long strings of motorway lights. I had to be sure. Now that Michelle and me had come together, maybe I was feeling like his dad or something equally barmy.

'Tipper ships for us, Lovejoy. Repros through the Hook.'

Does? No past tenses for poor old Tipper, RIP? Dutchie, for all his gormlessness, was looking better and better. I drew breath to exploit Dutchie's unawareness, but Tinker said helpfully, 'Your pal Tipper's snuffed it.' So much for tact.

The A90 had most traffic, so I bombed in on that while Tinker cheerfully narrated Tipper's tale to the stricken Dutchie. Parking the motor would be a nightmare . . . Too late I noticed the bloody toll bridge. Too tired for any more vigilance, I was in the queue and the man asking for the gelt. He could see Dutchie quite clearly, manacles, chains, block. No hidey nooks in a tourer.

'Fringe?' he said, nodding at Dutchie.

'Eh?'

'Your show.' He shook his head sadly. 'The council should provide proper places for the Fringe Festival. It's a disgrace.'

'Ta. We'll manage.' I tried to look brave but wounded.

'Good luck.'

And we were through. Fringe? 'What was he on about, Dutchie?'

Dutchie chuckled. His first ever. 'He thought we were performers. The Fringe Festival's unpaid art. It makes its way. Streets, bars, even bus stops, living rough.'

I cheered up. We were along Queensferry Road. Civilization and people—God, the people—lights, traffic. 'Shout if there's an ironmonger's.' Suddenly it was simple. I could buy a cutting file without fear. Part of our show's props. See how easy towns are, compared to countryside?

Signs directed us a different way than I'd intended. Older buildings, denser mobs, louder talk, songs, turmoil. I didn't want the old crate trapped in some sequinned cul-de-sac.

'There's a pub, Lovejoy.' Tinker had dried into restlessness.

We were down to trotting pace. I didn't fancy this at all. I wanted a zoom through the fleshpots, a rapid file session to lighten our load, then to go to earth while Tinker and Dutchie caught the Flying Scot south to safety. I'd follow later when I'd convinced our pursuers I'd escaped. But sedate traffic in a glare of road lights can be inspected quite easily—as indeed the pedestrians were doing, openly admiring our Mawdslay.

'Tinker. Got your medals?' A brainwave. The cunning old devil always carries them, and a mouth organ, to do a bit of busking if he's short of a pint and I'm not around.

He obeyed, smoothing them in place. A cluster of stilt-walkers followed us, striding and waving. A couple of girls in Red Indian costumes danced carrying buckets. A jazz band led by a pink donkey, I assure you, stomped jubilantly beside us, one of the players drumming on our side panel, a deafening racket. At a traffic light, me grinning weakly and trying to hum along to show we honestly were fringe people too, a lass in a straw boater stuck her head next to mine and screamed, 'Seen a gondola?'

'Er, no, love.'

'Soddation.' She climbed into the passenger seat. Tinker cackled. She seemed to wear little, black mesh stockings and bands of snakeskin. 'You can drop me off. You in the procession?' She lit a cigarette. Where the hell had she kept that? 'Or marching?'

'Well, er, you can see how we're fixed.'

'Ah.' She gazed round, eyes narrowing as she took in Dutchie's slavehood. 'Good, good. Rejection of imperialistic chauvinisms. The medals are genius.'

'Me wounds still hurt, dear.' Tinker started a shuddering cough. Sympathy always starts him cadging.

'Shut it, Tinker.' No exits down the side streets. All one way now, with the multicoloured mob a long winding tide. Police grinning, waving. A Caribbean dustbin band bonged to our right. A non-band of chalk-faced mimers played non-instruments alongside. Jesus. We were in a parade. My head was spinning. 'Lads, look for a way out.'

'I agree,' the girl groused. 'No political motivation. They're hooked on happiness. Perverts.'

I'd no idea what she was on about, but I made concurring mutters and simply drove in the worsening press. It was pandemonium. In front were handcarts, a lorryload of

Scotch bagpipers. All the shops were lit bright as day. Pirates dangled from lamp-posts, singing that chorus from *Faust*. A girl wearing a dog on her hat reclined on our bonnet with a weary sigh and popped a bottle of beer on a headlamp. Tinker whimpered. The dog looked fed up. Two ballet dancers danced outside a shoe shop, *Jewels of the Madonna* but I couldn't be sure because of the other bands. Applause. A youth dragged a floreate piano into the swelling parade, making placatory gestures to me to hold back while he made it. Wearily I waved him on. That said it all—Lovejoy, hot-rodding to escape, overtaken by a pianoforte. A poet de-claimed from a girl's shoulders. She was dressed as a skeleton and clutched an anchor.

'See what I mean?' Our girl was bitter. 'A waste of political potential.' She suddenly burst out laughing. The Mawdslay stank sweetly from her smoking. Oh dear. And Dobson's gaunt face among the pavement mobs.

'Lovejoy.'

'I see him, Dutchie.'

He was hurrying along the pavement, quickening when we could make a yard or two, dawdling in each hiatus. One overcoated bloke was with him. As long as we stayed with the carnival . . . A group of tumblers formed a sudden arch. The parade trundled beneath, to cheers. Our snakeskin girl sang tunelessly, head back.

'This bint's taking tablets,' Tinker croaked, disapproving. To him anybody stoned on drugs is 'taking tablets'.

Ahead a regular thumping sounded. A brass band. Correction: a military band, getting closer. Pipes. A cluster of actors froze an instant, took three paces, froze, dressed as vegetables. A pea pod, a cabbage, a possible lentil, a flute-playing celery. Fireworks lit the sky, hitherto the only turn unstoned. A bobby waved us on, veering towards somewhere distantly tall. The thumping of drums at long range. Our pink donkey's jazzy band bopped past as we got stuck behind the piano. I felt clammy. No sign of Dobson and his goon, but one bloke was stock-still on the pavement, keeping his eyes on us even when jostled. Depression and fear fought for my panic-stricken spirit.

'There's no bleedin' notes in that piano,' Tinker said.

'It's Jan The Judge,' our snakeskin said, happy herself now. 'He plays silence. The performance is in its nothingness.'

'What happens if he don't turn up?' Tinker was puzzling.

'Lovejoy. It's the tattoo.' Dutchie pointed. Searchlights swept the night. Pipers lined the battlements. A fusillade crackled.

Slower and slower. The parade was practically static now. Sweat poured off me. The Mawdslay, inch a minute, was trapped. Exactly as I hadn't wanted, there was no way for us to go. Behind us bands jigged, actors twisted and danced. Both sides were thronged with acts and noise. Giant puppets milled. Above us stilted actors and balloons. Something shattered the windscreen. Nobody noticed except me.

'Hey, your gondola!' I grabbed the girl, now floppy-limbed and crooning. 'Scatter, lads.' I was crouching below the dashboard, yelling. 'Tinker, hop it. Dutchie, stay among a band.' I hauled the lass sideways. More glass cracked. The Mawdslay trembled. The bloody donkey trod on my foot. Its band swayed past.

'Where?' She stood up, peering.

'Over there,' I yelled, fetching her down on me by a yank of her arm. The shots came from ahead but obliquely, so I spoiled a few syncopations by shoving my way through to the pavement. I couldn't even do that right. I had to step over three actors in evening dress in the gutter. A placard announced that they were the Drunken Theatre of Leigh. I tugged the snakeskin girl along, some protection. You penetrate crowds fastest hunched over and butting along at waist height. The trouble is you can't see. After a hundred yards a doorway, people shoving inside with such a tidal rip I got crushed along.

Brilliantly lit, wall labels and pseudo-Victorian illumination. Red plush, chandeliers. We were in a foyer. Cinema? Theatre? Thickset men in dinner-jackets on the door directing us, me included.

'No, mate,' I said, breathless in my terror sweat. 'You see, me and my bird are—'

He practically lifted me aside. 'Dressing-room there, laddie. She in the Supper Room? The Music Hall shares the same accommodation.'

'Where?' My girl's question was audible. A bell sounded two pulses. People began to hurry carrying half-finished drinks. A theatre's two-minute bell.

Applause burst out upstairs, amid catcalls. A xylophone began. I pulled the door. Two girls were just leaving, all spangles and scales. 'Jesus,' one said, disgusted. 'Not more? There's not room to swing a cat.'

'Sorry, love.'

The room was empty but looked ransacked. A ring of tired bulbs around a mirror, a lipsticked notice pleading for tidiness. Graffiti criticized somebody called the Dud Prospect Company for nicking make-up. My ears worked out what was the problem, finally got there. Silence. My adrenals gave a joyous squirt and relaxed: safety and solitude. I sat at the mirror.

'Right, love,' I said. Hopeless. 'Do me.'

'What?' She squinted over my shoulder. 'Are you on soon?'

'Five minutes.' I swept all the Leichner sticks and pots closer. 'Do the lot.'

'Bastard apolitical theatre managers.' She started me.

For the first time ever I didn't feel much of a clown. No clown's clobber, of course, except gloves and a weird hat. I'd sliced the fingers so they dangled, and scalped the topper into a lid. My face was chalk-white. Red nose, scarlet lips, lines about my eyes. I looked like nothing on earth. She'd done a rubbishy job, but I was grateful as I left, promising to send along any passing gondolas and vote something-or-other. She was carolling drowsily to her reflection, another smoke helping the mood. I turned my jacket inside out, and nicked some baggy trousers. Being noticeable was the one chance.

One of the evening-suited bouncers said, 'Hey. Other way,' but I kept going, down the foyer and out. The carnival was flowing on, over and round the Mawdslay. It stood there forlorn. No sign of Tinker or Dutchie. An overcoated man moved against the flow, finding refuge behind a pillar-box. I capered clumsily into the mob and drew a squad of ghosts trotting with a fife band. A jig. How the hell do you do a jig? I moved faster, advancing up the parade. I even caught up with my stilt walkers, jazz band, the silent piano man.

A policeman pointed me to one side. 'I reckon you're late, son.'

Thank God, I thought, prancing out of the stream. And saw Big Chas. And Ern. And Mr Sidoli's two terrible nephews. They were in carnival gear, flashing bow ties and waistcoats, striped shirts, bowlers.

'No,' I bleated in anguish. The bobby'd thought I was something to do with the fairground. Even as I whined and ran the familiar sonorous pipes of merry-go-rounds sounded.

'*Lovejoy*.' I heard Big Chas's bellow.

I fled then, down across the parade so terrified that cries of outrage arose even from those fellow thespians who'd assumed I was an act. I needed darkness now as never before. If the gunshots from Dobson's two goons had seemed part of the proceedings, a clown being knifed would seem a merry encore. I hurtled into a small parked van, wrenching the door open and scrabbling through. Two first-aid men wearing that Maltese Cross uniform were playing cards. I waited breathlessly, gathered myself to hurtle out of the front sliding door.

'All right, son?' one asked placidly, gathering the cards. 'An act, is it?'

'As long as he's not another Russian.' He gave me a grandfather's smile. 'No offence, laddie. They only come over here to do Dostoevsky and defect.'

'Aye. Always the second week—'

I swung the door out and dived. Somebody grabbed, shouted. Some lunatics applauded. 'How real!' a woman cooed as I scooted past, bowling a bloke in armour over. God, he hurt. Another carrying a tray went flying. I sprinted flat out, hat gone and trousers cutting my speed, elbows out and head down. I charged, panicked into blindness, among a mob of redcoated soldiers. They were having a smoke, instruments held any old how, in a huge arched tunnel with sparse lights shedding hardly a glimmer. I floundered among them. A few laughed. There was floodlight ahead, a roaring up there, possibly a crowd. Well it couldn't be worse. 'Here, nark it, Coco,' a trumpeter said, and got a roar by adding, 'Thought it was Lieutenant Hartford.'

A gateway and an obstruction, for all the world like a portcullis. I rushed at it, bleating, demented. An order was barked behind in the tunnel, and I'd reached as far as I could go. I was gaping into an arena filled with bands. Jesus, the Household Cavalry were in there, searchlights shimmering on a mass of instruments and horses' ornamentation. Lancers rode down one side. I could see tiers of faces round the vast arena. I moaned, turned back. Out there I'd be trapped like a fish in a bowl.

The soldiers formed up, marching easily past, some grinning. The drum major glared, abused me from the side of his mouth. The portcullis creaked. Applause and an announcement over the roar. The back-marker strode past, boots in time and the familiar double-tap of the big drum calling the instruments into noise. Gone. The entrance tunnel was empty. I couldn't follow the band into the arena, so I turned. Best if I tried to get to George Street. Those Assembly Rooms . . .

I stopped. My moan echoed down the tunnel towards the exit. Dobson stood there, pointing. Two goons, overcoated neat as Sunday, appeared and stood with him.

'Help!' I screamed, turning to run. And halted. Round the side of the arena gateway stepped Sidoli's nephews. Two more henchmen dropped from the tunnel archway, crouched a second then straightened to stand with the Sidolis. Big Chas walked between them. Five in a row. Both ends of the tunnel were plugged. I was trapped.

'Now, lads,' I pleaded, swallowing with an audible gulp. Blubbering and screaming were non-negotiable. 'Too many people have been hurt in all this . . .' The fairground men trudged towards me.

Dobson called, 'He's ours, tykes.'

'Ours,' a Sidoli said. The tunnel echoed, 'Ow-erss, owerss.' He was Sidoli's nephew all right.

No side doors in the tunnel's wall. I stood, dithering. Big Chas's line was maybe twenty yards away and coming steadily. Dobson's pair had pulled out stubby blunt weapons. I thought: Oh Christ. A war with me in the middle.

'Stop right there, Chas,' I said wearily. 'You were good to me. You've no shooters, like them. It's my own mess.'

And I walked towards Dobson. My only chance, really. And it bought me a couple of seconds. It bought me much more than that, as it happened. I moved on trembling pins towards my end. At least I now only had one army against me instead of two. More favourable odds, if doom wasn't a certainty.

'No!' a Sidoli shouted. 'Noh,' the tunnel yelled angrily.

Dobson backed smiling out of the tunnel entrance to where I'd first cannoned into the Guards band, his goon with him. I came on. They were in a perfect line. A stern warning cry, 'Loof-yoy! No!' behind me.

If I'd known it would have ended like this, in a grotty tunnel, I'd have marched out into the arena with the band and hared up through the crowd somehow—

An engine gunned, roared. It seemed to fill the tunnel with its noise. I hesitated, found myself halted, gaping, as a slab lorry ran across the arch of pallor, and simply swept Dobson and the two overcoats from view. And from the face of the earth. All in an instant time stopped. To me, forever Dobson and the two nerks froze in a grotesque array, legs and arms any old how, in an airborne bundle with that fairground slab wagon revving past. They're in that lethal tableau yet in my mind. Dobson's expression gets me most, in the candle hours. It's more a sort of let's-talk-because-there's-always-tomorrow sort of expectation on his face. But maybe I'm wrong because it was pretty gloomy, and Ern didn't have any lights on as he crashed the wagon into and over Dobson and his nerks.

Footsteps alongside. I closed my eyes, waiting.

Big Chas's hand fell on my shoulder. 'Lovejoy,' he said,

friendly, and sang, '*Hear thy guardian angel say: "Thou art in the midst of foes: Watch and pray!"*'

'I'm doing that, Chas,' I said.

Mr Sidoli was overjoyed to see me; I wasn't sure why. They gave me a glass of his special Barolo while I waited. I'd expected death. Unbelievably I was left alone on the steps, though everybody I remembered came up and shook my hand. The fairground seemed to have grown. There was no sign of Bissolotti's rival fair. Instead, a marquee boasted a dynamic art show, periodically lasering the darkness with a sky advert.

Francie rushed up to say everybody was proud of me. Her whizz kid was temporarily running the Antique Road Show. Like Tom the cabin boy, I smiled and said nothing, simply waited for this oddly happy bubble to burst.

It was twenty to midnight when I was called inside. Mr Sidoli was in tears. His silent parliament was all around, celebrating and half sloshed.

'Loof-yoy,' he said, scraping my face with his moustache and dabbing his eyes. 'What can I say?'

'Well, er.' Starting to hope's always a bad sign.

'First,' he declaimed, 'you bravely seize Bissolotti's main generator, and crush his treacherous sneak attack.' He glowered. Everybody halted the rejoicing to glower. 'And restrained yourself so strongly that you only destroyed three men.'

Scattered applause. 'Bravo, bravo!'

'Destroyed? Ah, how actually destroyed . . . ?'

His face fell. 'Not totally, but never mind, Loof-yoy. Another occasion, *si*?' Laughter all round. 'Then you cleverly tell the police it is my generator so I can collect it and hold Bissolotti to ransom.'

This time I took a bow. The nephews burst into song.

'And at the arena you bravely tried to spare my nephews then the risk when they go to help you, knowing how close to my heart . . .' He sobbed into a hankie the size of a bath towel. Everybody sniffled, coughed, drank. I even felt myself fill up.

'And you walk forward into certain death!'

I was gripped in powerful arms. Ern and Chas sang a martial hymn. Fists thumped my back.

When you think of it, I really had been quite courageous. In fact, very brave. Not many blokes have faced two mobs down. It must be something about my gimlet eyes. You must admit that some blokes have this terrific quality, and others don't.

Joan was watching in her usual silence. Her eyes met mine. Well, I thought, suddenly on the defensive. I'd been almost nearly brave, hadn't I? I mean, honestly? Joan smiled, right into my eyes, silly cow. She's the sort of woman who can easily nark a bloke. I'd often noticed that.

They'd have finished the auction in Tachnadray.

It was three o'clock in the morning before I remembered Tinker. Sidoli's lads found him paralytic drunk busking in George Street, Dutchie doing a political chain dance round his political granite block. Tinker said we'd all go halves. His beret was full of coins, enough for a boozy breakfast for us all.

CHAPTER 31

Countryside. No rain, no fog. And, at Tachnadray, no longer only one way out. Me, Duncan and Trembler were talking outside the workshop. They'd taken on half-a-dozen apprentices. From the quality of their work I wouldn't have paid them tea-money, but Duncan said they'd learn.

'Make sure you spread them about this time.' I meant the reproductions they were going to mass-produce. 'One each to East Anglia, Newcastle, Liverpool, Glasgow, Bristol and Southampton. Stick to one route and you're in the clag.'

'We've had enough trouble,' Duncan said with feeling.

'You didn't have any,' I pointed out nastily. After all, I was the hero. 'Okay, your son was a hostage, but safe. He's a McGunn.'

'There's no trouble for you now, Lovejoy, eh? I mean, those two men, and the others?'

'Tipper Noone? And the driver? No. Whatever the police find won't matter a bit. Dobson and his killers are dead.'

The vehicle was fixed by Ern, a spontaneous case of brake failure. The police could enjoy themselves speculating on the guns found on two of the deceased. I, of course, wasn't within miles. I sprouted alibis, Sidoli's doing.

'Wotcher, love,' I said to Elaine.

Elaine had a new automatic wheelchair. I said it wasn't as good as the old garden machine we'd sold at the auction. She'd bickered back that I didn't have to sit in it.

'Lovejoy,' she said, in that tuneful propositioning voice women use when they're going to sell you a pup. 'How'd you like to become a partner?'

'If that is a proposal of marriage, you're too plain.'

'Stop fooling. In Tachnadray.'

'It's not me, love. Trembler here will. It's time somebody took him in hand.'

That's what we'd been heading towards all along. Elaine turned her sea-bed opalescent eyes on Trembler. 'Will you, Cheviot?'

'He's been on about nothing else,' I said irritably. 'He's trying to work out how to word it. Nerk.'

Trembler tried to start a solemn contractual conversation. 'I'll have to think—'

'Me and Tinker did a draft contract for you after break-fast. And,' I added, 'my percentage of the auction profits you can spilt three ways—Tachnadray, and the families of the driver and Tipper Noone. How's that?' As soon as I'd made the offer I groaned. Still, easy come, easy go.

'Is Lovejoy serious?' Elaine asked.

'I'll do a list of exploitations. Pottery, prints, pressed flowers of Tachnadray, tartan novelties, photographs of the ancestral home. And you'll sell inch-square plots to tourists, fortune at a time, each with a great Sale Deed in Gothic Latin lettering, a sealing-wax blob on a ribbon. Postage extra. And "coin" tokens in fifteenth-century denominations. It's where greatness lies.'

'There's something scary about all this, Lovejoy.' But Elaine's eyes were shining.

You have to laugh. For the first time in her life she'd challenged the outside world, and won victory. Now she wanted the thrill of the contest over and over. There'd be no stopping Tachnadray now, especially with Trembler on the team.

'I'll come and check on you every autumn, Cheviot.' It was the end of an era. There'd be a sudden drop (I nearly said tumble) in Soho's sexploitation shares tonight.

They had moved away when Elaine paused. 'Oh, Lovejoy. Can I ask something?'

I walked over. Trembler moved politely out of earshot. Her eyes were radiantly lovely looking up at me.

'Lovejoy. Did you and Michelle?'

'Eh? Did we what?'

She blushed, a lovely rose pink. 'You *know*.'

'No.' I was puzzled. Then my brow cleared. 'You can't mean . . . ?' I was mixed furious and hurt. '*Elaine!* How can you ask that, after . . . after . . . you and me . . .'

'Shhh,' she said. 'I'm sorry.' My back was towards the workshop. 'I honestly didn't mean anything, darling. And thank you.' She blew a mouth and left smiling, beckoning to Trembler.

Duncan and I watched them go.

'She'll take him in hand, Duncan.'

'Aye.'

Michelle was there in the car, waiting to drive me to Inverness for the train home. I'd already said my goodbyes. Mrs Buchan had wept uncontrollably at the simultaneous loss of two prize appetites. I'd restored her to normal apoplexy by saying I had to get home because her pasties weren't a patch on East Anglia's. Mrs Moncreiffe was also sad: 'It was all so naughty, wasn't it?' she said, tittering. Tinker hates tittery women. Dutchie would be down again before long. I'd said so-long to Hector, his two dogs and the others. Robert hadn't looked up from shoeing a horse. I kept out of range in case he lobbed the anvil at me in farewell.

'Duncan. You'll say cheerio to Shona for me?'

'Aye. I will.' He knocked out his pipe, cleared his throat. Something was coming. 'She's always been headstrong, Lovejoy. She shared all the clan obsessions. Don't blame her.'

'I don't,' I said, with my sincerest gaze. 'But the road Elaine's taking is healthier. More open. More people.'

'Aye.' He sighed. 'My sympathy's with Jamie. It'll be a sorry union between that pair.'

'One thing, Duncan.' I pointed to the east wing, by far the weaker of the two. 'Ever thought of having a fire? Accidental, of course. Just before a sale, like that Norfolk business in the mid-'seventies . . .'

'Och, away wi' ye.'

He was laughing, as I was, as we left.

'Are you sad to be going, Lovejoy?' Michelle had waved to Duncan, said she'd be straight back after she'd dropped me.

'Not really. No antiques up here, is there?'

She gave a tight smile. After we'd reached that wretched bridge and were cruising on the metalled road instead of shaking the teeth out of our heads on the bumpy track, she shot me a glance.

'Lovejoy. Did you ever . . . you know, with Elaine?'

'I *knew* you thought that.' I spoke with indignation. 'I could see the bloody question coming. Look, love.' Bitterness now. 'If that's the best your vaunted woman's intuition can do I'd trade it in for guesswork.'

'Did you?' She slowed, to inspect my eyes.

'No,' I said levelly, with my innocent stare. I never try for piety because it never works. 'And if you count the tableware you'll find it complete. Anything else?'

'I was only—'

'Because I'm a bit scruffy and don't share your blue blood I'm the perennial villain. Is that it?' I was looking out at the moors, quite a tragic figure really, I thought.

'I'm sorry, Lovejoy. But you must realize—'

'You and the laird, okay. I did realize, eventually. But your main problem with Elaine is Trembler—forgive me, Cheviot Yale, Esquire—not me.'

She pulled at my hand. 'Don't be angry, darling. It's only natural anxiety. I didn't mean to offend . . '

We were three hours reaching Inverness. I forget what took us so long. Anyhow, before saying goodbye Michelle promised in spite of all my protests to accompany Dutchie on the runs to East Anglia with the reproduction antiques. She looked shy, new, voluptuous.

'You don't want me, love,' I said, thinking of Francie, Joan, Ellen, and Jo who would be desperate to hear how I'd got on. 'I'm even bad at hindsight.'

'Next month to the day, darling,' she said. 'I'll stay with you a whole week. I'm dying to see your cottage, and nobody need know. Here. For you.' She gave me a parcel, quite heavy. I know you're not supposed to, but I can't help palpating presents to guess what's inside. She saw me and laughed. My chest was bonging a definite chime.

The Mawdslay had gone before I remembered. I'd promised Ellen I'd stay on her houseboat down the Blackwater for a few days about then. And Sidoli's fairground was due through on its run south in that week. And Jo had hinted she'd have three half-term days to spare. And I'd Margaret to thank. And Helen. Oh God. Why is it that trouble always follows me, and never anybody else?

On the train I unwrapped Michelle's parcel. The lovely pair of snuff mulls shone as the fading light patched and unpatched the carriage windows. The milky silver gleamed in time with the train wheels, and then blurred. Bloody women. No matter how you try they always get you at a disadvantage, don't they.

One day I'll give everything up, I honestly will. As soon as I find out how.